DOLPHIN WAY

A NOVEL BY
MARK CANEY

DOLPHIN WAY

RISE OF THE GUARDIANS

First Published 2011
Published by AquaPress Ltd
AquaPress and the AquaPress Logo are Trademarks of AquaPress Ltd

ISBN: 978-1-90549-223-7

CONTENTS

For Anouk

ACKNOWLEDGEMENTS:

I would like to thank these patient individuals for taking the time to give me their opinions and help as I assembled this book: Anita Burgh, Chris Davey, Elizabeth North, Graeme Gourlay, Harry Bingham, Jon Coon, Jüri Gabriel, Kate Beal, Laura Taylor, Mike Seares, Sarah Fecher, Theresa Kaplan and of course, my family.

A NOVEL BY
MARK CANEY

DOLPHIN WAY

RISE OF THE GUARDIANS

The white gull snapped its curved beak deftly four times across a stone, as though to prepare it, to clean it, to sharpen it.

From a short distance away, Touches The Sky held his head above the water helplessly, watching the murderous bird. The inert form of a dolphin lay stranded on the sand of the little bay, well clear of the water, exposed to the intense heat of the tropical sun. Sky knew how that felt. He had nearly died that way once, many years before, and it would be a cruel and horrible death, your flesh drying and burning while the shocking weight of your own body crushed the air out of you.

The gull hopped nearer the battered dolphin, very close now to its nearest weary eye; sharply inclining its black capped head back and forth as it peered into it. Judging how helpless this creature was. If this should be its time. Sky leapt from the sea in frustration, letting out a rattling scream of anger as he crashed back into the clear water. The gull barely looked at him. It knew that the other dolphin was powerless to help its beached friend.

Sky surfaced again to watch the scene in nauseous horror. The battered body of Born Into Summer was completely inert apart from small movements of her eyes. The rake marks across her back and sides glistened with drying blood. Otherwise, her flesh was taut, dry. Her previously beautifully proportioned tail flukes had clear teeth marks and deep nicks in several places. Sky had never seen one of his kind so obviously abused by other dolphins before. He called her name once more, but she could not make a sound, would never reply. She did look towards him though, just for a moment, and there was the brief light of recognition there, perhaps of gratitude too. That at least a friend was close by at the end.

Sky recognised the moment when the gull made its decision. As it made the first strike, he dived. Dived deep and long, deep and long, shutting his own eyes tightly; trying to block out what he had just seen.

CHAPTER I

"Beware the tool makers. Once they have tasted the power to change, they will not cease until all is changed. There will be no balance, no harmony, no beauty, when the tools are at last laid aside."

As agreed, they swam in silence so that they would not alert their intended prey. Their powerful tails drove up and down as they sliced through the lazy swells, their smooth backs breaking the surface briefly here and there. Fleetingly, the rising sun gilded the fine spray from each expelled breath before it dissipated in the gentle tropical breeze. They kept in tight formation just below the undulating silver of the surface, their broken images racing above them. Below, they left no shadows. There was only the still depths of the open ocean, seemingly falling away forever in the frail light.

Touches The Sky held his position close alongside Deneb Rising. Like Sky, Deneb was a large and powerfully built young adult, and their leadership of the hunt had been unquestioned. From time to time Deneb made a low leap from the water to confirm the direction of the distant mass of excited seabirds. As he sliced back into the water, he ordered fine corrections to their course with small inclinations of his head. With a gesture, he urged the hunting party to greater speed as they closed with their quarry. Sky drove himself forward hard, trying to eradicate the memory of the scene on the beach the previous day. But he could not erase the image of that white bird with its cruel yellow beak — nor would he forget the final shudder that passed through Born Into Summer's body before she passed beyond the reach of more pain. Sky was still stunned by what had happened, and had happened so suddenly. Sky had always admired Born. She was outwardly serious, yet always serene. Like one who knows some fine secret — some special, wonderful truth that allowed them to see the minor troubles and dramas of daily life as being as inconsequential as they actually were. She had taught Sky and the others a great deal; fragments of knowledge, elements of control, glimpses of the deeper meanings of the Way. Warnings of errors to avoid, of Ocean's many natural dangers, and of the less natural ones too. The perverse, twisted logic of the Guardians, the strange, apparently self-destructive workings of the Walkers. But mostly, Sky remembered her complete trust in the Way. Clarity of thought; perfectly attuned to Ocean. All the self assuredness of one of the elders in one not much older than Sky himself. He remembered her full of life, skin smooth, eyes shining, ready to help anyone wishing to learn, and especially patient with Sky. Trying to make him take his responsibilities seriously, telling him that there must be more to his life than games from now on. He had never really understood. And then, unaccountably, she had been driven to that beach, to that waiting gull.

Sky was brought back to the moment by a sound. He glanced across at Deneb who looked back meaningfully at him without breaking the pace. He had heard it too: the faint buzz of another dolphin's sonar — they were not alone here. Sky listened carefully, and there it was again. Nearer still this time; and clearly just one lone dolphin — strange.

Sky tilted his body to one side as he swam so that he could look down. They had begun their sprint towards the birds barely able to see in the dim light, and without echolocation it had been almost like swimming blind. Now, the light was increasing and he could see the sun begin to penetrate the darkness of the deeper water. The wavering shafts of light picked out occasional tiny flecks of life in the clear water and hinted at the presence of the seabed far below him in the indigo depths. But apart from the rest of the hunting party there was no other dolphin in sight.

He broke the surface in a low leap, exploding from the water at the peak of the long swell so that he could look ahead. They were drawing close to the birds now and in the brief time he was airborne he could hear their screams. Some were bobbing agitatedly on the surface, some diving into the water, others squabbling noisily. Sky tried not to remember that lone gull on the beach. Tried not to feel anger at these other birds. They were just fulfilling their allotted role on Ocean. The sound of their screeching vanished abruptly as he fell back into the sea.

Suddenly, the dolphins' object appeared ahead of them through the blue of the water. A wall of living mercury: undulating, shimmering, an equivocal, giant beast. Deneb gave a pair of short jerks with his head and the party split into two; seven circling to one side of the silver cloud with him, six to the other led by Sky. As though in a well choreographed dance, they circled the shoal of sardines in opposite directions. They snapped at the fish to drive them closer. Three of the dolphins repeatedly dived to the bottom edge of the shoal where they sent up curtains of bubbles to panic the little fish into herding tighter together.

Before long the shoal was a densely packed shining ball, its members terrified and confused. While the other dolphins continued to force them together, two dived to the bottom of the shoal and with sharp, menacing movements began to force the sardines towards the impassable wall of the surface. Soon the shoal was as closely packed as it could ever be. The little fish were showing signs of fatigue as their multitude began to deoxygenate the water in which they swam.

Now, at last, Deneb broke the silence. 'Enough: let's eat,' he called in a strong voice. 'Who will dedicate this meal for us?'

No one replied.

'Come on then little brother, you do it!'

Sky smiled to himself. Although not really brothers, they were as close as if they were and it felt good when Deneb called him that. Like having a family again. He paused for a moment then called out clearly above the clamour: 'We thank Senx for these points of light that we may shine the brighter. We honour them for their gift to us this day.'

'Good!' Deneb Rising cried. 'Now let's eat, and quickly. We don't want the Cleaner to get too much from all our hard work.'

With that, two of the dolphins broke away from their circling and cannoned into the seething mass of fish, snapping up the sardines left and right. The tiny fish attempted to scatter, but they were too tightly packed and the dolphins proceeded to gorge themselves. Two by two, they broke away from their encircling patrol and feasted on the oily tasting fish, while their fellows kept the panicked shoal packed together at the surface. The seabirds wildly entered the hunt in earnest as the fish made the water surface boil.

Soon Deneb called out again above the clamour: 'How many have your lot taken Sky?'

'Sixty-three, no...sixty-five now,' Sky shouted back as he shot past, 'we're unstoppable!'

'Oh no you're not! We've had our shares of the quota already, and you need to take your last few morsels and we'll head home. The Council is going to be happy to hear that there's still some prey at least out here.'

They soon moved away from the writhing ball of fish which still swarmed about mindlessly. As the dolphins left, Deneb Rising called to Sky again. 'That was the best hunting in many moons.'

Sky nodded. 'And we're not the only ones to appreciate it. Look: just as you expected, they're here already.' He gestured downwards. There, could be seen several large, slender shapes rising from the depths, moving silently towards the shoal. One of them diverted leisurely from its path to snap up a falling fish tail, the others were moving purposefully; drawn by the traces of blood in the water.

Deneb watched for a moment then turned to Sky again. 'Never mind them, did you see him — the lone zeta?'

Sky was confused for a moment, then remembered them having heard the sound of a dolphin's sonar as they had approached the shoal.

'No, I didn't. Did you recognise the voice?'

'No. But he was Ka-Tse. We should keep an eye out for him.'

Sky nodded. Even though the stranger was Ka-Tse — a bottlenose dolphin like them — it was best to be wary. Very few dolphins would choose to travel alone so the stranger may well be an exile. There was usually some good reason for them to be alone.

They swam away, leaving the sharks to their business. Sky moved alongside another young adult male who was singing happily to himself. His pale grey stocky bulk contrasted sharply with Sky's dark, toned body. Sky tried to lift himself from the dark thoughts that were coming back to him again now the excitement of the hunt was over, and brushed against the other dolphin's side companionably. 'So, Muddy, you seem in good spirits.'

Muddy River Mouth's eyes beamed back at him. 'Oh, yes I am. I haven't eaten so well for a long time. I am going to make the rest of the clan just hate me when I tell them about this.'

'You're so full of fish you'll likely sink out of sight before we get there!'

The larger dolphin snorted. 'I can promise you that I could've eaten a lot more. I know we need to have them, but these quotas make no allowance for those of us who simply *need* more food.'

'Well, the Gathering starts soon. I'll personally request that you be allowed to talk to the Elders on behalf of special cases like yourself.'

'I wouldn't dare speak to them! Do you really think that they'd even listen to me anyway?'

Sky looked gravely at Muddy. 'Oh yes. They'd realise the seriousness of your situation as soon as they saw your poor, emaciated, little body before them.' Sky forced his eyes to smile a little. It was not Muddy's fault that Born was dead.

Muddy looked about to give Sky a nip on the tail when they both realised that Deneb and the others had halted just ahead of them. Sky stopped himself beside Deneb, keen to see what was happening; Muddy hung back cautiously. Sky immediately saw why they had paused. A single dolphin was approaching them hesitantly. He moved a little stiffly, awkwardly, like he still nursed some old wound. Although he had pale undersides and dark grey back like most of them, there was something unusual about the skin on his back; like an old mottled scarring just faintly visible.

He stopped, announcing himself formally.

'It is I, Rain Ending!'

Deneb replied on behalf of the hunting party, 'It is I, Deneb Rising of the Dune Coast Clan! My companions are also of that clan.'

The stranger dipped his head in acknowledgement.

'Greetings to you all. I hope your hunt went well.'

'It did, thank you. But you did not name your clan.'

'No…I have none. Have not had for many years now.'

Deneb glanced at Sky, a question in his eye. The others would be wondering too. Sky thought it best to put the question that was in all of their minds. He moved forward a little.

'It is I, Touches The Sky!'

'Greetings…Touches The Sky.' The stranger looked long and hard at Sky, staring almost rudely.

'Are you here because you wish to join our clan, Rain Ending?'

'No, that is not my intention. And I'm not an exile in case that might be a concern.' He still stared at Sky, making him uncomfortable. Then his gaze fell on Sky's right pectoral fin. The very tip of it was missing, the result of an injury he had suffered when he was very young. Nothing unusual: most dolphins had scars, so Sky thought it odd when the stranger commented on it.

'Touches The Sky, that injury to your fin — is it old?'

'Yes, from when I was small, I don't even know how it happened really. Why do you ask?'

'I just wondered…if it was something that bothers you…but obviously not. You must have a good Healer in your clan. And that is why I've approached you— I have an old injury — a very old injury — it's always caused me some trouble but recently it's become worse. If you have a Healer in the Dune Coast Clan I'd like to seek their advice. Just advice, that's all; then I'll be on my way.'

Sky and Deneb exchanged glances. There was nothing threatening about such a request. Deneb answered. 'We have two Healers at present and they are both skilled. We'll have to seek permission from the Council of course, but your request sounds very reasonable. Follow us back to our clan and we'll see if we can help you.'

Deneb asked two of the party to accompany Rain Ending in case he might have trouble keeping up with the group. He was a little slower and soon he and his escorts were trailing at the back of the company. When he was well out of earshot Deneb spoke softly to Sky: 'Do you know him, Sky?'

Sky had no memory of the stranger and shook his head.

'Well he seemed very interested in you. Let's keep an eye on him just in case. Any lone zeta is suspicious but the way he acted while he was speaking to you was strange. Very strange.'

'Do you think he might be connected with what happened to Born?'

'I doubt it. If it *was* other zetii that drove her on to that beach as you believe it would have to be more than one. And they'd have needed to swim much faster than he can. But that whole idea seems incredible to me! Zetii deliberately killing a fellow zeta? What about the Way?'

Sky screwed up his eyes then opened them again wearily. 'I know, it seems fantastic, but there are stories, these Guardians — they are supposed to be turning all the old rules upside down — corrupting the Way. Maybe it's something to do with them.'

'But, why? Born was such a lovely zeta, would never hurt anyone.'

'Look, Deneb, I *saw* her body! I saw the marks on her and I am sure they were made by zetii. Someone chased her, hurt her, and scared her so badly that they drove her up onto that beach. And then they left her there to die.'

Deneb looked at his friend compassionately. 'And you saw her end, my friend. It must have been hard, especially for you.'

'But why couldn't I have arrived just a little earlier — when I might have saved her?'

'Don't think that way. You had no reason to know anything was going to happen.'

Sky inclined his head in agreement. 'I suppose so. But now we know something *has* happened. Something that shouldn't be possible according to everything we've learned. Deneb, what's happening?'

Deneb looked at him sympathetically. 'Soon it will be the Gathering. There have been so many stories recently of food shortages and bizarre rumours about what the Guardians are up to. Maybe the Gathering will come up with some interpretations of the Way that can help.'

'Maybe. Maybe the Way isn't enough any more.' Sky felt slightly shocked at hearing himself say it.

Deneb looked at him gravely. 'Let's hope you are wrong there, for the zetii and for Ocean's sake.'

CHAPTER 2

"When the sons and daughters of T'ret returned to Ocean's waters they had the gifts of warm blood in their veins, milk for their children and vision without sight. They thereby had the strength to thrive in the Great Waters, but their greatest gift was the Way."

- The Creation Legend

The returning hunting party neared the headland of a wide, sweeping bay. The seabed rose to meet them as they approached the shore; the steep fall of the bottom mellowing into a gentle, sandy slope as they neared the land. Wave-filtered sunlight dappled the endless sand ripples that paralleled the shore; miniature reflections of the swells that had formed them. Lone hermit crabs toiled across the miniature dune fields, ducking sharply back into their borrowed shells and tumbling into the tiny valleys as the dolphins' shadows approached.

Sky and Deneb were at the head of the group, swimming side by side. They had spoken no more of Born's death or of the stranger who still trailed at the back with his escorts. Sky glanced at Deneb as they travelled. Typically, he looked quiet, concentrated. Deneb took his responsibilities seriously and seldom spoke spontaneously. Sky supposed that mainly came from the fact that his mother Silent Waters, was the clan leader, but he sometimes wished Deneb would relax a little more and have more fun. But then, he reflected, if Deneb said something, he had thought about it and he meant it. He was a strong individual and a good friend to have. Once again, Sky counted himself lucky to have been taken into their family.

Deneb tilted his head, listening. 'I think I hear familiar voices, Sky. Shall we announce ourselves?'

They made their signature calls:

'It is I, Deneb Rising!'

'It is I, Touches The Sky!'

Faintly came back:

'And it is I, Fades Into Dusk!'

Sky's spirits lifted as the owner of the call came into view: a young adult female, slim, but a powerful swimmer, with an intelligent face. Her graceful body was smooth and her skin shone. Just behind Fades Into Dusk, another female appeared; her companion from the perimeter patrol.

'It is I, Wakes Softly!'

As the others returned her greeting warmly, Sky noticed how the pretty, petite Wakes seemed to glow in Deneb's presence. She was a relative newcomer to the clan and had been painfully shy at first when she had joined them at the Academy, but now she was gaining in confidence and Sky had begun to notice her interest in Deneb. He wondered if Deneb was aware of it. She looked first at Deneb, then Sky as she softly said, "Everyone is talking about what happened to Born Into Summer. Poor Sky, you were the one who found her, weren't you?'

'What happened?' Dusk asked. 'Do we have any idea how she ended up on land?'

Deneb answered. 'Sky thinks other zetii may have attacked her, chased her ashore, perhaps.'

Sky tossed his head in negation. 'Not perhaps. They must have. I can't see another explanation for it.'

Wakes recoiled visibly. 'We never kill except to eat, not even the tiniest thing, – so zetii killing another zeta — no, it can't be!'

'Maybe it's possible,' Dusk said. 'If it was another species — one with a grudge against us Ka-Tse, maybe the Xenthos, say.'

Deneb gave a small shake of his head, and looked doubtful, but said nothing.

They lapsed into silence for a while, then Dusk tried to lift the mood.

'Tell us about the hunt,' she said. 'You were lucky— going hunting while we're stuck here just swimming up and down.'

Sky gave a small smile with his eyes, aware of what she was trying to do, and grateful. 'I'm sorry you two couldn't have been with us today, Dusk — in fact you missed fine hunting; the best this year.'

'I hope you've left us something,' she replied, 'We've been on patrol since midday and I'm famished. Some of the clan are talking about going back to look for your fish ball this evening but I can't join them; I've got to be somewhere else.'

Sky was about to ask her where; Dusk had been going off alone a lot recently and he missed her company in the group, but Wakes Softly spoke first.

'Was it a big shoal then?'

'Oh yes, and we left plenty of fish', Deneb replied, 'although the Cleaners were quick enough to move in after us. There should still be some left tomorrow, given that Muddy can't join the second hunt.'

The females smiled and glanced across at the larger dolphin to see if he had heard, but he was describing the hunt and his part in it in graphic detail to some of the others.

As they looked that way, Rain Ending passed behind Muddy with his two escorts, on their way to seek out an elder from the Council.

Dusk watched with interest, inquisitive as usual. 'Is that a new member for the clan?'

'No,' Deneb replied, 'he says he just wants to see the Healers. Has some kind of injury.'

'And then he's off again? What's he like?'

Sky answered. 'He claims he doesn't want to join the clan. Said he hasn't got one of his own though. And he's…a bit strange…but maybe that comes from being alone for a long time.'

'Is he an exile?'

'Says he isn't, but you can't be sure, I suppose. Maybe we'll find out more later.'

Deneb leapt from the water to gauge the height of the sun, and reappeared in a moment amongst an explosion of silver bubbles. 'Look you two, we've pretty much had our allowances for today — but why don't we swim along the eastern drop-off and see if we can find you something to eat as well?'

They readily agreed, so Sky, Muddy, Deneb, and the two females set off across the shelving sea bed towards the headland. Small coral heads started to appear, becoming larger as they neared the rocky promontory at the eastern end of the bay. Delicate, branching, stony corals gave shelter to myriad small fish; bright orange, metallic blue, velvet black, flashing silver. All darted in concert into the protective crevices of their homes as the dolphins passed, only to cautiously re-emerge once they had moved on.

As they reached the headland the bottom fell away steeply, becoming almost a vertical face. They followed this wall, staying near the surface;

looking for the fast swimming silver fish that dwell in that zone.

Sky placed himself just behind Fades Into Dusk who was at the front of the group, swimming close enough to feel the pressure waves from her tail. He admired her elegant, natural grace as she powered along. He made up his mind to try to get her to spend some time with him later, perhaps to play a game of memoranii or just to play tag with some of the other young ones. He needed to do something to get his mind back to where it was just a few days ago, when Ocean had seemed such a gentle place.

Just then, Dusk called back to the others. 'What's that up ahead? Something big in the water — not moving.'

Sky moved closer to her. Nothing could be seen yet, but then she had detected it by sound. He sent out a short burst of clicks in the direction she was looking. Yes, he could "see" it too. The reflected sound that came back from his sonar signal showed it to be a large, firm bodied animal; not a squid, probably as big as a dolphin...and then he could actually see it. 'It's a Cleaner', he said, 'and it seems to be dead.'

They cautiously circled the shark. It was not long dead; its sleek, blue-grey body had not stiffened yet. Its perfect, hydrodynamic shape now pointed skyward as it hung suspended from the long, vicious hook that was embedded in its open mouth. The line from the hook led almost to the surface where it was attached to another, horizontal line that extended out of sight in either direction.

'What happened to it?' Wakes Softly asked.

'Walkers,' replied Deneb grimly. 'Let's follow this and see where it goes.'

'What a horrible way to die,' she murmured, unconsciously moving slightly behind Deneb as though to protect herself from shark and hook.

They followed the horizontal line which was suspended just below the sea surface. Soon they came to another line and hook; this one empty but for some shreds of the now missing bait. But the next had another victim: a young Blue Shark. It was still very much alive and it thrashed against the pull on its jaws. This just drove the hook further into its flesh. It stopped for a moment, exhausted, staring at them with wide eyes, its dark pupils dilated.

They followed the line further. There were five sharks in all on separate hooks; two dead, one nearly so, the remaining two very much alive.

Muddy turned to the others, his expression troubled. 'Do they just leave them here to die?'

Deneb shook his head. 'No, they'll come for them eventually. They return to these things. But I wonder how many they take like this; they seem to be killing more and more fish every year.'

'They say that's why the hunting's getting so hard', Sky agreed.

Dusk rolled her eyes and snorted bubbles. 'Don't be so naïve, Sky! That's such a convenient explanation for everybody. The real truth is that it's not the Walkers, it's other zetii taking more than their share from the quotas!'

'No, I don't believe that we would...'

'Not *we* — not the Ka-Tse. I mean the deep water zetii; the Xenthos or Xa-Hana. They're not like us; they move around in those huge clans and eat everything they come across. Don't tell me they're following the quotas!'

Sky knew he should stay calm and back off, but this had become a familiar argument from her recently, and it frustrated him that Dusk believed this stuff. 'Come on, Dusk,' he said, gently, 'there's no proof — this is the kind of nonsense those so-called Guardians come out with.'

'Well it sounds like they actually realise there's a problem then!'

'Stop it,' Deneb interrupted. Talk about the issues if you want, but stop talking about the Guardians. There are good reasons why they're banished from the rest of us.'

Dusk was about to reply but stopped, her head tilted, listening. The water slowly filled with the distant, rhythmic thrashing of a propeller cleaving the water. The sound grew steadily louder, then slowed. Above them, they saw the shape of the boat silhouetted against the glare of the surface, its wake strung behind it. They could even make out the shapes of the men that reached down to haul in the longline.

One by one, the sharks were winched aboard the boat. Three, passively; two still fighting for life. But even as the last one was dragged out of the water, the sharks began returning to the sea, spiralling down from the surface towards the dolphins. But something was wrong. The sharks' bodies, already exquisitely streamlined by millions of years of evolution, were now even more so. Obscenely so.

Sky stared at the first descending form in confusion. It was hard to see against the light, and a darkening cloud spread behind the shark as it fell towards him. Behind it, the surface was broken again as the next shark entered the water, followed by its own expanding cloud.

The first shark fell between Sky and Dusk. Its body trembled and twisted weakly as it desperately tried to halt its fall into the depths. Its eyes looked uncomprehendingly into Sky's as it passed him. The next four sharks followed one by one, each like the first, with fins and tail hacked off. The dolphins watched in shocked silence as the bodies passed them, but as the last neared them, Sky spoke at last.

'This one is still alive too. Let's move it over to the wall at least.'

They gently pushed the shark over to the steeply sloping wall and found a sand covered ledge big enough to accommodate its body. It squirmed helplessly on the sand, blood still flowing freely from its wounds.

Wakes closed her eyes, then opened them slowly and looked at her friends, her expression pained.

'Why?'

'Who knows?' replied Deneb. 'Of course, the Walkers are wasteful, but this seems incredible. Why take just their fins? And why be so cruel?'

The shark was shaking slightly, its mouth opening and closing rapidly as it fought to breathe. Dusk turned to the others and spoke quietly, as if she was afraid it would understand her.

'We should kill it — end its suffering.'

'No Dusk!' Sky said. 'You know we can't. We mustn't kill except to eat.'

She turned to face him, her voice quietly angry. 'Don't quote the Way at me! Just look at it — we can't leave it like this!'

'And we can't just ignore the Way whenever it suits us! It's what makes us civilized — otherwise we'd be no different from those Walkers!'

'I'm not saying we ignore it all — we just need to realise that it doesn't answer all the questions any more — Ocean's changing, and if we don't change too we'll all end up like this Cleaner!'

Deneb moved between them.

'Both of you calm down. I think the argument's irrelevant. Look, he's almost gone now. I say we let Ocean take him back.'

The shark had stopped trying to swim and was still. There was a small flicker of life in its eyes, but it was a small, distant, failing thing. Like a stone dropped into the void and gently fading from sight. They lifted what was left of its body and carried it away from the wall, out over the darkening blue of the open sea. Without a word they let the shark fall. As they did so the flicker of light vanished and its eyes were left with only the peaceful, indifferent gaze of the dead.

They watched it tumble gently into the abyss.

CHAPTER 3

"Trust the words of a fool. Only the wise lie well."
- Traditional.

'There's just sand. Endless sand. And sand doesn't talk.'

'Keep swimming.' Sky pressed ahead faster, forcing Muddy River Mouth to keep the pace, hoping that the greater effort might discourage his complaining. But he knew that Muddy would never allow himself to make any unusual effort without at least a token show of resistance and reluctance. That was just Muddy and it did not mean a thing.

'Why are we doing this, Sky? Alright, so Born was stranded on the beach near here, but that was days ago now. You think that someone is going to be still hanging around here? There's nothing here!'

Sky said nothing. It was true that the area was barren. Just a flat, shelving seabed, a continuation of the white sands of the shore stretching far out under the sea, the small ripples in the sand the only blemishes on an otherwise bland space. That was why so few dolphins from the clan came this way; there was just no reason to. But Sky had dragged the reluctant Muddy along to try to find something, anything, to explain what had happened to Born; what had driven her onto that beach and why.

'Sky, we need to stop and find some food. I am so hungry, I could eat...'

'Quiet!' Sky stopped swimming so suddenly Muddy almost careered into him. 'Listen!' he hissed at Muddy.

Faintly, the sound of two female dolphins' voices could be heard ahead. They were young, not yet adults, and bottlenose dolphins like Sky and Muddy. Sky flicked his head to Muddy in a signal commonly used in a hunt — *close in silence*. They approached the voices cautiously then Sky stopped them as a huge shape loomed into view at the edge of visibility. The wreck of a large metal ship lay partially on its side in the sand; decaying rusty plates, cables and containers beside it. Corals and sponges were growing on various parts of the hulk, gradually absorbing the intruder into the world in which it had fallen. The voices were coming from the other side of the wreck. Sky and Muddy surfaced to take a breath, then Sky led the way to the near side of the ship where they stayed motionless, listening. Sky could hear the young dolphins clearly at last. He glanced at Muddy, who tipped his head in silent acknowledgement. Sky knew these voices: one was Bellatrix Unseen, one of the younger students he and Muddy helped to teach at the Academy. The other was the same age and new to the clan, she was called Shining, but he could not remember her full name: something Shining, anyway.

Bellatrix was speaking now, quickly and full of enthusiasm as always, but in the loud conspiratorial whisper of a child trying to keep an exciting secret. 'He's late again! I hope he is going to turn up this time! Are you sure he meant today, Shining?'

'Yes, that's definitely what *we* said. But you never know with him. I don't think he hears half of what we say.'

'Let's go up and see.' Bellatrix led her friend to the surface where they both finned hard with their tails, lifting their heads high above the water to look out into the clear air. Sky took advantage of their temporary inability to hear to speak to Muddy. 'They shouldn't be here on their own! Who are they meeting so secretly?' Before Muddy could answer the two young dolphins dived down again to the other side of the wreck, chattering excitedly. Sky and Muddy hung back in the shadow of the ship's keel. They could clearly make out Bellatrix's voice. 'So he did remember! He's just late as usual. I wonder if he's going to try to scare us again today!'

Sky swam cautiously upwards until he could just see through the thin branches of a red gorgonia, which swayed gently back and forth on the upper rail of the ship in the lazy swell. The two young dolphins were looking expectantly out into the blue away from him. Sky heard the sound of the approaching dolphin's ranging sonar, then saw him appear and approach the two females. He was not much older than them, and Sky was sure he had never seen him before. His head was slightly misshapen, flattened on the top and one side, as though it had been squashed somehow as a baby, and the eye on that side was partly closed. He spoke slowly, his voice flat and dull. He seemed to need to concentrate hard to get the words out. 'You still here. I said you must go.'

Shining shook her head vigorously. 'We told you, we can't just go! The Council decide where the clan goes, and they are not going to move it now with the Gathering coming up.'

The strange youth dipped his odd head for emphasis as he spoke again in the same stilted way. 'Is Gathering that troubles start. You go before Gathering. Go now.'

Bellatrix interrupted. 'But you still haven't told us why! We can't tell our mothers we just want to go without a reason!'

The youth spoke more forcefully still. 'Don't tell then! Just go before bad things happen. Go before Gathering'. Then, pleading, 'Promise you go.'

Sky sank slowly back to Muddy's side and indicated for him to take station behind the gorgonia, then swam quietly around the bottom of the wreck till he was on the opposite side of it, behind the three young dolphins who hung above the wreck, absorbed in their conversation. When he was directly behind the strange young male, Sky rose up into view, saying as gently as he could, 'It is I, Touches The Sky. And I think you had better tell *me* about these bad things.'

The three young dolphins spun to look at him in shock, the male looked terrified and turned to bolt, but as he did, Muddy's bulky body loomed up above the edge of the ship in front of him. He turned back to look again at Sky for a moment, then to Sky's horror he shot into an opening in the wreck, disappearing into the darkness of the ship's inside. Sky darted to the opening but did not dare to go in.

'That young idiot! If he gets lost or trapped in there he'll drown! Muddy, see if there's another way out.' His friend swam swiftly along the wreck, using sharp bursts of sonar to scan the surface as he went. Sky turned back to the two females. 'You two are both from the Dune Coast Clan. You know you are not meant to be here! Who is he?'

They looked at each other, frightened and guilty. Bellatrix answered at last. We are really sorry, Jeii. We didn't think it was so wrong. His name is Sand In Rain.'

'So his clan call him Rain?'

Bellatrix looked embarrassed. 'He says they call him "Sand In Brain". It's why we come here — we're his only friends. We call him Sand though.'

Sky looked at them hard for a moment before going closer to the darkness of the opening into the wreck. He called into the darkness: 'Sand! Come out Sand! We're not going to hurt you.'

Muddy reappeared. 'There are no other openings big enough for a zeta to pass through that I can find. He needs to come back out this way or not at all.'

'I don't think he will answer you, Jeii,' Bellatrix said, 'he's not allowed to speak to zetii from other clans.'

'He needs to come out of there soon. He must need to breathe by now.' Come on, let's all go up, maybe that will encourage him.' Sky led them all to the surface to take air, keeping his eye on the dark opening in the wreck. But there was no sign of the strange youth. 'Muddy, I'm going to have to go in after him.'

'No, Sky, you don't know what you will find in there! There could be some kind of Walker trap or something. It's not natural for a zetii to be in an enclosed place like that!'

Sky knew that full well and dreaded going into the hole. Getting trapped underwater was every dolphin's worst nightmare, maybe even worse than getting trapped on the land. 'I know, but I have to go. It's our fault he went in there, we scared him. And I think he may know something important.'

They dived down again and Sky entered the hole cautiously, leaving the others at the entrance. He called the youth's name again: no reply. Had he passed out already?

Sky went deeper into the wreck, relying more on his sonar as the light fell away. Shafts of light came in to dimly illuminate the space, coming through round apertures in the higher side, but they were too small for a dolphin to pass through. As he moved past the debris inside the ship, slowly billowing clouds of silt rose from the bottom, blinding him. The metal and other strange materials sent back confusing multiple echoes from his rasping sonar bursts, and he began to feel disorientated. He turned to look for the light from the entrance, but found to his dismay that a great wall of silt was following him. There were small patches of light here and there, but which one was the real opening? He began to feel panic rising in him. He was starting to feel the need to breathe. He should just go — Sand must have lost consciousness by now — must be dead by now. But no. He would go just a bit further, just to the end of this space. Then he heard a soft return to his sonar; and a moment later he could dimly see the shape of Sand, pressed against the side of the wreck, his eyes blank as though already dead.

'Get out!' Sky called urgently.

The youth stared at him blankly then moved his head sideways slightly in a negative gesture.

'Get out now or you'll die in here!'

Again the blank refusal.

Then Sky, remembered what Bellatrix had said to him about Sand. 'You don't have to speak to me. And I won't tell anyone I've seen you. I promise!'

The screen of resignation lifted slightly from Sand's eyes and he focused on Sky for a moment. He looked about to pass out.

'I promise,' Sky repeated firmly. Sand seemed to relax a little so Sky moved forward and pushed him into the silt cloud in the direction he hoped the exit lay. Sand swam with difficulty and seemed disorientated. Sky pushed him ahead of himself, hoping the opening was in fact this way. He knew there was no chance that Sand would make it if they were going the wrong way, and he was not sure he would either. He called out: 'Muddy! Help me! We are lost!'

'Here! You are not far now, I can hear you!'

With relief, Sky swam on, and Muddy kept calling encouragement, his voice getting louder, until at last, through the cloud of soft mud, Sky saw the light of the opening. He pushed Sand out ahead of him and then they both made the surface to take great gasps of beautiful air.

When they had recovered, they joined the others at the bottom again near the wreck. The young females circled nervously; Sand rested with his tail on the bottom, impassive but body full of tension.

Sky turned to Bellatrix. 'I know he does not want to speak to me. So you ask him. What is going to happen at the Gathering? Who is behind this?'

Bellatrix looked very nervous but turned to the inert form. 'Sand, what will happen at the Gathering?'

He looked at her sullenly. 'Bad things. Zeta fight zeta. Maybe worse.'

'How worse?'

'Maybe kill.'

'Kill!' Muddy exclaimed. 'We don't kill other zetii. It's against the Way to kill except to eat! That's impossible!'

Sand looked at him angrily. 'Not true! Sand heard it is already happening.'

Sky glanced at Muddy and motioned him to be quiet. He nodded to Bellatrix again.

'Who wants to make this happen, Sand?'

'Sand must go now.'

'First say who, Sand.'

He looked around fearfully, then dropped his gaze to the seabed. 'My clan. The Kark Du says it must happen. He will make zeta hate zeta. We must do it or we die, he says.'

Sand was looking more and more upset and Sky was afraid that he might bolt at any moment, maybe back into the wreck. 'Kark Du?' he enquired gently.

'That is the name we give leader. Our father and our master.'

'Who are "we"?'

'Sand must go!'

Sky spoke gently to the young dolphin, trying to calm him, 'Alright, you can go if you promise to come back and speak to me. When can you come?'

Sand looked at him mutely.

'When would you normally meet him again, Bellatrix?' Sky asked.

'The next new moon, at sunset. But are you going to tell the Council about this Jeii?'

Sky glanced at Muddy for consent before replying. 'Well, not yet anyway. Not if Sand promises to come back. Alright Sand? Come back then and you and I will talk some more. Promise that and you can go, and I will not tell our Council about your friends.'

Sky held the frightened stare of the youth for a long moment. Sand looked deeply distressed but finally lowered his eyes in what seemed to be acknowledgement. Sky decided that was the best he was likely to get.

'Just one last question before you go: who are "we"? Who are your clan?'

Sand looked at him in panic. 'We...they are...Guardians! And they kill me too if they know I speak like this.' And suddenly he turned and was gone, swimming at speed out to sea.

CHAPTER 4

"For countless millennia, Ocean nurtured all the zetii; delighting in the strong, tolerating the weak. Now the times of plenty draw to an end. Only the true followers of the Way will prosper. The Ka-Tse are Ocean's favoured sons and daughters. Others shall not eat until they are satiated."

- The 'Seer' Stone Eyes (13,222 -13,264 post Great Alluvium).

He was being crushed by his own body. The unfamiliar weight of it driving his chest against the hot sand. Every breath a struggle. Sunlight burning his back, his skin stretched dry and tight. The tide had ebbed away leaving him and the rest of the clan in this alien world, their grey bodies scattered across the beach like giant, wave tossed pebbles. He was glad at least that his mother was beside him. It soothed him at first to look into her clear eye. There was some sand in the corner of that eye, and it looked wrong, unnatural. A drop of thick liquid carried some of it down her face. He wished he could help her get rid of that sand, it must be hurting her. At first he'd thought that she was trying to comfort him — was trying to speak to him. But he couldn't hear her. Had heard nothing since the terrible noise had begun.

At first it had been exciting; they'd gone up to look at the strange machines. Odd, angular shapes protruded from the massive grey bodies that sped through the water driven by the noisy, swirling blades. He'd been frightened by those, but riding the huge pressure wave in front of the *machines with his father and older brother had been fun.*

Then the sounds had begun. Shattering pulses of sound that shook his chest and seemed to split his brain. He'd been terrified and had looked to the adults for guidance, just wanting them to stop the pain, make everything right; like they always did.

Father and mother had led him and his brother in a fast swim towards the land with the rest of the clan. There were no words of comfort, or none that could be heard. They couldn't even navigate with their sonar; the awful sound pulses dominated everything; so they just fled through the turbid water.

They had blindly followed the rest of the clan up into the shallows and then through the surf of the beach. As they stranded among the waves they were at last free of the terrible, mind shattering pulses and they flopped about in confusion. The retreating sea left them there as Senx rose in the sky, pouring his burning heat onto their backs. Heat like he'd never experienced — the sea had always caressed it aside before.

He'd tried to talk to his mother in his childlike way but he never knew if she'd heard him. She'd tried to smile with her eyes but he saw hints of a strange, disturbing terror there. He remembered watching her blowhole open and close, taking reassurance in that even when the bright light of intelligence began to fade from her eye. As Senx reached his zenith and the heat grew beyond all endurance, the bodies around him fell still one by one. He'd still thought that everything would be alright, that father would come and help them back into the sea; make life go back to normal. Then he noticed that his mother had stopped breathing. Her sand coated eye stared blankly through him and for the first time in his short life he found that it was possible to be completely alone.

Then there was nothing for a long time; mind drifting, body crushed, the bright, merciless eye of Senx burning into his own. Then they came to him, or he thought they had. Maybe he just dreamed them. Moving upright with apparent ease, in spite of the oppressive weight of gravity. And making complex sounds to one another — almost as though they were talking. Strange others who caressed him reassuringly and looked into his eyes with compassion. The sand harsh against his belly as they pushed him back into the waves. He'd tried to swim onto the beach again to be with his mother. There was nowhere else for him to go in Ocean. But they must have pushed him back into the water with their gentle insistence. Back into a world of solitude that seemed more frightening to a young child than that beach of death...

'Wake up Sky!'

After a long moment's confusion he opened his eyes gratefully to see Muddy's concerned face peering at him in the half light of the pre dawn greyness. 'I was dreaming...'

'I gathered that. The same dream I suppose?'

'Yes — the beach...I wish I could get it out of my head.'

'You probably never will. For that kind of thing to happen to a little kid — losing your parents, your brother — it must have been a huge shock.'

'But I don't really remember much about it; how I got off the beach, how long I was alone, how I survived...'

Muddy tipped his head in a shrug. 'Well it's no secret how you were found. One of our hunting parties came across you half dead in the shallows, right? Silent Waters can tell you all about that.'

'Yes, she has of course, lots of times. I think I mean more *why* I survived. Why *I* survived, not the others.'

'Don't start getting all morbid this early in the day. Come on, let's find something to eat, that'll take your mind off it.'

Sky smiled to himself. Eating was Muddy's solution to a wide range of problems. He followed the broad form of his friend across the bay. Below them, the familiar expanse of rippled, shallow sand fell gently away. A slender garfish darted off in panic above them as they approached; its shining silver body blending perfectly with the underside of the surface. They ignored it, looking for a meal that would be easier to catch and more palatable. Occasional pale fan worms snapped their delicate circle of arms down into the sand as the dolphins passed above them, then slowly re-emerged once they were well past. The rising sun coloured the rolling dunes behind the shoreline a warm pink, in striking contrast to the deep blue of the sea. They surprised a small group of cuttlefish in the open and Muddy snatched two before the rest jetted off from sight.

Muddy muttered a belated thank you to Senx before turning to Sky again. 'What's the matter, not hungry? They're delicious — and no nasty sharp spikes or bones.'

'Yes, I know. And I will eat soon. I was just wondering about what that strange Sand character told us.'

'Yes, he was very strange. Mad would be a better word. All that stuff about zetii killing each other! That can't be true.'

'Are you so sure, Muddy? What about Born Into Summer? Something caused her death. And Sand said he had "heard it is already happening".'

'Oh, come on, you can't believe that the Guardians can somehow make the zetii break one of the most basic teachings of the Way after a million years or whatever it is?' Muddy looked troubled. 'But if they could...what would it be like?'

'Ocean is a very different place now, Muddy. Maybe they could change things with everything in such a mess. Maybe that's *why* they are doing this now!'

'I don't want to believe it. All this stuff about Guardians must be exaggerated. Where's the proof?'

Sky was about to reply when three dolphins shot out of the blue, emitting short blasts of navigational sonar as they came. Sky recognised them from the clan; all young males, not really friends of his but they had always been amiable enough. Now though, they careered past Muddy and deliberately bumped into Sky, one each side then one from below, striking him roughly.

'Hey!' Muddy called, 'what are you doing? You hit him!'

'Then he shouldn't be where he doesn't belong!' came a reply, and they were gone, as fast as they had appeared.

Sky stared after them, very shaken.

Muddy looked at him in concern. 'Did they hurt you?'

'No — no not really. But what was that all about? They were so aggressive; what have I done to them?'

'I've no idea, that was really weird.' Muddy looked around nervously. 'Well, I think they've gone for now at least. You sure you're alright?'

Sky nodded.

'Let's get away from here then; let's get back to the clan.'

After they had swum for a while, Muddy looked over at Sky again. 'You look depressed. Still thinking about those idiots?'

'Yes. But also about yesterday. The Cleaner — what Dusk and I were talking about.'

'Arguing about you mean. You two always seem to argue these days. More than old lovers.'

'Well, that's *not* the reason as I've told you before.' Sky kept pace with Muddy as they swam slowly inshore. 'Don't look at me like that — I know what you're thinking. A year or so ago I thought that maybe there was going to be something between me and her. But it never happened, alright?'

'That's because you always just wait around hoping everything will work itself out. You have to take some initiative Sky! She'd have been perfect for you.'

'I know that's what everyone thinks, but she's changed. Dusk has such strange ideas now. You heard her yesterday; she's openly questioning parts of the Way — I don't feel I have a connection with her any more.'

'Look, I don't get into all the deep thinking stuff like you do, but a lot of Ka-Tse are questioning the Way these days. In fact *all* kinds of zetii are questioning it from what I hear. Ocean has changed and the Way is ancient. It doesn't seem to have all the answers like it used to.'

Sky leapt high from the water as they swam, trying to clear his head. He exploded back down through the surface again, a cascade of silver bubbles following him as he powered back alongside his friend.

'I'm not talking about questioning details of the Way; there's nothing wrong with that. After all we're meant to do it as Novices aren't we? Even more so if we qualify as Initiates of the Way. No, I mean that she really seems to be arguing against some of the basic principles. If she goes on like this she could get into a mess. That's how ordinary Ka-Tse like you or me end up getting seduced into the Guardians.'

Muddy's normally amiable features started showing signs of irritation now.

'Sky, just forget it. You're imagining things again. Listen, I know how important it is for you to finish this last year at the Academy well. Here's my advice: keep away from Dusk if you can't avoid talking about philosophical things — it always ends in a fight and I hate having to listen to it. Now, no more about this please; here's the clan.'

As they closed with the shallow water near the shoreline they found themselves in the happy confusion of the Dune Coast Clan. The water was full of sound as the dolphins moved about in sociable groups; playing, flirting, hunting. Sky realised that there was at least one more family present now that had returned to the clan after having been away for a couple of years. He tried to remember how many that made their number now; he guessed at about sixty-five: a big clan. He and Muddy threaded their way through the groups and among the small isolated coral heads that protruded from the sand. Then there was a signature call he knew at once, with an odd, urgent edge to it: 'It is I, Deneb Rising!'

They replied with their own calls and Deneb appeared, his pale eyes showing concern.

'Sky, my mother wants to see you immediately. Follow me.'

Sky took station alongside Deneb who led him in silence away from the crowds and along the coast where the sandy beach turned to a harsh rock face that fell almost sheer into the water. A narrow vertical fissure in the cliff face continued downwards into the water where it widened, its two inward facing walls dropping away out of sight. They approached this, and as they drew closer, Sky could see the slight form of Silent Waters suspended almost motionless between the towering stone walls, the wavering shafts of sunlight from the surface making her pale skin seem to glow against the dark shade of the cliffs. Deneb signalled to Sky to continue alone and turned to leav

Sky approached her, troubled. In spite of having been raised by her since he was only two, he still shared some of the awe that most of the clan had for their leader. He had never been summoned to see her in this way before, and he struggled to stay calm.

'You wanted to see me Prime Mother?'

'Yes, come closer, Sky.' Her rich, melodious voice would have sounded as composed as ever to most listeners, but Sky detected something: a faint echo of alarm that made his stomach tighten in concern. He stopped in front of her, the two of them hanging almost upright in the rock recess; moving their tails gently to hold position.

'Sky, you are doing well in your studies.'

'Thank you Prime Mother, I try. I enjoy most of the lessons.'

'Your teachers tell me you have great promise. This is your last year as a Novice; if all goes well you will soon qualify as an Initiate of the Way. But there are heavy responsibilities attached. We Ka-Tse have always expected the highest personal integrity of our Initiates: they should not merely be able to quote the Way. They should embody it.'

'I understand that, Prime Mother, and I want to do exactly that. I do believe in the importance of the Way— it's allowed us to live in harmony with nature for a million years after all. I *want* to try to embody its teachings.'

She nodded slowly, as though to herself. 'I believe that you do. But I have learned something today that will make others question your right to become an Initiate — will make them want to argue against it in fact.'

Sky stared at her in confusion. She continued, picking her words carefully.

'We have had a visitor. He came to seek help from the Healers, they did what they could and he has gone now.'

Sky nodded. It was Rain Ending of course, the lone dolphin that had approached their hunting party.

Silent Waters watched him intently as she continued. 'Sky, you always told us that the rest of your clan died that day on the beach.'

Sky felt as though his heart had stopped.

'Yes...they did...I was sure they had.'

'This visitor told us he was from your old clan. And he was not the only one to escape. He said that a few others survived too.'

'What happened to them?'

'He said they went separate ways, too few to make a clan. But he knew that a couple of them had been angry at what happened — were in despair. He had heard that they turned to those abominations that we do not even speak of. They joined the Guardians.'

Sky suddenly felt very cold. 'Why are you telling me this, Prime Mother?'

She looked up towards the surface for a moment and closed her eyes, then looked directly back at Sky, her eyes piercing. As if trying to read his thoughts; see inside his mind; find the truth.

'He said that one of them was your father, Sky.'

CHAPTER 5

"I love you for what you are
Though your heart bears scars
From life's harsh tempests
I would not wish it unblemished
Each wound carved your strength
Suffering gave you wisdom
These flaws make you perfect"
- From the Arcturus Love Sonnets

Fades Into Dusk made her way through the bustle of the clan towards the eastern end of the bay. She kept to the edge of the groups of dolphins who were variously talking, telling stories to the young or preparing for a night hunt. As she reached the coral headland at the edge of the bay she waited, pretending to search among the sand patches for hidden fish as the perimeter patrol went by. Once she judged it was clear, she slipped around the headland and set off parallel to the coast, relaxing as she distanced herself from the clan. The sun was dropping below the low dunes on the land, a great red disc. The few strands of cirrus cloud were turning a deep purple and the sea was darkening. Once she was sure she had slipped away unseen she began to sing to herself as she swam and occasionally leapt from the water, sometimes spinning quickly in mid-flight as she loved to do.

She kept swimming for hours, while the water gradually turned first to velvet black then slowly lightened again as the bright white moon rose; almost a complete disc. Soon she did not even need to use her echolocation to navigate and used only occasional bursts of sound to look ahead. Eventually, after several hours swimming she reached the steep sandy shelf with the familiar, distinctive rocky arch protruding from it. The moon was almost at its zenith so she was just on time. She could feel her pulse quickening. Because she was excited to be here? Or because it was wrong? She made her signature call: 'It is I, Fades Into Dusk!'

There was no answer.

Storm Before Darkness was not here yet. Or not coming? He had missed two of their meetings before and had always had excuses about emergencies that had come up that needed his attention. Rationally, she knew that it was likely that there would be such demands on his time given his responsibilities, but both times she had dreaded that it must mean he was tired of her and was bored with meeting her. He seemed so different from all the males in her clan. He was obviously admired by his followers, and he had such clarity of vision. There was no vagueness about him, he knew exactly what he wanted to achieve in the world. She found that very attractive. She also found *what* he wanted to achieve rather frightening, but that was exciting in a way too.

Everything she had learned at the clan told her that what Storm Before Darkness and these others said was wrong, and when she was listening to Cloud Passing or Silent Waters speaking she was almost convinced again that it *was* wrong. But when Storm spoke and became impassioned she was swept along by the precision and ruthlessness of his arguments. When she heard him she doubted the Way; doubted it could help them any more.

She called out again, 'It is I, Fades Into Dusk!'

Silence.

She remembered when she had first met him. She was with two other females from the clan on their way back from a hunting trip. They heard the voices of some other dolphins calling to one another. They were Ka-Tse like those of the clan, but they spoke with an odd dialect, it sounded harsher and more purposeful than the speech she was used to. Her friends were nervous and wanted to leave before the strangers became aware of them. But she was curious and in spite of their protestations she insisted on holding back when they left. She had then silently approached the sound of the strange voices and drew closer. At the edge of visibility she could see it was four dolphins; males from their voices, in a circle on the sand, their heads low.

She could make out some of their words and it was clear that one of them, an exceptionally large, dark skinned dolphin with a pale scar over his right eye, was their leader. He looked and sounded authoritative and he spoke with the ease of a natural and unquestioned leader. She had encountered dolphins with an aura of power before, but they had all been elders of the clan, and it arose from the respect accorded the wise. This one spoke of action, and the power was also a physical one. She was strangely attracted and disturbed in equal measure.

She had been about to leave when he had become aware of her. She saw his eyes lock onto hers and it had felt like she had been struck a blow. She had started to swim off but he called to her to wait. It sounded like a command, and she had stopped dead without making a conscious choice to do so.

He had left his companions and swam over to her. Once he had established she was alone, he had wanted to know what she had heard. He must have soon realised that she had really heard nothing of consequence. Their conversation had been one sided, almost an interrogation, but he seemed to soften when she answered more of his questions about herself. He seemed interested in the movements of her clan and genuinely fascinated to learn that she was in training as a Starwriter. She was flattered by his attention and so, at his suggestion, accompanied him on a swim over the shallow sand; their course following the lines of the ripples. She was intensely curious, as it soon became clear to her that he was a leader of a clan, even though he could only be a few years older than she was. She had not heard of such a young male taking that role and was quietly impressed. She was also impressed by the way he spoke and his sure, precise movements. He radiated strength. When they separated and he suggested they meet again she agreed. At that point she knew little about him, but soon they were secretly meeting regularly. She was probably already more than half in love by the time she found out what his clan called themselves. That had been a shocking day for her and she had tried to stay away from him for a while, but the lure was too great, and in any case, she reassured herself, their relationship had never gone further than close companions. She had explained that such a thing was impossible now, and he seemed to understand that. But he knew her circumstances would be different soon and he had been quite clear that he had expectations for that day. She did not know what she would do then.

Where was he? She called again: 'It is I, Fades Into Dusk!'

A long pause.

Then, faintly, a voice from the night: 'And it is I, Storm Before Darkness!'

CHAPTER 6

"The child will have long to think on the mistake that the parent made with so little thought."
- *Carried Westward (12,214 – 12,242 post Great Alluvion)*

A large swell rolled towards the shore, born in the deep open sea, a vestige of a far distant storm. Above the deep waters the great liquid monsters lifted and fell benignly, sleep swimming ponderously towards the land. After their long journey, the sudden resistance of the small coral reef woke them with a shock; they reared up in outrage and crashed down in white violence.

Lying on the sandy bottom on the inshore side of the reef, Sky watched the huge breakers crash down at the surface above him, driving great billows of white into the clear water. He had lain there a long time; watching, thinking.

'It is I, Deneb Rising!'

'And I, Wakes Softly!'

Deneb's dark form appeared in front of Sky, his serious face showing concern. Wakes hung back at a short distance to give them a chance to speak privately.

'We've been looking for you little brother,' Deneb said gently. 'You've been gone a long time.'

'I needed some time to think. It's been such a shock.'

'Of course it has. Come on, swim with us, I can hardly hear you with all this noise. Let's go down where it's quieter.'

Sky slowly followed Deneb and Wakes into the calm of deeper water, reluctant to leave the clamour of the waves; the comforting caress of the swell.

'Whatever everyone else thinks Sky, nothing has changed for me. I will still treat you like a brother and I'm sure my mother will still treat you like her son. You're still the same zeta.'

'Maybe I'm not though. I've gone through my life thinking my family was dead, now it seems my father may still be alive. And a Guardian! If half of what is said about them is true they're bad enough. They say they condone killing other zetii sometimes and that they follow a perverse form of the Way; saying it was only really meant for us Ka-Tse or something like that — that the other kinds of zetii are inferior.'

Wakes shook her head. 'Even if that's all true, it doesn't matter. *You're* not a Guardian.'

'The rest of the clan won't be as reasonable as you though — after all my father might be! Deneb, I have to know, I want to ask him what would make him do such a thing!'

'Well, you can't! You know the penalty for any kind of contact with them. You'd be crazy to risk everything now when you are almost at the end of your studies.'

'Alright, alright, I know that makes sense, but I really need to know more somehow...'

At that point Sky trailed off. Ahead of them were five adult males from the clan. Sky made his signature call:

'It is I, Touches The Sky!'

Before Deneb or Wakes could add theirs, and without any proper reply to Sky's call, the largest of the males said, 'Don't you mean "It is I, Son of a Guardian!"'

Sky recognised him as Last To Speak. One of his daughters was Bellatrix Unseen, who Sky had seen at the wreck and who sometimes attended the classes that he helped to teach at the Academy.

Deneb advanced towards the older, larger dolphin; deliberately placing himself between Sky and him. 'How dare you speak like that! There's no proof of this. And even if it is true it's not Sky's fault.'

Last To Speak snorted. 'Don't come on high and mighty with me, boy. Just because you're the Prime Mother's son doesn't give you any authority over us.' His companions circled around them, watching the exchange without comment but clearly following it with interest. Sky was shocked by the animosity but felt he had to defend himself. He moved closer.

'Who told you this story?'

'Everybody knows it now. And maybe you haven't done anything wrong yet, but I think it's just a matter of time. Like they say, "no stronger current than the father's blood in the child's veins". I think the Council should get rid of you now before you do any harm.'

Deneb replied before Sky could, his voice cold but angry. 'Fortunately the Council are able to make their decisions based on facts, not emotions. That's why zetii like you aren't on it! Come on Sky, let's go.'

They left the group of males behind them, Last To Speak's voice just reaching them as they moved swiftly towards the headland: 'We'll be watching you, Guardian's son! The first sign of you turning bad and we'll drive you out of this clan in a tailbeat!'

The three friends swam around the headland into the clan's bay. The western end of the bay was quite calm, but the breakers boomed against the other side of the protecting headland, sending fountains of fine spray to hang briefly in the bright, tropical sunlight.

Deneb slowed the pace at last and turned to Sky. 'Don't pay too much attention to them.'

'No you mustn't Sky,' Wakes agreed, 'I'm sure most of the clan won't think that way. It was good that you two stood up to those idiots. Deneb, you really put him in his place.'

Deneb gave her a small smile but turned back to Sky, serious as usual. 'Sky there's something else too isn't there? I talked to Muddy today.'

Sky had been wondering what to do about Sand and his story, after all he had promised him not to tell anyone that he had spoken to him. But now he told Deneb and Wakes what had happened. 'Don't tell anyone else yet though, please,' he finished, 'I need to find out more first.'

Deneb inclined his head in agreement. 'Very well. Let's go and see mother though. Wakes, why don't we meet you again after we've seen her.'

They found Silent Water in the shallows, laying on the sand; meditating.

They waited a short while nearby. She must have become aware of them as they could tell that she was slowly raising herself up through the levels of consciousness, making small movements, then slowly opening her eyes. Without apparent effort, she drifted to the surface, took a brief breath, then settled back to the seabed. 'You look troubled. Has it begun?'

Deneb glanced meaningfully at Sky, who spoke first. 'Has what begun Prime Mother?'

'Prejudice and bullying from the foolish. It is inevitable I am afraid. No need to answer; I see that it has.'

Sky nodded, his eyes downcast. She continued. 'There are some in every clan that can think for themselves, make their own judgements, accept and embrace change. Then there are others whose horizons are close by, who find a false courage in unthinking conformity.'

'What should I do?'

'Probably best to do nothing. If they see that you are hurt, it makes their sport all the more rewarding. Remember that their opinions are of no real value. Seek out the company of those with open minds. In time you will see they are the ones that really matter and are truly respected by the wise and the good.'

'And my father — what about him being a Guardian? What will happen to me now?'

'I hope that there is no need for anything to change. I have spoken with the Council and we have agreed that whatever your father may have done, you have committed no fault. But Sky, do be careful. There will be many who are suspicious of you now, who will look for any hint of an error. I cannot protect you if they find one.'

'Prime Mother, I really need to know more about my father.'

She drifted up again to breathe; sank back again thoughtfully. 'I can understand that. But if he is alive and has become a Guardian, you must not try to meet him. You know that any kind of deliberate contact with them will result in exile.'

'Could I at least try to find the zeta who brought the news about my father? Perhaps he could tell me more about what happened that day on the beach — to explain why.'

She paused for a while, considering. 'I do not like this at all, Sky. There will be many zetii who will be very suspicious of you now, looking for reasons to expel you from this clan. Do you understand?'

Sky nodded. 'Yes, but I really have to know more — to find out where I've come from.'

She looked at him for a long time, her eyes full of compassion. 'Very well, when your studies permit you can try and find him, but do not spend too long searching, he may be anywhere by now. And you are not to go alone. Now go and try to forget about this for the moment.'

They left and made their way back to where they had left Wakes Softly. She was playing with a pufferfish, teasing it as it swam in irritated circles around a boulder. She looked up with shining eyes as Deneb approached.

'Did she have anything to say about it?'

'She'd anticipated something like this happening and warned Sky to be careful. But she's given him permission to find out more about his father.'

The three of them began a gentle cruise along the shoreline, swimming close together as they talked. Wakes looked at Sky in concern. 'Sky please do be careful! You know how impetuous you can be sometimes. I hate all this — why is everyone behaving so oddly lately?'

Sky glanced at Deneb questioningly who tilted his head as a shrug. 'Who else is behaving oddly, Wakes?'

'Well…those bullies attacking you, what happened to Born, the Walkers killing those Cleaners in that awful way, and then the night I saw…' She trailed off her eyes frowning.

'Saw what?'

'I'm not sure exactly, which is why I hadn't meant to say anything until I had a chance to try and check things properly.'

'Come on, Wakes,' Deneb prompted her. 'You've got us curious now; you'll have to say more.'

She smiled at him. 'Well, I'll tell you *what* I think I saw, but I don't think I should say *who* I thought I saw. A couple of days ago, I was looking for Dusk. It was getting dark when I saw her; she was with some of the other trainee Starwriters and they were practising or something. They were in the shallows in a kind of rocky depression, so that they could see the stars without being disturbed by the waves. When I got there they had already dropped into that trance they go into and the Dreamweaver had started to chant the stuff they had to memorise; old historical stuff, I think. Of course, I didn't want to disturb them, so I was about to leave, when I noticed an older zeta watching them from behind the rock.'

Sky interrupted her. 'Do you mean this zeta was close enough to hear what they were saying?'

'I am pretty sure he would have been. In fact it looked like that was what he was trying to do.'

'But they're not allowed to do that,' said Deneb 'Who was it?'

She looked at him apologetically. 'I'm not certain. It was too dark. But I think that it was a zeta from the Council.'

'A Councillor! Who?'

'I don't think I should say, as I'm half guessing really.'

'What happened then?'

'I was curious, and so I watched for some time from the edge of visibility, but from where I couldn't hear the Starwriters. Eventually, he left; very carefully and quietly, as though he didn't want to be seen. I followed him. Maybe I shouldn't have, but it seemed so strange. He swam east from the clan a long way and eventually he stopped by a rocky outcrop. Soon another zeta came. A big, younger male. They talked, but I couldn't hear what they were saying — they kept their voices low.'

'So did you see where this other zeta went?'

'No. At one point they stopped talking and looked around — looked in my direction! I was terrified that they may have seen me as the moon was coming up so I came back to the clan as fast as I could.'

Sky looked at her seriously. 'Wakes, that *is* really strange. Tell us who you think it was.'

'I don't like to, as I'm not certain. And you know what the Way says: "Let the accused hear the accusation first."'

Deneb moved closer to her. 'It was brave of you to do what you did. And you're right not to want to spread rumours if you're not sure. But something is very wrong here. Promise me that you will tell Cloud Passing when we see him next for lessons.'

She smiled back at Deneb gratefully. 'That's a good idea. I'll talk to him. He'll know what I should do.'

Sky saw how closely the two of them were swimming. He noticed that Wakes had brushed her pectoral fin gently against Deneb's side at least twice now, as though by accident. Sky smiled to himself and decided he should leave them alone. 'I'm supposed to meet with Cloud Passing myself now. I'll see you two later. Hopefully we can find out what this little mystery is all about soon.' He left them to their swim and headed back towards the clan. He wondered if they had even noticed him leave.

CHAPTER 7

"Fear not endings
Without beginning and end
Nothing can be whole."
- Unseen Crystal (12,001 - 12,026 post Great Alluvion)

As Sky made his way across the shallows through the waking bustle of the clan, one of the new family groups passed him, swimming slowly together in synchronisation, often gliding between their short excursions to take breaths at the surface. One of the resident clan females swam with them. Sky overheard her discussion with the senior female of the visitors.

'…and did you come across any others?'

'Only once; a group of young males. We were afraid they might cause trouble so we moved on quickly, and they didn't bother us. We also passed a large clan of Xenthos who were heading east, far beyond our range.'

'Did they tell you why?'

'We tried to speak to them but you know how odd their speech is. I think it was due to a lack of hunting, but that always seems to be the reason these days. Anyway they're a strange sort so who knows?'

'Strange indeed. And of course, they say that they're stealing our share of the quotas.'

The visitor shook her head. 'I don't know about that. But we certainly saw the lack of hunting. It seems there are just no fish left in Ocean some days. I think the Walkers are to blame, not the Xenthos. You know how they are taking everything with their hunting machines.'

'Well, no doubt the Grand Council will be talking about these things soon enough. And what brings you back to us now?'

'It was mainly for the young ones. They need better education than we can give, so we'll probably stay at least until the second equinox. My youngest wants to become a Starwriter! I've tried to tell her the amount of study that will mean but she is too young to understand yet. At least she has an ambition! So, we'll be here for some time, and we wanted to get here for the Gathering in any case.'

'Oh yes, it would be a shame to miss a Gathering. There are so many things planned for it! You must get your young ones involved in some of the recitals. Let me find you someone from the Academy who can help you…'

Hearing this, Sky veered off to one side abruptly before the speaker might turn and see him. He swam as quickly as he could without, he hoped, appearing to be escaping. He reassured himself that he really did have to go to his meeting and that he had no time to listen to what was likely to be a long explanation of the merits of the children and a listing of their many artistic talents. He made his way to the appointed end of the bay and looked for Cloud Passing.

He found him slowly gliding in the shallows with his misty eyes half closed, apparently deep in thought. Sky watched him from a respectful distance for a while, and marvelled at the way he spent so long submerged between breaths, easily exceeding the six or seven minutes that was the limit for most dolphins. His slight body was covered in small scars like many of the older dolphins, but Sky noticed that he seemed to be acting noticeably time-worn of late. When he did swim to the surface for air, it seemed as though the movements pained him and his breathing seemed laboured. It hurt Sky greatly to see him like this. Cloud Passing had been his teacher and mentor for many years and he had more respect for him than any other dolphin. He hoped that one day he might reach the level of oneness with Ocean that the old dolphin had clearly attained. Sky knew that the old dolphin would have been deeply hurt by the death of Born Into Summer too. She had been a favourite student of his, and had spent much of her free time acting as an assistant to him. Sky drew closer. 'Greetings, Cloud Passing-Jeii.'

The old dolphin opened his eyes fully and turned slowly to peer at him.

'Greetings, young Sky,' he said affectionately. 'I see you got my message.'

'Yes, Jeii, but am I disturbing you now?'

'No, not at all.' He looked thoughtfully at Sky, his misty eyes kindly. 'Silent Water tells me that you have had some strange news.'

'Yes, Jeii.'

'How do you feel about it?'

'I feel...confused. I hate the thought that my father might be a Guardian, but if I even have a father still...'

Cloud Passing nodded. 'Of course. Most zetii of your age take parents for granted. But if you have never known a parent, it is inevitable that you must wonder what they were like.'

'Exactly. If he is alive I would like to know more about him, even if it's only to find out I don't even like him; I just want to know.'

'Have you spoken to Silent Water about this?'

'Yes, today. She said I can try to find the zeta that told our hunting party about him, when my studies allow it.'

'Alone?'

'No, she said I should not go alone.'

'Very wise of her — as always. Sky, you must be careful. I sense there are some events on your near horizon that will be hard for you to cope with. You will need to rely on your training and instincts to deal with them. Let me see...yes, you can take a few days for this, but you must return by first dawn after the new moon. And you can take one of the other novices with you.'

'Thank you Jeii, I'll take Muddy River Mouth if he'll come.'

'I am quite sure he will, you are all such a close group. Which reminds me, I have been meaning to tell you: I have enjoyed teaching you and your four friends immensely. I think you have been probably the brightest group of Novices I have had the pleasure to work with for a long time. I shall miss our lessons.'

'You must know that we look forward to your lessons the most, Jeii. Anyway, we have a few more moons of lessons still to go, and then you'll have a new group of Novices to test your endless patience next year.'

The old dolphin looked wistfully at Sky, a faint smile in his cloudy eyes. 'No, I am afraid that I won't be leading any classes next year.'

'But why not, Jeii? Are you sick?'

'I am not at my best. But you know that; I am sure you all must have been aware for some time that I have been unwell, it is an unfortunate side effect of getting old.' He slowed as he came alongside a large isolated boulder and paused to peer at a small, red, hermit crab that was laboriously picking its way through the low algae towards the top. He seemed deep in thought for a while, then seemed to come to a decision. He turned to Sky and said gently, 'Sky, you were always one of my best and most favourite pupils. Let me share something with you. You will be one of only a few I have mentioned this to. It is not a secret; I am just not in a hurry to tell everyone just yet.'

Sky nodded without a word, wondering what he was about to hear. He had not seen his teacher quite like this before, and he felt a cold shiver of anticipation that something bad was coming.

Cloud Passing looked once more at the small crab which had almost reached the summit of its boulder. The crab became aware that it was being watched and stopped its climb. Its unwinking black eyes stared expressionlessly at the old dolphin for a moment. It seemed to sense he was no threat and began its climb again, only to stop, as it discovered a discarded shell. The shell was somewhat larger than the one it currently inhabited and the crab examined it carefully, reaching inside with its claws.

'It looks like he is growing out of his current home', observed Cloud Passing. 'Time to move on to something better.'

'Jeii, you were going to tell me something.'

'So I was. Sky, I have been thinking a lot lately. It has been a long time since I made a deep dive down to the dark waters. I think I should like to make one more.'

'Jeii, you don't mean...'

'Hush a moment Sky. I had thought of arranging this in a moon or so when this whole Gathering business is over with. But I discussed it with Silent Waters, and she seems to think it would be appropriate to incorporate it into the celebrations. I am very flattered of course, and do not wish to appear pretentious...'

Sky could not stay quiet any longer. 'Jeii, no!'

'Touches The Sky! I am surprised at you', Cloud Passing said in mock reproof. 'As a scholar of the Way you know that it is every zeta's right...'

'Yes, of course I know Jeii, but...'

'There cannot be any buts. However, I do have a problem.' He looked hard at Sky for a long time, as though he was searching for the right way to put something. 'I had thought that I had all my duties properly discharged in preparation for this. But, now things have changed.'

Sky waited; confused.

Cloud Passing continued, apparently choosing his words carefully. 'You have learned a great deal about the Way, and are a good student.'

'Thank you, but I still have so much to learn, Jeii.'

'Hmm. So tell me, how would you like to change the Way?'

'Change it? But...that's an impossible question, Jeii. It can't be changed...

it's the immutable teachings of the ancients.'

'Did I ever tell you it was "immutable"?'

'Well, no, I don't think so, but everybody knows...'

'Everybody likes to think that, of course. But Ocean changes over time, and the Way needs to adapt to those changes sometimes.'

Sky was confused by this idea. He had always believed that the Way was a perfect set of truths; an unwavering code for behaviour. If the zetii followed it, all would be well. And now Cloud Passing, of all zetii, seemed to be implying it could be changed! 'But, Jeii, who decides if it should be changed? The Council?'

'No. They deal with more pragmatic matters. There are others who have been entrusted with this task, entrusted since our histories began, since the Way was first codified.'

'How are these zetii chosen?'

'They are not only zetii, Sky. Some are of the Great Wanderers, for example.'

Now Sky was really confused. He knew that there was some level of communication between some of the dolphin species and whales, but he had thought it was at best very basic. Now, Cloud Passing was saying that the Great Wanderers were involved in changing the Way! 'Why are you telling me this, Jeii?'

'The ones given this task are known as the Aligners of the Way, or more often just the Aligners. There is normally at most one member in each of the larger clans of zetii. It so happens that I am an Aligner.'

Sky looked at his teacher with a new respect. 'I have never heard of them, Jeii.'

'No, you would not. Very few know of their existence, even less of their identities. In this clan, just a few of the Council members know that I hold this honour. But I have a problem. It is the duty of each Aligner to arrange for an apprentice who may take over their duties when they are gone. I had someone that I was very confident of, and spent much time preparing her for the role. But now she is dead.'

'Born Into Summer?'

'Yes, exactly. I had high hopes for her. And it is a tragedy that she should have died. Because she was a wonderful zeta of course, but also because she was to take my work forward now that I must go. And it is a great blow to me that she died so suddenly and at such a vital time. But now I need to find someone else. And that someone must take on the obligation with little help from me as I do not have much time. I am quite unwell you see, Sky.' The old dolphin quietly waited expectantly.

Sky hardly knew what to say. 'Jeii, are you asking me?'

'Yes, Sky. I have chosen you. It is a heavy thing to bear at the best of times, but it will be far worse for you I am afraid. I am not going to be able to help you much, and I fear that Born's death was no coincidence. She may have been killed because of what she was about to become. If that is true, then you are also at risk. Therefore you must tell no one of this. And I will tell only those that absolutely must know. I know what you are thinking, Sky. You are not worthy, there must be others in the clan, and so on. It is what I would expect you to say. But you will have to trust my judgment more. And I believe you are the best one to take on this task. Please accept it.'

Feeling he was diving into a dark pool of unknown depth, Sky tried to keep his voice steady as he replied, 'Very well, Jeii. Thank you for honouring me so.'

'Good. Oh, and one other thing. When the day comes for my Darkening Dive, I was hoping that I might ask something of you.'

'Anything Jeii, you don't have to ask.'

'Well, you have always had a fine singing voice Sky. I wondered if you might sing me a particular song that day.'

Sky smiled sadly at him. 'Of course, Jeii. I shall sing it with all my heart.'

CHAPTER 8

"Feed them hard truths as you would feed them
a sour meal — in small bites"

- The 'Seer' Stone Eyes (13,222 -13,264 post Great Alluvium)

She was alone again in the warm tropical night, gliding through a velvet sea to her forbidden lover. The swell lazily lifted and fell about her, casually tossing breakers onto the nearby shore. Dusk could hear each one drawing itself up — like, she imagined, some huge eel: dragging a mouthful of coral fragments, shells and sand into its jaws before idly lunging forward and spewing it back onto the steep shelf of the beach.

Although the full moon would come up later, for now it was very dark; yet the starlight alone was enough to allow her to clearly make out the white beach whenever she leapt from the water. She leapt often that night. She leapt for the sheer joy of it. She leapt to see the stream of bright phosphorescence she created as she fell back into the welcoming water. She leapt to admire the beauty of the night sky.

Dusk took a special pleasure in looking at the sky. Of course, like all dolphins she used the stars as her calendar, clock and compass; but she had studied them in much greater detail than most during her apprenticeship as a Starwriter. She enjoyed being able to name almost every point of light she saw. On this perfectly clear night, the most distant white cloudy belt of stars stretched in a band from one horizon to the other, marking the edge of the galaxy in which Ocean floated. Dusk even made out one of the "New Stars" — strange, tiny points of lights moving swiftly across the sky. They were not stars at all of course, but their origin was mysterious. The Starwriters' meticulously kept records showed that they were a recent phenomenon: only in the last fifty years or so had they started to appear. There were various theories about them, including some that Dusk considered far fetched, like that they contained visitors from the stars who orbited Ocean in great shining, water filled orbs. She thought that the more likely explanation was that they were connected somehow to the Walkers, but what their purpose might be no one knew.

She arrived at the rock arch where they usually met. She was just on time, with the upper edge of the moon beginning to appear above the sea surface. Soon the whole disc was up, painted a dirty orange colour by the sand and dust blown from the land. She made her signature call: 'It is I, Fades Into Dusk!'

Silence. She hated it when she was here alone, calling into the night; not knowing what the silence meant. She always tortured herself with possibilities.

He was not coming.

He did not even remember — she was so unimportant to him.

He was with someone else.

He was dead.

He wanted to end it.

She tried to imagine how she would act to each scenario if it was true. She tried to work out which one was worse.

She watched the moon rise by the height of its own diameter nine times. As she counted each one she called again. The oppressive silence of the replies was louder each time. At the tenth diameter she gave up and started swimming slowly towards the area where Storm Before Darkness' clan usually spent the night. That was how she named them to herself. Storm Before Darkness' clan. His clan. She shook her head. That was not what they called themselves. She was just trying to trick herself with words, not naming the thing of her fears, like she had done as a child. It was like the time she and her two best friends had resolved never to say the names of the great black and white pack hunters. The older children would try to frighten them with stories, but the three of them had agreed that if they never said the monsters' names out loud, they would be safe from them.

Now she was making the same pretence with Storm and his clan. And she wasn't a child anymore. So she would just have to face facts and call them what they were: the Guardians. She was meeting and talking to

Guardians, directly against the clear orders of the Grand Council. Punishment: exile.

But at least, she told herself, she was not *swimming* with the Guardians — not a member of their clan. Storm had tried to persuade her, but she resisted. Claimed that she must finish her studies. He did not argue too fiercely against this — he seemed to be encouraging her to finish her Starwriter training in particular, and she appreciated his understanding. He was thoughtful that way.

Now there were voices in the water ahead. She moved up into the shallows and could see clearly now where the moonlight reflected from the white sandy patches. She disturbed a little foraging reef shark which moved quickly aside, concerned that it might become a meal itself.

She could make out a number of dolphins still on the bottom— one here and there occasionally rising slowly to breathe — all of them clearly asleep. She stopped using her sonar to avoid disturbing them. A little further was the source of the voices: seven young adult males had just returned from a night hunt and were talking in low tones about it. She was about to swim past when one broke away and approached her.

'Hey, beautiful, where's your manners? Aren't you going to announce yourself?'

Her first reaction was to try to avoid this obviously flirtatious approach but then thought that if Storm could not be bothered to turn up to their meetings he could hardly complain if she spent time with other males.

'It is I, Fades Into Dusk!' She knew that protocol demanded she should have properly added "Of the Dune Coast Clan", as she was greeting a member of another clan, but then she felt almost a member of this clan. Almost, but not quite.

'And it is I, Catches In Air! And you can call me Catches. Why haven't I met you before?' He swam next to her, trying to gently direct her course away from his friends who trailed idly behind them.

'I like to spend time alone sometimes. And I'm new here. And enjoying a swim by myself, thanks.'

'Pretty name for a pretty girl. Did you change it when you arrived?'

Dusk shook her head. It was common for many of the Guardians to choose a new name when they joined — "everything changes when you become a Guardian" they said.

He carried on, 'There seem to be lots of new clan members recently. At last all these zetii are coming to their senses.'

'They hope to start a new life here I suppose.'

'They realise there's no other choice! They're tired of the indecision of those ancients that ran their old clans. Not only that, they're starting to realise that their precious Way is dead.'

She glanced at him sharply, unsure if he actually meant that or if he was just being provocative to show off.

'Is it dead then?'

'Well, the version that most zetii grew up with is. All that stuff about living in harmony with the environment, the Ka-Tse keeping their proper place, self sacrifice for the good of Ocean — all that. Of course the Guardians still have the Way, but it is the new Way, with the Ka-Tse in their *real* proper place; as the dominant species in Ocean. Now, why don't I take you for a swim along the shore just over here?' He started to press against her side to try and guide her away from the clan.

She snapped her jaws at him in exasperation. 'I said no! Tell me more about these other zetii instead — those not Ka-Tse. What happens to them now then?'

Catches gave up trying to redirect her physically, but stayed close to her side as he continued sulkily. 'The Seer told us the Way was never meant for them. They're smaller than us, weaker than us — and stupid mostly. They need to keep in their own corners of Ocean and stay out of our ranges.'

'I see. And what if they don't want to?'

'Drive them out of course. If we have to. We can do it.'

'Just the Guardians? There are so many of the others.'

'Of course! But when all the Ka-Tse join together against them we can. Can't we stop talking about this stuff and just go for a little swim? I know this lovely little bay near here...'

Dusk shook her head. Inside she was shocked at this youth's aggressive beliefs. Surely he was just boasting and did not really believe this nonsense?

'It's hardly likely that the Ka-Tse are suddenly all going to join together against the other zetii though, is it?'

'Oh yes, it is. And not far off. Kark Du has it all planned. He said that...'

He suddenly cut off as one of his friends bumped him hard from the side. Catches turned to him in anger but the friend whispered something urgently to him. He turned back to face her, wide eyed, suddenly quiet. She prompted him: 'You were about to tell me what Kark Du said?'

The friend answered instead. 'Greetings, Fades Into Dusk. If you're looking for Kark Du Storm Before Darkness, I know that he was called away urgently to meet a messenger. He may not be back till dawn.'

'I see. Thank you, that's helpful.'

He dipped his head slightly and led the still stupefied Catches In Air away.

Dusk paused for a moment, then decided she had better leave. She turned and made off away from the Guardians, towards her own clan. She thought about the strange conversation with the youth Catches. It had been different from any she had had with a Guardian before, they always seemed a little careful of what they said. Catches had said disturbing things. She was sure he must have just been showing off. Storm had made some harsh statements about what needed to be done, but always justified them with the crisis that forced them. He was fond of quoting: "Hunger makes the bitter fish sweet". He had never said anything to her about dominating the other zetii. Yes, that must be it. Catches was just a typical young male, showing off to impress her for the usual reason that young males showed off. All that stuff about driving out the other zetii — he must be exaggerating.

CHAPTER 9

"Anger sullies the pure heart."
- Forgotten Thunder (8,111 - 8,159 post Great Alluvion)

A fresh south easterly had been building the sea swell, and large, rolling breakers crashed against the lonely beach. Sky and Muddy raced along the rearing edge of the breakers; enjoying the fleeting novelty of a vertical wall of water beside them. Just before each wave broke, they could clearly see out from the face of it and make out the tall palms on the shoreline that were being buffeted by the gusty wind. The dolphins darted through the mayhem of the surf zone; only their finely tuned reflexes and sheer power stopping them from being thrown bodily onto the beach.

Muddy was the first to tire. 'Come on Sky, let's go deeper now. That was great but exhausting. I need something to eat, we've been swimming since dawn.'

Sky followed Muddy reluctantly into the calmer depths and they searched for food as they continued their swim eastwards parallel to the shore. Sky begrudged any delay; he badly wanted to find Rain Ending, and was acutely aware that he had only a limited amount of time in which to do so. All they had to go on was that he had mentioned to one of the clan's Healers that he tended to stay around a large isolated coral reef near the coast in this direction. Sky knew that they might well not find him at all, and the delay while Muddy looked for food chafed at him.

Eventually they located enough small bottom dwelling fish to meet Muddy's immediate needs, and Sky was able to persuade his grumbling companion to resume their fast pace eastwards.

It was almost dark when they reached a large area of coral rising from the sandy seabed a little off the shore.

'This fits the description,' Sky said. 'Now, will he be here?'

'Well, I hope you're not expecting to start looking for him now. I'm exhausted after that swim. Let's just see if there are any titbits to be had and then get some sleep. We'll search in the morning.'

'Muddy, I've only got two days to find him in! You sleep if you have to, I'm going to start going around the reef. I'll wake you at midnight and you can help me.'

Muddy complained bitterly at the thought of so little sleep but eventually agreed. Sky left him and followed the edge of the reef around until within a couple of hours, he was back to where he had begun, having seen or heard no sign of other dolphins. Muddy lay resting on the sand, occasionally half drifting, half swimming upwards to breathe without waking. Sky surfaced to look at the night sky: it was still not midnight, so he snatched a little sleep himself.

A while later, Sky woke from a troubled dream. He had been confronting his father, a dimly seen, unclear figure, who had been angry with him for some reason. Sky had the feeling that his father had left because of him; something he had done wrong; and he had wanted to make amends somehow. But his father wouldn't speak to him or answer his questions. At last his father said in a strange voice: "It's out of alignment with the new Ocean. Out of alignment. That's why they're all dead. Out of alignment." He was still repeating that as Sky rose from the strange dream.

Sky woke Muddy and they searched the surface of the submerged reef for the remainder of the night, easily navigating in the darkness with their sonar. In the morning they searched the nearby coastline, but with no sign of the lone dolphin. That afternoon Sky suggested they try the deeper water out to sea from the reef, and so they crisscrossed the upper regions of the deep water far from the shore. It was there that they finally heard the distant but distinctive rapid clicks of another dolphin's sonar. They followed the sound and to Sky's great relief it was Rain Ending.

'It is I, Touches The Sky of the Dune Coast Clan!'

'And I, Muddy River Mouth of the same!'

'And I, Rain Ending!'

The older dolphin looked at the two friends suspiciously. 'Have you come all this way to find me? I suppose your curiosity is aroused young

Sky?'

'Yes it is. I was hoping you could tell me more about my family, my old clan.'

'A zeta does not choose this life because of his love of conversation. I am not a great one for explanations. In fact talking of any kind. I'd rather be on my way.' He nodded to them and then turned as if to go.

'Wait! That's hardly fair. You were ready enough to speak to other members of my clan about me! Do you know how much trouble you've caused me?'

The other paused, reflecting. 'Well, yes, that's probably true. It was not my intent, just the surprise at seeing another survivor…after so long.'

'You recognised my name?'

'Vaguely. But it was the missing tip of your fin that reminded me. I was nearby when you lost it.'

'Really? I never knew how it happened — it was before I can remember and there has been no one to ask.'

'Of course. It was a simple enough thing; as a little one you strayed too close to a big triggerfish nest. The owner gave you a good bite and a scare. Your mother was mortified I remember.'

'My mother? You knew her?'

'Yes, and your father. Come on then you two. Swim with me and I'll tell you what I remember.' He turned and started to swim again then suddenly jerked to a stop, his back arched and eyes full of pain. He twisted in torment and began to sink into the depths. Quickly, Sky put his head beneath him and, with Muddy's help, lifted him to the surface to breathe.

Rain Ending lay there panting for a short while then the spasm seemed to pass and he slowly relaxed. Soon he could move again. 'Excuse me. A problem I have with my spine. It comes more often these days, but usually passes quickly.'

'Is that why you wanted to see our Healers?' Muddy asked.

'Yes. They have suggested some changes to my diet and exercises that will alleviate the pain and help to reduce the severity of the attacks. No cure, unfortunately.'

When he was recovered enough they swam on together and Rain Ending seemed to try to answer Sky's questions as well as he could. He had known Sky's parents; not well, but thought them to be well liked zetii who fitted in with clan life. He had been amongst the clan the day they had heard the terrible sounds, and had found himself stranded on the beach like the others but close to Sky's father. They had been on a different part of the beach to most of the clan and although he had expected to die there, the waves there had eventually lifted him off, along with two other dolphins. One of them was Sky's father.

'Was my older brother one of them too?'

'Your brother? What is his name?'

'Still Bay. He was a couple of years older than me I think.'

'Then no. I didn't know who the other one was at the time; you have to understand we were very confused and couldn't hear properly for weeks, so we didn't talk then. But I heard the other's name later…when I heard where they had gone…I don't remember what it was but it wasn't Still Bay, I'm sure of that. I'm afraid your brother stayed on that beach with your mother.'

'And what did you hear about my father?'

'That he was heartbroken at losing all his family. Heartbroken and angry — very angry. He wanted to blame someone, anyone. He came across the Guardians. Their strange philosophy must have appealed to him somehow while he was in that state — gave him a way of rationalising things while he was desperate to find a reason for it all. Maybe it gave him a focus for his anger.'

'So it's true,' Sky murmured, half to himself, 'my father is a Guardian. I was dreading hearing you say that.'

'Well, it gets worse,' Rain Ending replied grimly. 'Last I heard he wasn't just a member of the Guardians. He was the leader.'

Chapter 10

"When no dawn is looked for
Comes the full weight of night
Ocean spares not a favour
If you've no strength to fight"
Last Pebble (5,155 - 5,189 post Great Alluvion)

Sky and Muddy followed at a distance behind Rain Ending as he swam out over the deep water of the open sea, looking for shoals of small fish to eat. Muddy shook his head vehemently. 'Knowing what you do know, don't even think about trying to find your father! You know what would happen. Any deliberate contact with the Guardians means exile. And don't think it wouldn't happen to you — there are zetii in the clan just looking for an excuse to blame you now.'

'But I need to know, Muddy! I've got to try and see him somehow!'

'No! You can't do that! Look, why don't you ask Rain to help you? He's had some kind of contact with the Guardians in the past, maybe he still knows how to reach them and can ask for you?'

'Alright, that's worth a try. But if he can't do it I will, and I don't care about what might happen.'

They caught up with the lone dolphin and put the idea to him. 'Yes, I do know where they used to be, but I'm not prepared to approach them again. They've got some strange, dangerous ideas. They have their own codes about not speaking to outsiders, and the penalties for doing so are harsh.'

'But I just want to know if my father is still there.'

'I don't care. I'm afraid, and I don't mind admitting it. I wouldn't put it past those Guardians to kill me if they thought I was a threat.'

Sky wondered if he was exaggerating. 'Kill another zeta? But that's against the most basic teachings of the Way! You can't be serious.'

'I am. They don't follow the Way as you and I know it. They have twisted it according to the teachings of Stone Eyes — he's long dead but they call him "the Seer". He said that the Way was only meant for Ka-Tse that follow his teachings. According to him all the other zetii are inferior and pretty much expendable if need be. Forget all the traditional stuff about zetii living in harmony with Ocean. They say that Ocean has changed and the Way has changed too. They're ruthless, and I've heard that sometimes they will kill other zetii.'

Sky remembered Born Into Summer, laying helpless on a burning beach; that deadly gull poised beside her.

Muddy broke in to the conversation. 'Can't you just try and find out if Sky's father is still with them, though? If you don't, I know that Sky is going to want to do it himself, and he's going to end up exiled or worse.'

'No, I've told you, there's…wait…something's coming.'

The other two listened, and soon could all hear it: a number of big creatures coming closer at speed. Sky sent short bursts of sonar in the direction of the sound. They all listened to the reflected echoes.

Sky articulated their thoughts. 'Fish. Big ones, at least forty. Moving fast. Coming this way.'

A few seconds later a shoal of yellowfin tuna appeared out of the blue. The powerful silvery fish were all large adults, the biggest almost as large as the dolphins themselves. They took station under the dolphins and followed their progress, the darker upper surfaces of their bodies making them harder to see from above, only the occasional flash of silver showing them clearly whenever one fleetingly turned to inspect some passing fragment in the water column.

Rain Ending looked relieved. 'Well, they can follow us if they want, but we don't know where the food is either.'

Sky and Muddy stayed with Rain Ending as he continued his swim over the depths, trying to persuade him to change his mind and help but he was adamant. The tuna kept their silent station below them, hoping the keen senses of the dolphins might lead them to food.

The two friends were about to give up and leave when a new sound grew in volume. The distinct thrumming sound of a boat's engine, and then the sound of a second, smaller but faster boat.

The dolphins leapt from the water to look. The larger boat had protruding structures at the back of it and something was trailing in the water behind it. As they watched, it stopped heading directly for them and turned as though to commence a curve around them. The smaller boat veered away to the opposite side of them, moving fast and bouncing from wave to wave, the roar of its engine like a gigantic, angry insect. It raced loudly occasionally as the boat bounced from the waves.

'What are they doing?' Rain Ending asked.

Sky was worried at first; the sounds of engines always reminded him of the awful time his clan had been driven onto the shore by the pulses of sound. But these were different machines, smaller than the giant monsters they had seen that day, and brightly coloured, not all grey as they had been. 'Maybe they saw us and have turned like that to avoid hitting us?'

Muddy shook his head. 'I don't like it. Why would they go with one on each side of us like this? And what's that stuff coming out of the back of the big one?'

'You're right, it's strange. Well we don't have to stay here and watch them, let's just go and leave them to it.'

The dolphins started to swim off in the direction the boats had come from. The larger one continued to circle around behind them. The smaller one abruptly turned around and shot ahead of the dolphins, its engine roaring. They could see the vivid white wake above them as it blasted in front of them. They instinctively turned away from it and swam faster, making frequent leaps to check where the boats were. The speed boat kept cutting across their path, confusing them. Below them, the tuna still followed them but were sharing the dolphins' growing agitation and darting about nervously.

The dolphins were turned back by the fast boat three more times while the large boat completed its great circle around them, then suddenly the small boat slowed to a halt.

'Come on,' Muddy called nervously, 'they seem to have given up — let's get out of here!'

They set off away from the boats, the tuna following them, but then Sky saw a line of small floating objects ahead of them in the water. 'Look out! There's something up in front of us!' The net appeared in front of them underwater suddenly, a great wall dropping out of sight to either side and below them.

'Go back the way we came!'

They turned and sped back towards where the boats were, veering off to one side of the larger one. It was busy lifting something back aboard. Moments later they were faced with another vast net wall. They turned and there it was again. Sky realised with horror that it was all around them: a continuous circle.

'It's shrinking!' Muddy cried. 'They're making it smaller!'

'Go down,' Rain Ending panted out, 'let's go under it!'

They dived down through a confused mass of tuna that were darting in terror in all directions. Twice, Sky was violently bumped by one as he swam downwards. Then he could see the net below him as well. He almost gave up, but then realised that it was moving, closing. 'This way! Maybe it's not closed yet!'

He led the other two in the direction that part of the net was moving. The sound of working machinery came clearly through the water as the heavy cable drew the base of the net shut. Then Sky could see clear water through the shrinking opening at the bottom of the net. 'Come on! We can still get out!' He darted through, Muddy close behind him. They turned to look at the enormous net above them, the tuna swirling within it in confusion.

'Where's Rain Ending?' Sky asked.

'He was just behind me — he must still be in that thing…'

'I'm going to get him.'

'Sky you can't — the Walkers will get you!' But Sky had shot back into the opening of the net calling Rain Ending's name. Inside, he was immediately confused. The visibility had dropped with the water full of bubbles, scales, and other debris. The mesh walls were getting closer, forcing the fish closed together and he had to fight his way past several panicked tuna as they shot out of the turbid water at him. Then his sonar picked out the subtly different reflection of the body of a dolphin amongst those of the giant tuna. There was Rain Ending, his body racked in a spasm. Sky rushed to the dolphin and began pushing him downwards to where he thought the opening should be. The other dolphin resisted weakly. 'No, leave me, save yourself; I can't move now.'

'Come on, you have to! This way!'

Sky pushed him ahead through the silver madness of the tuna. Soon the floor of the net was in front of them. He swam on but it seemed to go in all directions. The net was closed!

He was ready to give up, and desperate to breath, when he faintly heard Muddy's voice.

'Sky, where are you? Sky, quickly, it's about to close!'

With a final effort he pushed the other dolphin in the direction he thought Muddy's voice had come from, and then he could make out the bulk of his friend at the rapidly shrinking opening of the net. He pushed the weakly moving Rain Ending through the opening then forced himself through as the cable constricted the base around his body. For a moment his tail was caught in the net, then with a violent jerk he was free.

They watched from a distance at the surface as the tuna were dragged struggling onto the boat and flopped about in their death throes on the deck. Rain Ending's spasms had almost passed and he could support himself again at the surface unaided. 'You saved my life. And you nearly got yourself killed for me. Why?'

'I didn't have time to think about it. It just seemed the right thing to do.'

'I don't know how to thank you, Touches The Sky.'

Sky paused, then faced him. 'If you want to thank me, find out what has happened to my father. That's what I want to know more than anything.'

Rain Ending nodded slowly. 'I'll do my best, but it will take a while. Look for me at the Gathering. I'll find you there and tell you what I've learnt.'

'Thank you. This means a lot to me. But please be careful. Now we must go quickly, tomorrow is the new moon and I have to be back with my clan by dawn!'

Chapter 11

"Honour the teachers: shapers of our future."
- Second Rainbow (8,127 - 8,159 post Great Alluvion)

Dusk, Muddy and Sky met at the west end of the bay for their lesson. Deneb soon appeared, looking concerned. 'Do any of you know where Wakes is? I've been looking for her since yesterday postnoon and can't find her anywhere.'

None of them had seen her, so Sky tried to comfort Deneb. 'She may have just gone off for a night hunt with some friends and gone too far. Or maybe she forgot we have lessons today. She'll probably turn up soon.'

'That's not like her. She's always on time, you know that.'

'Yes, that's true, I guess. Well, if she's not here by the end of our lessons today, we'll all go and search for her, alright?'

Cloud Passing then appeared from seaward, and they greeted him deferentially. He paused a moment to be sure he had their full attention. 'You have a full day today. We will first attempt to further our understanding of the Way by continuing our discussion of the Right to Life and its principle exceptions. Then, you will be teaching some of the young ones until half-postnoon. And please remember that tomorrow morning Green Wave Falling will be guiding you all in the development of your breathing and heartbeat control exercises, so I suggest you get some practice today. Any questions?' He paused and looked at them quizzically, although it was obvious that he saw them only vaguely. Sky stole a glance at Muddy who was looking uncomfortable. He knew that Muddy hated the lessons with Green Wave Falling, their strictest teacher. And Muddy had never excelled at anything involving control.

Cloud Passing peered at them again. 'And where is Wakes Softly?'

'We don't know, Jeii. We're going to look for her later.'

'Hmm. Well, we had better begin. Now, where was I?'

'Cloud Passing-Jeii,' Sky ventured, 'a few days ago Dusk, Deneb, Muddy and I saw something strange, something…bad. Can we discuss it before we start your lesson today?'

'Well, I cannot see why not. "Accidental lessons are remembered best" as the saying goes.' He began to swim stiffly to the surface then momentarily froze, a look of pain in his eyes. Sky looked at him in concern but the old dolphin had himself under control again. He carried on up, took a breath and then dropped back to them gently, saying, 'Swim with me.'

They fell into formation with the elderly dolphin, pacing their movements to exactly mirror his. He led them parallel to the beach, moving slowly and often gliding with his body motionless. Occasionally they rose as one to take a breath at the surface, where their exhalations flashed silver in the clear morning air.

Sky described their experience with the sharks that the Walkers had cut the fins from, trying, in accordance with his training, to be factual in his description, without making assumptions or interpretations. The other Novices remained quiet, only occasionally inclining their heads in agreement. He finished his story, and their teacher swam in silence for some time, his eyes almost closed. Eventually he spoke.

'Well, that was a lesson I wish you had been spared, but I am afraid that what you saw is not an uncommon event anymore.'

Sky could see that Dusk was clearly desperate to say something. When she did, she was obviously forcing herself to keep her emotions under check. 'Jeii, how can Ocean ever stay in balance when the Walkers act like this? We Ka-Tse can have all the quotas and rules we like — this makes it all a sad joke!'

'Well then, Deneb Rising, what do you think we should do about it then?'

'I don't see how we can do much more than we already are, Jeii. The Seekers monitor the levels of prey pretty well and try to manage the stocks, but maybe there should be more cooperation with other zetii species. We're all supposed to be trying to conserve Ocean's resources but we don't work together anymore.'

Sky tilted up his chin, indicating he wished to speak. Cloud Passing nodded to him. 'Jeii, why don't we invite representatives from other zetii species to the Gathering? If we speak to them we may find that they have just the same problems as us. Maybe we can agree ways to work together to solve them.'

Cloud Passing looked thoughtfully at him and slowly nodded his head slightly. Dusk made a small explosive noise and blew a small burst of bubbles from her blowhole. They rocked lazily towards the surface.

'Yes Dusk?' Cloud Passing inquired gently. 'You have an opinion about this I think?'

'We don't really know what the other zetii are doing Jeii! Many of us think that the blue water zetii are flaunting the quotas, taking more than their share. How would we ever know? They spend their lives out above the deep waters moving about in those huge clans: hundreds, even thousands strong. When they move into an area they must take everything! Someone has to stop them!'

'Dusk, we don't know that,' Sky reasoned. 'You know that there's no proof that's true.'

'And no proof it isn't! It fits the facts — everywhere there's a shortage of food, the Ka-Tse are going hungry, but you don't see any fewer of those Xenthos or Xa-Hana.'

'But they're still zetii like us! They're entitled to hunt just as we are, as long as they're reasonable in what they take. If we just dominated them because we feel like it, we'd be just like the creatures we despise!'

Cloud Passing interrupted: 'That is enough you two, this is getting far too emotional. This is not how I would expect to hear two scholars of the Way conducting a debate!' Sky and Dusk looked suitably contrite as he continued. 'I am not hearing suggestions as to what should be done. Fades Into Dusk? What are your thoughts?'

'Jeii, I know the Way has served us well for thousands of years, but it just doesn't seem to have all the answers anymore. I'm afraid that if we just blindly follow it, the Ka-Tse are going to die out. There's too much competition for too little food.'

'Hmm. And Touches The Sky?'

'I know times are difficult Jeii, but I don't think we can consider deviating from the Way. It's what makes us special, what has allowed us to live in harmony with Ocean for so long. I don't think the problem is the other zetii species, I think it's the Walkers.'

Cloud Passing looked grave. 'The Walkers are a strange anomaly on Ocean. All other life forms we have ever known have been constrained by the self limiting workings of the Cycle of Life. Somehow they have moved outside of those boundaries and have apparently somehow acquired great power without great wisdom. They lived in harmony with the Universal well enough for many thousands of years. Then they discovered how to create machines and manipulate their environment to their own ends. Now we simply do not know what may happen. Some of us believe the Cycle of Life will somehow correct their actions as it always has in the past with rogue species. Others are afraid that they are already too far outside the reach of the Cycle and that Ocean must suffer a great catastrophe in the next few hundred years; perhaps much sooner.'

'So what do *you* think should be done, Jeii?' asked Deneb.

'Well, it is not for me to decide alone, but I can assure you that this is a subject that will be debated at length at the Grand Council meeting during the coming Gathering. Which reminds me. We have a vacancy for one of the Voices on our clan's Council at present. You may know that I have held the post of Voice of the Others for some time — one of four Voices we have represented in our Council at present. I have spent much time meditating on the problems that we have just discussed, and I intend to make a suggestion to the Council, which I think many will find radical. My post demands that I do my best to represent the views of all other species but it seems to me that it is time to let one of the other zeta species actually come along and speak for themselves.'

'Can we trust what they will say, Jeii?' Dusk asked.

'*Not* speaking to them only increases what mistrust already exists. I think it must be worth trying. Now, I notice that Touches The Sky made a very sensible suggestion along these lines in our little debate just now.'

Sky wondered where this was going, and felt reluctant to accept this credit. 'Well, Deneb started me on that thought, Jeii.'

'Be that as it may, it so happens that the current holder of the Voice of Youth has just retired; I am afraid she does not really qualify to hold it any more. So I believe that Sky might enter that position on a trial basis and be able to contribute something useful.'

'Me at a Council Meeting, Jeii? I wouldn't know what to say…'

'Nonsense, you are a smart fellow, you just say what you think — or rather, what you believe the younger generation think. That is the point of that Voice after all: otherwise it would just be me and the other scarred old bags of bones — making decisions without taking into account the wishes of half the clan.'

'But some of the clan are going to object, surely…with the gossip about my father…'

'I think this is the best way for us to demonstrate that the rules of the clan still apply. It is your father that is accused, not you. This may help to stop some of the rumours. Now, what do you say?'

Sky was awed by the responsibility he was being offered. He wondered if this was somehow linked to Cloud Passing's plans for him as an apprentice Aligner. He looked at the others to see their reaction; Muddy winked at him encouragingly. Sky steadied his racing heartbeat with an effort, 'Jeii, I'd be honoured to accept then. I just hope I can represent the younger generations properly.'

'I am sure you will be fine. And you only have to worry about those around you, of course; the Voice of the Unborn has to speak for the needs of future generations. 'Now, let me see where Senx is in his travels, I fear it is getting late.'

They surfaced and Cloud Passing gauged the height of the sun.

'Indeed, time for you to go to your respective classes. Fades Into Dusk, you will take first echelon students for group foraging practice. Muddy River Mouth, take the second echelon and give them an introduction into the art of the Starwriters...'

Muddy interrupted as politely as he could, his voice pleading. 'But Cloud Passing-Jeii, might it not be better for Dusk to lead that lesson? I could easily lead a foraging lesson but she is in apprenticeship as a Starwriter, and could teach it so much better. I know so little about it compared to her.'

'And that is precisely why I have assigned the subject to you. They only need an introduction; you will manage. Now, where was I? Ah yes, Deneb Rising, assist Dusk to control her class, please — they can be a little wild at that age. And, Touches The Sky, take the third echelon and guide them in an appreciation of the Shades. Apparently they plan to present a harmonic chorus using them for inspiration at the Gathering. When I heard them practising yesterday it was ghastly. Even with my eyesight I could see they were quite out of mood with the light...'

They were interrupted by the arrival of another dolphin. 'Cloud Passing-Jeii, I am sorry to stop your lesson, but one of your Novices has been found.'

Cloud Passing looked at the messenger in surprise. 'Is it Wakes Softly? Is everything alright?'

'No, I'm afraid not, Jeii. You had better see for yourself.'

'Jeii, can we come too?' asked Deneb urgently, 'she's our friend.'

'Yes, of course — you may all come.'

They were led some distance to the east of the bay. A few of the clan's members were guarding the spot, their demeanour grim.

Wakes Softly was in a depression in the rock. Her body was covered in parallel cuts, and was discoloured where she had suffered blows to her side and head. Her eyes stared lifelessly at them.

The messenger spoke with compassion to them. 'I'm sorry, she must have been your friend. She has a lot of internal injuries; she must have been hit by something several times very hard. That was what killed her. We think she must have died recently, earliest last night, as the scavengers haven't found her yet and...'

'That's enough!' Deneb cried. 'Could you leave us alone for a while?'

Cloud Passing nodded sympathetically. 'This is another terrible tragedy. We'll leave you to your grief for now.' He led the messenger to one side, his expression pained.

Deneb moved beside Wakes cold body and pressed his head beside hers, talking quietly. 'What happened to you, little Wakes? Why did you have to be alone to face this?'

Dusk, Muddy and Sky waited in silence. After a time, Deneb returned to them. 'What did this?'

'A Cleaner?' Muddy ventured.

'No. They bite much deeper. They wouldn't leave her intact.'

Then maybe a pack of krakars?'

'No. None have been seen around here for a long time. It's too warm for them here, and they would do much more damage. Only one kind of creature kills like this.'

It was Dusk who said it out loud. 'Zeta? You mean another zeta killed her? That's unthinkable!'

'Deneb turned to her. 'Not necessarily one zeta. Maybe several zetii. They would leave teeth rakes like that, they would kill by ramming another creature. They'd have to be big zetii too, like Ka-Tse.'

'But that's absolutely against the Way. It can't be true. Maybe she was hit by one of the Walkers' crafts.'

Then Cloud Passing returned to them. 'I shall miss Wakes Softly. She was full of life, with great potential. Now she is taken from us too soon, just like poor Born Into Summer was. We must arrange the farewell ceremony for her. Fades Into Dusk, please go back to the clan and return with any who should attend. Who will say the last goodbye above the Abyss?'

Deneb spoke: 'Her only relative here is her mother. If she will allow it, I'll carry Wakes Softly with her and say the last goodbyes in her company.'

'I think she will appreciate that. And then the only thing we can do is get back to our lives as best we can. We'll carry on with the Academy tomorrow. We can discuss this more later.'

Sky looked across at Deneb, who was staring at Wakes' body, his eyes full of pain. Sky felt nauseous. This was the second of his friends he had seen die unnaturally. And, unthinkably, unimaginably, other dolphins looked likely to be the reason. What was going on? Tonight was the new moon. He had an appointment. Maybe he would find out then.

CHAPTER 12

"See hunter measure and compare
Shoal waits in fear, each one aware
He focuses: the choice is made
All hearts but one no more afraid
The prey her dance of death begins
While erstwhile friends silently sing"

Third Wave Breaks - (3,001 – 3,043 post Great Alluvium)

Sky swam in gentle circles at the surface, often lifting his head to look across the wave tops for signs of the young dolphin with the distinctive, misshapen head. At first, if he had come from the west, Sky would not have seen him; the glare from the dropping sun reflected harshly from the sea, tossing bright balls of light from the peaks of the wavelets. But soon Senx changed from his fierce white daytime guise into the indolent red giant of day's end, and lowered himself lazily into the pliant horizon.

Sky hung above the wreck, waiting. Hoping that Sand In Rain would come again, as he had seemed to promise he would. Hoping that if he did, he would reveal something more. About Born. About Wakes. About these dangerous plans of the Guardians.

The sun settled lower, painting the dunes of the shore a deep orange-red. The tropical darkness came hard on the tail of the retreating daylight, but

Sky could still make out the wreck clearly against the white sand of the seabed. He dived down to swim alongside it. He wondered why the Walkers made these devices. Why were they charging about the sea in these noisy metal monsters? What was the point of it? Sometimes you could tell; sometimes they hunted; taking from the waters. But often, the biggest of these things just thrummed their way from one horizon to the next with no pause, no apparent purpose. Sometimes, Sky had seen the Walkers moving about on them in their strange, jerky way, but he had no idea what they were doing in their great machines.

The sound of someone's sonar stopped him. The light was very dim now, the new moon giving no real light. But he saw a dim shape at the edge of visibility — a small dolphin on the landward side of the wreck. It must be Sand In Rain. The newcomer hovered about there above the seabed. Sky made his signature call: 'It is I, Touches The Sky, of the Dune Coast Clan!' No reply.

He advanced slowly towards the figure. As he drew nearer it retreated away from him into the shallows slowly, often turning to look back at him. Sky swam forward steadily but carefully, not wanting to scare him again. 'Sand, it's me, Sky. Don't be afraid. I just want to ask you some questions.'

Sky swam a little faster, but the small figure sped up too, so he slowed again. Sky surfaced briefly when the youth went up to breathe and looked above the water. In the twilight, he could see they were entering a narrow bay, so they would have to stop soon. The sand on the beach glowed an almost luminescent white in the last of the light. Then Sky realised that this was *the* beach. The one where Born had died. There was a rocky headland dropping into the sea here, and the slight figure disappeared behind it, just ahead of Sky. It was now so dark that he could see a trail of yellow-green specks of light behind the dolphin where he was disturbing the tiny, bioluminescent creatures in the plankton. Sky rounded the corner and stopped, confused. There was no sign of the smaller dolphin, even though he had not been far ahead. He sent out streams of sound and listened for reflections but there was just the rock of the wall face and the softer sounding shelf of sand. Something made him turn around towards the open sea behind him. He was not aware of hearing anything, but he turned quickly, some inner sense warning of something wrong. Seven or eight streams of yellow-green light were approaching at speed, one much nearer than the others. In a moment he had an impression of them: the up and down strokes of their tails showed them as dolphins, but not like the small creature he had followed into the bay; these were big, powerful dolphins. The nearest one came straight at him — Sky lunged to one side as the other's rostrum crashed a painful glancing blow against his side — a blow that would have crushed his ribs had he not moved. Sky leapt out of the water, momentarily confusing his pursuers, but as he exploded back into the black water he saw them turning and coming at him again. Sending out blasts of ratcheting sound to locate him. Sky fled in confusion. 'I am Touches The Sky! Why are you doing this?'

His only answer was a harsh laugh and a call back in a rough voice: 'And we are going to help you spend some time a little closer to that sky soon!'

His pursuers had spread out now and Sky realised that they were between him and the open sea. They were hemming him into the small bay. He realised with horror that this must have been what happened to Born Into Summer, that she had been driven high up onto this same beach and left to die. Then his fear mixed with anger. He had to escape somehow. To tell others what was happening. To find out who these strangers were and stop this madness. He suddenly veered and swam away from the nearest big dolphins towards the shore. They took a moment to follow him. No doubt they had expected him to try and break out for the open sea between them, not to head for the impassable wall of the shore. This gave him enough of a head start to get out of visual range, so they could not see his trail of light; but they knew there was nowhere for him to go. He heard two or three harsh laughs again as the hunters slowly closed in on him. Again that rough voice came to him through the water,

'Come and join us for some fun, little fish! The other meddler was boring too. She preferred lying on the beach to playing our games!' Several more jeering laughs followed.

Sky sped close inshore to one end of the small bay. Soon he was in barely enough water to swim, up against the rocky headland. It was a high rock wall, totally impassable. He made a small leap, and could just see in the failing light that the other end of the bay was blocked in the same way. He was trapped! He could hear the ranging sounds from his pursuers, it sounded as though most of them were waiting at the narrow opening of the bay while three more were closing in, searching for him, hunting him down like prey. He swam fast along the shore, his belly brushing the sand in the shallow water. The hunters' sonar was louder. Sky did not think they would have detected his exact location yet, but he knew they would be on him soon! He approached the other end of the bay. There was no way out. Should he die on the beach like Born had? Or fight? Attacking another zeta was wrong, but defending yourself? Sky decided he would rather swim out and have them attack him. Sky looked out for a moment at the pale expanse of sand, still clearly visible in the starlight. It looked perfect, sterile, peaceful. Almost invitingly tranquil. But he'd almost died on a beach before, he could not face that slow, lingering death. Sky could hear all the hunters closing now, moving slowly and purposefully, confident of their success. They knew he had nowhere to go. This was the end. He heard the sonar of two of them move behind him, they were sweeping the along the shoreline now. They would be on him in a moment.

Sky lifted his head above the water for one last look at the sky. The rocky wall of the nearby headland could not be seen, but he could clearly make out its outline by the absence of bright stars where its mass blackened his view of an otherwise perfectly clear night. Then Sky realised that the headland was not quite a straight wall of rock. There was a small kink where the rock met the water, close beside him. It formed a small alcove in the rock wall at sea level and by moving closer to it he realised that there was a shelf of rock above the water there, maybe two or three times his body length above the water. Sky did not really think about what he did then. There was no time to. The sound of the hunters was so close, they would pick him up with their sonar at any moment. He just leapt as best he could from the shallow water. a mad, desperate leap, contrary to every instinct in his body, up through the clear night air, and then falling down onto the unknown, unnatural, cruel harshness of the rock. His body slammed down hard onto the rocky shelf and he had to stop himself screaming out with pain. The shelf was small, barely enough to hold him and he twisted sideways in the strange environment to stop himself falling back into the water, the rocks cutting painfully into his belly.

Sky lay still on the rock shelf, breathing with difficulty. Below him he could see the twin streams of green luminescence of the lead hunters sweep past him and then stop as they reached the wall of the headland, in apparent confusion. He guessed that a command must have been given, as he then saw the multiple trails of the other hunters start to move inwards, and the party started to comb across the small bay, hunting for him. Sky lay as still as he could, in agony. He could feel open wounds on his chest and pectoral fins oozing blood.

He watched the hunters sweep back and forth the small bay, at first methodically, then with increasing speed and agitation. He felt his skin drying out and tightening. The sharp rocks cut into his flesh and he fought the urge to move to try to gain some relief from the pain. Blood trickled from a deeper wound in his belly where a sharp point of rock had sliced into him. He eased himself away from it a little but the wound continued to bleed and dripped into the water below him slowly from a point on the rock shelf.

The trails of light from the hunters converged briefly then fanned out again, each moving to an equidistant point close to the shore. There, each one stopped, waiting. One was directly below Sky. He saw the large shape of the dolphin come to a stop there and then he heard it come to the surface to breathe. He could just make out the wet skin of its back at the surface dully reflecting the starlight. Then, Sky also saw another, closer wetness. The line of his own blood glistened slightly on the rock beside him. It oozed slowly to the edge of the shelf. A new droplet of blood formed there, and swelled, was about to fall...directly above the head of the hunter below. Sky watched it in horror as the heavy drop of blood separated and fell away, seeming to fall so slowly towards the dark figure, but just then the large dolphin settled down to the bottom again, and the fall of the blood droplet was lost in the swirl of his descent and the gentle movement of the swell against the rock.

The hunters stayed motionless for a long time, listening, waiting. Sky lay in agony. His blood continued to slowly ooze across the rock and fall; drip...drip...drip. If the hunter came up now he must hear it. Then there were a few glimmers of green light below him again. The hunter was moving again, slowly rising up to the surface again.

Drip...drip...drip. He would surface directly under that point. Sky's own blood would betray him. Now Sky could just make out the shape of him slowly approaching the surface, he was almost there, still moving quietly, still listening for the sounds of his prey. Sky watched another drop of his blood fall exactly over the shape of the rising dolphin. Then he twisted himself; leaning all his weight towards the wound, pressing down hard against the sharp blade that was the rock. He felt the sharp stone enter the wound again and he fought against his instincts to press it harder, yet more deeply into himself. He thought for a moment he was going to black out with the pain, but pressed all his weight against the point. He felt the sharp rock enter deeper into the wound, the blood continued to flow past it, then, as the stone spread his flesh wider it slowed, blocked. He heard the hunter below surface. A thick drop of blood slowly swelled at the edge of the shelf, directly above the waiting dolphin. Sky could see the slow line of his blood that fed that dangerous droplet. He pressed against the cruel rock in agony and the line of blood slowed. The droplet hung, quivering slightly in the faint breeze. Suddenly, as one, the hunters turned and sped out of the bay. Sky watched the light trails of their passage as they shot off into the distance. He eased his weight off the rock, wincing in pain as the point of stone pulled from his wound. The blood flowed freely now. Then, with an effort, he jerked his body several times until he tipped sideways, banged painfully against the harsh edge of the shelf, then rolled over the edge and fell gratefully into the water. He was hurting. He was bleeding. But he was alive.

CHAPTER 13

"Most assume that the Way is inviolate, unchanging. But it guides the zetii through Ocean's waters, and Ocean changes with each passing moon. So, the Way must adapt. A doctrine that will not adapt to change is a doomed doctrine."

- From the 938ᵗʰ Congress of the Aligners.

'What strange currents have carried us here? Are there not perils enough on Ocean that we must now kill our own kind?'

Cloud Passing closed his eyes and was quiet for a long time, deep in thought. Sky waited alongside him patiently. He had gone to find the old dolphin directly after his encounter in the bay, and had explained why he had gone there and what had happened. His mentor had listened in silence for the most part, but his pale eyes showed grave concern. At last he opened his eyes again.

'I am so glad that you are safe, young Sky. But I fear that I may have brought this upon you. Born Into Summer was my designate to take on my role as Aligner of the Way. She died suddenly, and it now looks as though she was killed. Then I appoint you, and now you are almost killed in the same way. This seems more than a coincidence.'

'But what about Wakes, Jeii? She was not an Aligner, was she?'

'No, she was not. So perhaps there are other factors here. But I am very concerned for your safety.'

'Should I tell the Council about this then, Jeii?'

'No…no, I think not yet. We have the Gathering starting here shortly and there will be a secret meeting of Aligners then. Let us wait until I can find out what they have heard before we decide what to do. I do not want to draw any more attention to you than necessary for now.'

'And can I tell my friends?'

'For now, tell no one. I am sorry, that will be hard on you, but I am not sure who to trust at present, and it is best if no idle stories are spread. Hardly anyone knew that you were my new designate, I had sent a message to another Aligner and told just a few key members of the Council.'

'So you think I was attacked because I am to become an Aligner, Jeii? And do you think that they were Guardians?'

'I think they must have been Guardians. And it is possible that they just learned of you from this Sand youth, but that hardly seems a reason to kill someone. So yes, I am concerned that they are targeting the Aligners.'

They both surfaced to breathe then glided back down and continued their slow swim. Sky tried to absorb the enormity of this. The Guardians actually did condone zeta killing zeta. And they were trying to harm the Aligners. And now he was a target for them, but he had no idea what the reason was.

'The Guardians, Jeii — why would they care about the Aligners?'

'Ah. Well, it seems that the Guardians have a new leader. He is taking this perverse philosophy of theirs further than ever before. You know that they have always believed that the Ka-Tse are somehow superior to other zetii?'

'I understood something like that, Jeii. Based on the teachings of that Stone Eyes, right?'

'Yes, their "seer". Well, now we think they are trying to create conflict between the zeta species. And they know that many are dissatisfied with how the Way seems to be less and less relevant to modern Ocean. That suits their plans. If the Aligners are successful in adapting the Way to the changes we are seeing, then much of the discontent they need to feed on may go.'

'But if that's true, aren't you at risk yourself, Jeii?'

Passing Cloud smiled. 'Perhaps. But they probably know that I am not long for life under Senx anyway. So why bother killing off an ancient who is going to be making his last dive soon?'

Sky winced at that reminder — the dolphin who had been most like a father to him was going to make his Darkening Dive soon.

'Jeii, there will be less kindness and wisdom in these waters when you are gone. I shall miss you so. You will not be forgotten.'

The older dolphin's misty eyes smiled back at him.

'And I shall miss you too. But to live well and memorably we must recognise the importance of not only *what* we do but *when* we do it. We must know the proper and best times to do things. When to speak; when to keep silent. When to take action; when to wait patiently. When to create; when to disassemble. When to live; when to die. I am approaching such a time, that is all.'

'But, Jeii, you can't go now,' Sky pleaded. 'What about my becoming an Aligner? Won't you wait for that at least?'

'I have thought about that, of course, but the answer is no. When I meet the others at the Gathering I am going to make arrangements for someone to continue your training, you will just have to be a little patient. But there is one small lesson I should like to give you now. Just in case anything should happen to me, I want to teach you something that will allow other Aligners to identify you.'

Passing Cloud rose slowly to the surface, indicating that Sky should follow. There, they lifted their heads above the gentle swells and the old dolphin looked towards the nearby land. A pelican was perched on a rock studying the water below it. Then it stretched out its grey-brown wings and flapped up into the sky, its pale head pulled back to better balance the weight of its large bill. It circled above them ponderously, studying the clear water below.

'Sky, occasionally you will meet another zeta who may seem in some way unusual; remarkable, let us say. Most may not notice this, but you have unusual powers of perception, which is why I have chosen you. Look for a sharpness of mind, for thought behind the words, for layers of meanings. When you meet such a zeta you should use this recognition protocol. There are many such coded tricks that we Aligners use to recognise one another, but this is one you can easily apply.'

'Yes, Jeii.'

The pelican quickly turned in its flight and fell towards the water, its wings drawn back behind it, its bill knifing into the water ahead of it. After a moment, it resurfaced, flicking its head upwards to better position its catch. A flash of silver in the bright sunlight and its bill snapped shut.

The older dolphin turned to Sky. 'Can the hunted trust the hunter?'

'Jeii? I don't know…'

'That is alright, Sky. I want you to ask me that question.'

'Oh, I see. Uh…can the hunted trust the hunter?'

'The hunted can trust that the hunter will kill.'

Cloud Passing lay at the surface watching the pelican, as it flapped awkwardly upwards from the water and started its circling again.

'If someone answers you with exactly those words, you will know they are one of us and that you can trust them. Now, you have a lesson to conduct I think. The little ones will be waiting for you. Go swiftly, and take care! The Guardians may try to find you again. Be watchful, and do not leave the clan on your own!'

CHAPTER 14

"For nothing surprises Ocean
She has brushed eternity and seen all, felt all.
Look to her depths to see the waters of life flow
Where you are carried now
Where you may be carried tomorrow"
- Dust On The Wind. (4,560-4,586 post Great Alluvium)

As Sky headed for the coral head where the third echelon class should be waiting for him, he passed a large turtle lying in the seagrass. With an effort it twisted its head and pulled up a mouthful, sending up a cloud of silty sand that drifted away gently in the slight current. The turtle turned the food slowly in its mouth and swallowed with a stoical expression. Its eyes did not follow Sky. Their lenses looked crystalline, white. Sky thought it probably blind. Although turtles could live to an immense age, Sky guessed that this one was near the end of its life. It reminded him of Cloud Passing, who also had that look about him now, the look of one who is ready to depart. He thought about their recent conversation; his teacher had spoken of a "deep dive down to the dark waters." Sky remembered yesterday's ceremony, how they had let Wakes Softly's broken little body fall down, down, down into the cold depths. What must Cloud Passing have thought seeing that? He would make his own Darkening Dive. And soon. He tried to imagine what that must be like. Last night he had been close to death. But that had been

84

sudden, unexpected and he had been desperate to escape, to live — to survive at all costs. But one day he might make his own Darkening Dive. Swimming out over the blue, over the great fall, nothing to see or hear below. What would you think about?

About what you had done.

About what you wished you had done.

About what you had done and wished you had not.

Then his thoughts were broken by the sound of his class ahead of him. As he approached, he could make out the five young dolphins and he made his signature call: 'It is I, Touches The Sky!'

'Greetings, Touches The Sky-Jeii,' came the response from his class.

Sky nodded, slightly, he was still not used to being referred to as a teacher and the 'Jeii' honorific continued to thrill and alarm him slightly.

'Greetings, class. Are your minds open today?' Sky concentrated on keeping his voice calm, trying to keep a sense of normality in spite of the madness of the last day and night.

'Yes, Touches The Sky-Jeii.'

Formalities over, Sky went on to explain the lesson: 'Today I'll try to teach you more about the Shades of Blue. Who can tell me why we study them?'

Lost In Moonlight, a small, pretty young dolphin, and one of his brightest students, answered him; her voice full of enthusiasm for the subject. 'The Shades are aids to meditation and the discovery of truth. They are also used to divine the future!'

'Very good, Moonlight. They certainly are fine aids to concentration and encourage oneness with Ocean. However, while many believe that the Shades of Blue can foretell events, a Seeker would probably dispute that there is hard evidence that they can.'

'Oh, but I believe they can, Jeii, and my mother does too. She says a friend of hers foresaw the death of the last Prime Mother with the Shades.'

Sky was taken aback at her conviction and wondered how Cloud Passing would handle this situation. Eventually he said, 'Well, you'll each have to make up your own mind about that. Let's consider the theory for now.'

Sky paused, then, trying to impart some of the gravitas of his own teacher, said: 'Swim with me.'

His class fell into synchronisation with him. He kept them near the surface as he led them away from the shore, towards the depths. His mind wandered, still playing out a Darkening Dive in his head.

You would take a last look at the cliffs, the dunes, the grass; the harsh strangeness of the land...

He forced himself back into the moment and spoke to his class: 'The colours of the waters are divided into three major groupings. These were probably originally derived from the effects of weather and environment. In fact, some of the Shades are not blue at all of course, but greens, browns or even reds.' Sky looked at the young dolphins' keen faces, and turned to one of the two he and Muddy had last met by the shipwreck with the Guardian youth, Sand. The same youth who had apparently betrayed him last night. 'Tell me, Bellatrix, why would the water be green?'

'Because of the tiny plants growing in it, Jeii?'

'That's right,' Sky agreed, 'And when would we find water with a brown Shade?'

'When we are close to the land,' another answered confidently.

'Correct. Water carries soil and other matter from the land in rivers and darkens the sea. The third type is the clear, blue water of the deep sea. Beautiful to look at, but not much lives in it. Incidentally, that is probably where the saying "In death there is clarity" originally comes from.'

Again, the intrusive voice in his head.

And in that clarity we'll seek Death.

'Today we obviously have that kind of water, and in the reading of the Shades it is said to imply Risk or Decay. Now, these three environmentally derived categories are known as the Krumas, and in the art of reading the waters they primarily indicate situation, background, or history.'

The class appeared to listen attentively as Sky spoke. He hoped his charges were noticing the subtle alterations in the hues around them as they moved over the deeper water. He continued his explanation of how each of the Krumas was subdivided into nine divisions representing the varying hues of the Krumas: the Tonellas. These were interpreted as representing direction, location, or sequencing of events. Then he explained how the quality, direction and intensity of light were defined into seven categories that indicate the degree, volume, or speed of events. He paused to see if he may be boring his class, but they seemed absorbed by his words.

'At this stage I don't want you to concern yourself with trying to read the waters, nor even trying to identify the exact definition of a particular Shade. It will be enough for now if you can learn to be receptive to the Shades, and can be aware of the change from one Shade to the next.'

Sky brought them to the surface to breathe. 'Now, we'll make a deep dive and then slowly ascend. Let's dive in silence. In these surface conditions we should see shafts of light that will reveal several of the subtler Shades. As we descend, I want each of you to close down the peripheries of your minds and bodies as you've been taught. We're aiming for the fourth level of consciousness now, but you must still be receptive to what your eyes tell your mind. Now prepare yourselves for a long dive.'

The students stilled themselves at the surface, breathing deeply, calming their bodies' need for oxygen. Sky watched them for a while but then found himself looking down; down into the depths.

There would be no bottom. At least none any living zeta could reach. How long would you prepare yourself for? How many breaths to take? How long would you want it to last?

Then he realised they were watching him expectantly. He cursed himself. They would have passed the peak of preparedness to dive — lost their concentration. He led the students in a hurried dive — messy — wasteful. The wound in his belly gave him a jolt of pain. He descended with his students just behind him.

You would start like any other dive. A dive to hunt, a dive to chase a lover in play.

As they fell, Sky softly intoned the names of the Shades as he recognised them, and listed the traditional meaning associated with each. The students swam silently alongside him. From the corner of his eye he noticed Lost In Moonlight looking especially concentrated. He began: 'This is *Ndria-axi*, meaning Joining, Reunion or Reconciliation. Now, see this change, this means Towards The Familiar or Regressing. Look, another change here,' Sky murmured, indicating the shafts of light that now wavered around them, 'this would suggest Something of High Import or Great in Scope.'

A good Shade for a Darkening Dive.

At a little over fifty metres depth he levelled out. There was no sign of the seabed, which was still far below them. He looked at each of the class in turn, trying to assess their mental state. They looked good: calm, slightly withdrawn, yet with their eyes still alert. He signalled for them to stop swimming. He wanted them to pay attention now; this was a depth these young ones rarely visited, for many of them it might be their first time. The water was a deep indigo around them, falling away to blackness below.

It's not frightening down there seen from here. Inviting, really. Like the welcome cool of the air on your back, when you lay at the surface on a summer night after a long day.

Far above them a cloud covered the sun, diffusing the light.

'The south facing light shafts prevail now, meaning Unexpected or Feared, and look what happens as that cloud begins to cover Senx: this would be read as being Towards The Unknown or Extending. Lastly, see this subtle change in the depths here: it would usually be read as Separation or Dispute.'

Separation. That would be an appropriate Shade. But wouldn't you hope for the Joining Shade now? How much further would you be able to go? Maybe there are more Shades to see down there, that the living have no names for.

No. There is only one kind of light down there: the colour of the Void. Utter blackness. The colour of nothingness. The colour Born sees now. The colour Wakes sees.

'Jeii! Jeii!'

He snapped back into the moment. Lost In Moonlight was calling him. He suddenly realised that since he had told them to stop swimming they had been sinking. He did not know how deep they were now, only that it was deep — too deep! He looked in the direction she was gesturing and saw that Bellatrix was losing consciousness, her young body tilting sideways, her eyes glazing.

'Alright, everyone! We're going up! Take your time, stay calm, follow your training.'

He put his head under Bellatrix and lifted her, bringing the class up as fast as he dared. If he made them swim too fast they would burn up their remaining oxygen and pass out. Too slow and it would run out anyway.

'Jeii, is Bellatrix going to die?'

Is Bellatrix going to die?'

'Hush now. Stay relaxed. Just swim.'

It seemed an age to the surface. And Sky tortured himself with guilt the whole way. These young ones were in his care. Their parents had trusted in him. *They* had trusted in him. He had been obsessed with thoughts of death and now here death was, swimming amongst them!

Don't die, don't die, don't die. Please don't die.

The water grew lighter, the surface nearer, nearer, then the light cracked open and they were there in the full sunlight.

He shouted at her and prodded her harshly. 'Bellatrix, wake up! Breathe, Bellatrix! Breathe, now! Bellatrix, breathe!'

For an eternity there was nothing. Then she shuddered violently and took a gasping breath. Slowly, she came back to consciousness. She looked at her classmates then at Sky. 'I'm sorry, Jeii, I missed some of what you said at the bottom of the dive.'

He almost laughed in relief. 'Don't worry. I'm just glad you're alright. We're going back to the shallows now.'

Soon the students were chattering away happily. None of them seemed to realise how close catastrophe had been, including Bellatrix herself. They all acted as though this was normal. Sky was still in shock. On the swim back Lost In Moonlight spoke to him earnestly. 'Touches The Sky-Jeii, you said at the beginning of the dive that because of the clear blue water here this Kruma means Risk or Decay, doesn't it?'

'Well, those are two possible meanings of this Kruma, yes.'

'So, today the Shades foretold a situation of decay, then some kind of reunion, a meeting with familiar things, probably a lot of them. It must mean the coming Gathering! And then something unknown but somehow frightening happens and there's some sort of conflict and separation!

'Moonlight, that is just one interpretation; an experienced reader of the Shades might come up with something quite different from what we saw.'

She shook her head vehemently. 'No, that must be what it meant, it was so clear. Something bad is happening to us. My mother said as much, after those two zetii died so strangely...'

Sky interrupted her. 'I think that's enough about that. Talk to Silent Waters about what the Shades meant when she has a moment,' he said eventually, 'she is able to interpret them far better than me. And don't look so sad, it's just the colours of the water in the end. Now, lessons are over for today.'

They made their farewells and departed. Sky was left confused. Should he have emphasised a logical approach and argued against Moonlight's interpretation of the Shades? What if the Shades really did foretell the future?

He looked down. The clear blue water fell far into the darkening depths, overlain with wavering shafts of light. A Separation or Dispute. Of Great Import.

CHAPTER 15

"The heavens hold all knowledge"
- Traditional

Sky found the other three Novices waiting for Green Wave Falling around midday. Sky stayed nearby, half listening, still going over his own near disastrous lesson in his mind. At first they spoke of Wakes Softly, tried again to guess what had happened. At last Deneb said, 'Well one thing is certain. I'm going to tell my mother what Wakes told Sky and me.' He went on to tell Dusk and Muddy of Wakes' story, how she had seen an older dolphin listening to the Starwriters and then meet another dolphin secretly. Eventually, they lapsed into an awkward silence, which Muddy eventually tried to lighten by relating his experiences that morning with the second echelon class. Sky lost track of the account for a while, busy with his own concerns, then focussed again as Muddy became more agitated.

'Then Pebbles kept asking me "But how *exactly* do Starwriters remember all that stuff, Jeii?" and of course I had to bluff it and say things like, "well that is too advanced for our current lesson", but I really have no idea! It was awful!'

'Well we don't remember it exactly,' Dusk said. 'It would be impossible to order it all in your mind properly. It is often fairly meaningless stuff you know; just data.'

'And that is why you somehow tie the data to astronomical events, right?' Muddy asked.

'We use astronomical events because they are so reliable and precise. Some Dreamweavers have experimented with other repeatable events like tidal movements, coral spawning and even volcanic eruptions to entrain information, but they are only suitable for imprecise, more generic data...'

'Hold on,' an exasperated Muddy interrupted, 'never mind all the exceptions to the rule, how do the basics work? How can I explain this to a class?'

Dusk closed her eyes and thought for a moment. 'Well, try putting it like this. We have all this information to record somehow, ranging from the findings of the greatest Seekers in history to dull data about prey stocks, Council resolutions and so on. It would be impossible to remember so much information reliably, especially when some of it may not be accessed for perhaps centuries at a time. So, the Dreamweavers entrain the data with cosmic episodes.'

'Oh, they "entrain the data with cosmic episodes", do they?' repeated Muddy stonily. 'That is *not* an explanation!'

'Alright, alright; let me think for a moment.' Dusk shot to the surface and leapt high, falling back through the mirror of the surface with barely a splash. Sky watched her leap and noticed again how beautifully sleek and muscular her body was as she effortlessly swam back down to them.

'We wait for a specific event in the night sky, such as the passage of a planet over the constellation of the Cleaner, for example. The Starwriters who will be recording have to be in the seventh level of consciousness in preparation for the event, so everything must be timed perfectly. The Dreamweaver who is in charge of the recording then starts the song she has composed for that session'.

'Does the Dreamweaver sing alone?' Muddy asked.

'Not always; for more complex, multiple layers of data, other Starwriters may help her with the harmonies that entrain additional information. They won't be in the Seventh Level of course, so they're not actually recording.'

'But why a planet? Why the Cleaner's constellation?' pleaded Muddy.

'Those are just examples, fish-brain!' said Dusk. 'Any event will do as long as one part of the universe is moving in a unique way in relation to another. That is why events like the lunar eclipses are so useful to us. We even have some songs that have been passed on from generation to generation of Starwriters that mean nothing until a particular comet comes by every hundred years or so and allows us to get the data out again.'

Deneb stirred at last, as Muddy had obviously hoped he would. 'That bit is extraordinary. I watched part of a Starwriter song once. They were reading from the sky at a time near the equinox when the moon was passing some star I think. A Dreamweaver chanted this strange song without words and the Starwriters stared at the moon through the whole thing for an age. When they came back to near consciousness they just poured out information — ancient stuff, from the First Millennium I think it was.'

'Exactly,' Dusk said. 'Once the information is woven into a song we sort of absorb it into our subconscious. We say that we *dream it in*. I can't consciously access the information I've taken in as a Starwriter. The only way to get it out is to see exactly the right alignment of stars or whatever at the same time as you hear the unlocking song. For more complex information the Starwriters sometimes enter into a form of shared consciousness so no single one of them may have understandable data – but I can't do that yet.'

'Isn't that what the Calculators do too?' Deneb asked. 'Somehow they are able to link their thinking together so that they can handle more complex computations. I suppose they speak to each other somehow, but if you watch them it seems they are just chanting together in a trance.'

'Something like that, I really don't understand how they do it. And it's no good asking them, they're mostly very strange to talk to. Anyway, enough about all that, it's too much like being back at the Academy. Sky, what have you done to yourself?' She stared at the fresh wound on Sky's underside.

'Oh, it's nothing really. I was stupid; I made a jump near the shore and landed on some rock.'

'Really? You are not usually that clumsy. So, how did your lesson go today?

Sky related his dive and Bellatrix's narrow escape. The others listened in silence.

"That's really not good,' Deneb said. 'Bellatrix is Last To Speak's daughter. I hope he doesn't get to hear about this.'

Sky had forgotten that Last To Speak was Bellatrix's father. He remembered how aggressive he had been to him when the rumours had started about Sky's father. 'Do you think he'll do anything about it?'

'I hope not. He might try and twist things to make you look bad. I guess we can only wait and see.'

Muddy tried to comfort him. 'Sky, these things happen. The younger ones can black out suddenly sometimes. That's why they have to make their first deeper dives under supervision. You did the right thing: you saw her problem and you brought her up. Everything was fine in the end.'

'But I didn't see her fast enough. I wasn't concentrating properly. If I had been, I might have seen the signs and...'

Dusk interrupted him gently. 'Sky, you are always so hard on yourself.

How did the lesson end up? Did they learn anything about the Shades?'

'Well, they are a bright group, especially little Lost In Moonlight. But the Shades foretold gloomy events, and she seems to take them very seriously'.

'What did they say?'

'Essentially, that there would be some kind of important meeting followed by conflict with everything set on a background of decay or danger.'

'Danger!' Dusk said. 'Well, that fits with what happened to Born and Wakes. And the meeting would be the Gathering, and the conflict might be the debates about the lack of food and why it's happening.'

Muddy broke in: 'That's what the Guardians are using to recruit new members to them. That the Za-Hana or the Xenthos are stealing our food and we have to take action against them; even kill if need be.'

'That will do!' A stern voice broke in. The Novices spun around to see an elderly dolphin behind them staring at them icily. Both his voice and his stiff posture carried authority. His body carried a number of old scars but, most noticeably, the tip of his dorsal fin was missing from an old wound, making it look oddly stunted.

'Greetings, Green Wave Falling-Jeii,' they intoned penitently.

'Greetings, class. It seems your minds are far *too* open. Guardians! Killing! Muddy River Mouth, do you learn nothing! You know very well that the Way expressly forbids the killing of other creatures except for food, and that therefore includes the Za-Hana and the Xenthos. They may not be of our species or speak our tongue, but they are still zetii. They breathe air as we do and their tails parallel the sea surface as ours do. This is sacrilege!'

Muddy looked crestfallen.

'But I was only repeating what others have said, Green Wave Falling-Jeii.'

'*Which* others precisely?' Green Wave demanded pedantically, his eyes burning.

'Well, um, North Wind said it openly just a few days ago.'

'And North Wind would do well to take his ideas to some other clan before he suffers banishment from this one! There is a zeta heading for exile if ever I saw one.'

He glared at them all.

'May I remind you that you are supposedly Novices seeking oneness with Ocean! You cannot deviate from the Way in any detail: it has been our path throughout history and it forbids such thoughts. I am particularly surprised at you taking part in this, Deneb Rising. What would Silent Waters say?'

'My mother has always encouraged free thought, Jeii,' Deneb answered, meeting his disapproving stare with a steady gaze.

'Does she now? Well, there will be a chance for all of you to express your free thoughts later today. You will all come with me to meet the Prime Mother and explain yourselves this half postnoon! Now, we move on to our lesson for today. The mind must control the body; only then can it control itself! We will begin with cardiac control. You will dive to the seabed below us and I will begin to count. Synchronise your heartbeats with my voice. I will slow my counting and you are to keep your heartbeats in pace. Take a breath and join me at the bottom. No one surfaces without my permission. Let us see if we can expunge these base thoughts with a little suffering.'

CHAPTER 16

"To be remembered as great we must recognise when to begin the new and when to end the old."

- The 'Seer' Stone Eyes (13,222 -13,264 post Great Alluvium)

They approached the still form of the elderly dolphin that lay on a small patch of seagrass. Green Wave signalled the four Novices to wait by a rocky outcrop that protruded from the sand close by. He moved closer to her and sank to the seabed a little way from her, apparently to wait for her to end her meditation.

Sky watched her carefully. Silent Waters was the nearest thing to a mother he had had for most of his life but he still shared much of the reverence that most of the clan had for her. Now she was lying motionless on the grass, her half-closed eyes fixed on a small hole under an isolated rock. Sky could just make out that there was a small octopus at the entrance of the hole, its eyes fixed on hers. Green Wave continued to wait respectfully.

A single Parrotfish approached the outcrop beside the four Novices, its brilliant blue and green body flashing brightly against the dull brown of the rock. It eyed their still forms warily and seemed to decide that they were no threat at present. The Parrotfish inspected the desultory coral cover of the rock and selected one section of low growth. It darted forward and snapped off some stony coral polyps with a loud crunch. Fragments of limestone rained down from it as it continued its patrol of the rock.

At last Silent Waters roused herself slightly and spoke. Sky, who was the nearest of the four Novices, could just hear her.

'Greetings, Green Wave Falling.'

'Greetings, Prime Mother. Were you about to eat?'

'No, not at all; I do not eat these creatures, they remind me too much of some of our fellows.'

Green Wave nodded slightly, as though he was unsure as to whether or not this may be a joke. She continued on, her gaze still fixed on the octopus.

'They are clearly highly intelligent, yet each one has no thoughts beyond the survival of itself and perhaps its young. No concerns for conservation of Ocean's resources, no concept of the Right to Life, of ethical behaviour. Why do we alone carry these burdens?'

'We act in accordance of the Way,' he replied stiffly, 'The zetii were chosen to act as guardians of Ocean.'

'Ah, yes, guardians. But not *the* Guardians.'

Sky thought Green Wave Falling looked uncomfortable at this, but he continued, his voice in a low tone. Sky could still make out what was said though. 'The so-called Guardians are an abomination of course. They are corrupt and flout the laws of the Way.'

'Laws? What about the spirit of it?' She raised herself from the seabed and turned to look at him full on. He shifted slightly under her clear, quizzical gaze.

'I do not concern myself with trying to divine the spirit of the Way,' he replied evasively. 'The histories we have provide clear enough guidance'.

Silent Waters replied, but as she did so the Parrotfish took two more mouthfuls of coral with loud crunches. Sky stared at it in annoyance and only heard her completing her point:

'…have never seen Ocean as sick as we see her now. Forces beyond all experience are at work. Perhaps new interpretations should be considered. You know that some will be saying as much at the Gathering.'

'The Way has served the Ka-Tse and other zeta species well through the millennia,' Green Wave replied obstinately. 'We cannot deviate from its teachings.'

'I am not suggesting deviation,' she smiled, 'but we must listen to these new ideas and consider the *spirit* of the Way as well as the histories. The Way did not spring into being instantly. The first guidance was created by the wise zetii of the ancient times and over the ages other wise zetii supplemented that knowledge, adding more interpretations and advice. Just because words are ancient does not make them infallible. The wise ones of old could not foresee every possibility, nor should we presume that the ancients had a monopoly on wisdom. The ones who monitor such things for us...'

Another explosive crunch beside Sky's head drowned her out. In exasperation, Sky opened his eyes wide at the Parrotfish and made a small snapping gesture at it. The little fish darted away but then stopped. Somehow it seemed to sense that Sky could not move at present. It came back to its feeding spot, and, while eyeing Sky, took another loud bite. Sky could not help but imagine it had a smug expression in its eye as it did so.

Green Wave had apparently redirected the conversation in the meantime, and was now talking about the Novices.

'...your son amongst them, talking about heretical things, even zeta killing zeta.'

'Indeed? And what did you do?'

'I castigated them of course. It is wholly inappropriate for them to be speaking that way, especially your son. He may well be leading the clan one day!'

'Perhaps there may be value in talking to them about it. In my experience, true belief comes from understanding, not received dogma. I see you have brought them here, let me speak to them.'

She swam over to the Novices accompanied by a stern faced Green Wave Falling.

'First, let me say how sad I was to learn of Wakes Softly's death. We are trying to find out what happened, of course, and if we learn more we will tell you. I am deeply disturbed that we have had two seemingly unnatural deaths so close together, and if you think of anything that might explain them you must tell me at once. But now you are here because your teacher tells me that you have made statements that contradicted the tenets of the Way. Muddy River Mouth, is this true?'

'Prime Mother, we were only discussing the things that everyone speaks about these days: the lack of hunting and why it is happening. I just repeated what they say the Guardians believe.'

Green Wave snorted. 'You see Prime Mother! Shameless! Advocating their beliefs is forbidden!'

She nodded slightly towards him. 'Yes, thank you for reminding us of what is forbidden, Green Wave Falling-*Jeii*. And it seems to me that the key expression here is advocating. Agreeing with the ideas of the Guardians may be a reason for exile but discussing them is not. Do you agree with them, Muddy?'

'Absolutely not, Prime Mother!'

'I am glad to hear it.' She looked each of the others in the eye. Deneb looked back steadily; Dusk smiled slightly and looked away. She last looked at Sky. He found it hard to hold that look; it seemed to see straight through the lens of his eye and into the back reaches of his mind. He wondered if Cloud Passing would have told her about his experience with the Guardians. Then she spoke again. 'Your first lesson tomorrow should take the form of a debate, I think. Each of you can explain one of the tenets of Guardian belief as you understand them and defend it as best you can. The others can apply counter arguments. Green Wave Falling will act as moderator.'

Green Wave Falling said nothing, but Sky thought he looked deeply unhappy with this outcome. Silent Waters changed the subject: 'It is useful that you are here in another respect though. A Council Meeting is about to begin. I have received a nomination for a replacement Voice which I have accepted. Councillor Green Wave Falling: Touches The Sky is our new Voice of Youth.'

The older dolphin bowed slightly to Sky, and murmured something that might have been congratulations or welcome, or perhaps something else completely. His eyes looked cold and hostile to Sky.

Silent Waters dismissed the other three Novices, and led Sky a short distance to where the Council meeting was to be held. Green Wave trailed behind them. Sky stayed parallel to her as she swam and made brief excursions to the surface. He listened attentively as she briefed him about his role at the meetings. This seemed simple enough; most of her guidance related to the proper etiquette to be observed when addressing other Council members, what to do if he wished to speak and so on. However, for the time being, Sky resolved to say nothing unless he was asked.

They reached the appointed place and almost immediately Cloud Passing and five other elderly dolphins approached, making their signature calls.

After an exchange of pleasantries, including a special welcome to Sky, they formed a rough circle at the seabed, each of them upright with their tails brushing the swaying sea grass. Silent Waters declared the meeting open, slipping into the traditional dialogue style of a Council meeting.

'The Council considers a request from the Voice of the Others. The Council recognises the respected Councillor Cloud Passing.'

Cloud Passing, long-time holder of the post of Voice of the Others, moved to the centre of the circle, 'This zeta gives thanks to the Council for their consideration and reports that the Voice of the Others wishes to invite an ambassador of the Xenthos to speak to the Grand Council at the coming Gathering.' He backed into the circle circumference again.

Green Wave Falling raised his head slightly. Silent Waters nodded imperceptibly and he entered the circle.

'May the Council be informed as to why the Voice of the Others makes such a request? No zetii other than the Ka-Tse have attended a Gathering in a thousand years. Surely it is the function of the Voice of the Others to speak on behalf of all other species. What would it serve to have Xenthos present? Councillor Cloud Passing's wisdom is renowned — he can speak very well for the Xenthos.' He returned to the circle.

Another councillor asked permission to speak and was bidden to enter the circle. Sky recognised him as North Wind, the present Voice of Change. The middle aged dolphin edged forward with his distinctive, awkward finning action. North Wind had been born with a deformed spine which caused his tail flukes to twist out at an unusual angle. It was a disability that would have caused the early death of most dolphins, but North Wind was a fighter. Sky knew him as an outspoken individual who was often openly critical of some of the Ka-Tse traditions. But here in the Council he spoke in more moderated terms.

'Many have said that the Xenthos and Xa-Hana have ignored the quotas and are plundering the principle fish stocks. It is true that the Walkers can also be blamed for this, but we cannot control their actions. If the Xenthos break their word with the quotas, then how may we expect truth from them at a Ka-Tse Gathering? This would seem a waste of the Grand Council's time.'

He withdrew and another, an elderly female, moved into the centre.

'While this request may be unusual, in such it fits the times. The Grand Council will again consider the matter of the quotas. While the Voice of the Others has the duty to speak for all Ocean's creatures, there may be merit in hearing from the Xenthos themselves in this case. The situation is becoming dire as you all well know.'

Silent Waters turned to Sky. 'The Council would know the thoughts of the Young.'

Sky hesitated, wanting to say that he could not be expected to know what all the young thought, but Silent Waters had briefed him on this very point. He should speak as though he did know; using his judgement to try to put forward the views of the younger generations as best he could.

'The Young are fearful for the future. There are deep concerns for the Ka-Tse: the poisons in the water, the new sounds, the sicknesses. But the most immediate problem is the lack of hunting and there are natural suspicions towards the other zeta species. There must be merit in hearing one of their members speak so that we can judge their integrity rather than guess at it.'

Sky backed into the circle. Silent Waters gave him a brief, encouraging smile with her eyes then tilted her head towards the surface. As one, they ascended to breathe then reformed the circle at the bottom.

No more requests were made to speak, so Silent Waters moved into the circle herself. 'With due attention paid to these worthy considerations, it is now proposed that the Council respectfully accedes to the wishes of the Voice of the Others and extends this clan's hospitality to the Xenthos envoy. Do any members of this Council dissent?'

None spoke.

'The Council therefore asks the respected Councillor Cloud Passing to make it so.'

'This zeta is honoured to carry out the wishes of the Council,' he replied, inclining his head respectfully.

Silent Waters closed the meeting, and they all made their farewells. Sky was about to go when she called him back. 'You spoke well at your first meeting Sky.'

'Thank you, Prime Mother. But I didn't understand why there is so much resistance to hearing from the Xenthos.'

'When a clan experiences hard times its members look for someone or something to blame. It suits many Ka-Tse to be able to have a simple answer to their predicament. Ordinarily that might be harmless enough, but as you know, there are forces at work trying to poison their minds. Saying that we must take action against the other zetii to stop them taking more than their fair share. I have never heard of a situation like this in our past and I think it very dangerous. And speaking of danger — Cloud Passing tells me that he has selected you for more than just the task of being a Voice.'

Sky looked at her anxiously. Did she mean the Aligners of the Way?

'Yes, Sky, I am one of the few that know. And I think we must guard the secret more closely than ever before. The Aligners keep the Way alive. They ensure it adapts to the needs of Ocean and the zetii. There are those that do not want the zetii to be content, especially not the Ka-Tse. It suits them to have discontent among us, so they may seek to disrupt the work of the Aligners. Born Into Summer died out of her time, and she died at a very bad time for us. She was to be our Aligner. Sky, you must take great care to keep secret what you are to become. I fear for you.'

Her eyes dropped to the wound on his belly, but she said nothing more. Sky wondered if she had been told about last night.

'But, I have no real idea what I am becoming, Prime Mother. And Cloud Passing says he has no time to teach me!'

'Cloud will have a plan. Trust in his wisdom. But trust no one else lightly! You must be careful, Sky!'

Chapter 17

"Name the young with care
Listen to the waves
Observe the stars
Will this one
Ride the surf
Or fight the current?"

- Traditional: the "grandmother's advice" from a Naming Ceremony

Sky was fully awake with the first light of the next day and swam over to Muddy, who was close by. Muddy was clearly still in the semiconscious state that dolphins sleep in, occasionally gently swimming to the surface to breath, with one eye partially open. Sky nudged him gently to no effect twice, then, despairing, gave him a sharp jab in the ribs.

'Ow, why do you always have to do that?' Muddy complained.

'Because it's the only way to wake you up! You'd still be dreaming by the time Senx fell again if I let you.'

'No I wouldn't, I'd be starving by then. But I *was* dreaming just now. And what a dream! I was with that lovely Moon Above Antares; we were alone in the shallows, just brushing alongside each other at first, then she turned that sweet, smooth belly towards me and...'

'Yes, thanks, I can imagine what happened next,' Sky interrupted. 'Can I remind you that as a final year Novice you've several more Moons of chastity to endure?'

'*Don't* remind me please,' Muddy moaned, 'it's killing me.'

'Well, I know how to take your mind off it. Let's find ourselves something to eat.'

They cruised the shallow water around one end of the bay, searching for food. There were several small coral heads protruding from the sand and swarms of bright orange anthias darted back into the shelter of the coral as they passed. Soon things started to look more promising, however, and they both intoned a quick thanking to Senx for those that must be sacrificed that they might live. In one spot they found a good sized shoal of fusiliers. The dolphins managed to snatch several of them as they rocketed into its midst, when the shoal exploded in a panic of metallic blue bodies.

Later, Muddy discovered that there were a few flat fish buried just below the sand. Invisible to the eye, they reflected the dolphins' sonar distinctly and were easy enough to spot. As they found each one, they gave it a short burst of high power sound to stun it before snatching it up. There were several there, and as no quotas had been set for that species they could hunt without restraint for once. An hour after sunrise they had fed quite well and swam back to the bay, taking turns to leap from the water as they swam.

As they entered the bay and began to hear the chatter of the clan, they made their signature calls. An excited young dolphin approached them and called: 'Muddy River Mouth-Jeii, come play with us!'

'Some of my students from yesterday;' Muddy explained. 'Shall we spend a little while with them?'

'Why not? It's full moon now so let's enjoy our day off. Let's see what they are doing.'

The young dolphin led them to where a sandy depression fringed with rock and broken coral created a natural amphitheatre where five young ones were playing. They had a long strand of green algae and one by one they would take it centre stage and show off to their friends. The others circled about and called encouragement or good-natured insults to the performer depending on the show they put on.

The two older dolphins watched one shoot in to take her turn, neatly hooking the algae on the tip of a pectoral fin. She swooped and dived with the translucent green strip strung out alongside her as a banner; she only finally lost it when she attempted to spin around her own axis and it slipped off her fin.

'Me next!' called a petite but exuberant dolphin of about a year and a half old. Sky recognised her as Pebbles Rolling, a bundle of energy and always talking. She chose to hook the strand on her dorsal fin; a much harder trick, as it was then behind her line of sight and the dorsal fin slopes back more than the pectoral.

'Watch this, watch this,' she called, trying to swim forward at speed with her back arched and her nose towards the sand. At first it worked but when she tried to add a rhythmic rocking back and forth, she soon lost it.

'Muddy! Muddy! Muddy!' the group chanted and he looked sheepishly at Sky. 'They obviously like you,' Sky said quietly to him. 'Let's see if we can do a double act! You hook it from below and stay level; I'll do the fancy stuff.'

Muddy barrelled under the algae with Sky just behind him and hooked the strand on his dorsal fin. At the same moment, Sky swam over him and flipped onto his back so that the tip of his dorsal fin was pressed against Muddy's. Off they swam at speed with the green banner trapped at the join between their fins, Sky on his back, both tails pumping up and down in unison.

The young dolphins cheered in delight as the pair did a lap of the depression in formation, only losing their strand as they peeled apart at the end of their circuit.

'Oh, Muddy River Mouth-Jeii, please, please teach us how to do that!' cried Pebbles.

Muddy gave an embarrassed sideways look at Sky, who was smiling to himself. 'Well, some other time perhaps— Touches The Sky and I have important things to do just now.'

As they left the noisy group trying to emulate their trick, Sky whispered, 'What important things would they be?'

'Nothing of course, but I wanted to leave while we still look good. You know very well that you did all the work in that trick; I just swam along the seabed! Should I have said something?'

'Well, your students seem to think the world of you, and I see no reason to disillusion them. Come on, let's look for the rest of the clan, it's nearly noon.'

They swam back along parallel to the shore, following the lines of the ripples in the sandy areas. Soon they came across nine young adults who were trying to out do each other with their bubble art creations; practising in preparation for the competitions to be held at the Gathering. Deneb Rising was amongst them.

As they arrived, one left the seabed, catapulting herself upwards, shooting through the silver barrier of the surface. The other dolphins watched the broken image of her grey body cartwheel through the air until she fell sideways back through the surface. At that moment she shot in a half-roll diagonally downwards, dragging a tunnel of silver behind her which gently drifted upwards behind her.

The others cheered her on, and then quieted as Deneb took his turn. He, too, started his leap almost vertically, and with great power, jumping eight times his body length above the water. He re-entered with almost no splash, but immediately executed a series of rapid, tight loops, exhaling air from his blowhole as he did so. The resulting bubble painting was a near-perfect spiral of dancing bubbles which swirled in his wake.

Sky joined the others in congratulating him on such a fine creation, 'You will take all the prizes with a dive like that Deneb, no wonder you get the pick of any hunt — you get faster every time I see you!'

'Then you'd *all* better learn to swim like our esteemed "leader-in-waiting" or get used to being hungry!' Sky recognised the owner of the gruff, mocking tone before he turned to see North Wind. 'Instead of making pretty pictures, you would all do well to concentrate on the real business of the Gathering: finding a way to stop our children having the food stolen from their mouths!'

Deneb, unfazed by North Wind's usual aggressive manner, confronted him. 'And what do you mean by that?'

'You know very well what I mean: other zetii, those pretty Xenthos and oh-so happy, leaping, Za-Hana are flouting the agreed quotas and taking our food!'

'There is no actual proof of that,' Deneb reminded him, ever the diplomat, 'many think that the real reason for our current problems are the Walkers.'

'Current problems?' North Wind sneered, 'This is not a *current* situation, lad, this is the decline of zetii civilisation that you're all witnessing. Have you understood nothing of the Seekers reports? Everything is bad — the fish stocks are depleting at a rate they can't recover from, the water near the coasts is turning to poison, the very air is being damaged, and Ocean is warming up like never before. What's going on? Do we have to wait for another Great Alluvium before anyone realises that we should have done something?'

Sky noticed that a few of the young dolphins around him seemed to be listening attentively and nodding as though they agreed with this rhetoric. He interrupted: 'So, what would you have us do?'

North Wind turned to him. 'Ah, yes, young Touches The Sky, our newest Voice. Now, you always seemed like a moderately intelligent young zeta; can't you work it out? We can't just float about like plankton, hoping the other zetii species will see reason. We have to make them understand that they *have* to comply. It's no good asking them to please be nice! They are parasites in our range, they would eat *us* if they could!'

Sky went on, realising a cracked edge was entering his voice, 'So we do what? Use force? Attack them? Kill them even? Like the Guardians want? What about the Way?'

North Wind gave a hollow laugh, evidently pleased that he was getting to Sky. 'You expect me openly to countenance what the Guardians preach? I would have thought you — with your family connections — should know the penalties. To openly endorse their philosophies or make any contact with them means exile! Pah! They may be pariahs to us, but that does not mean that every thought they have is bad!'

He swam off in his awkward way before any of them had a chance to reply.

'I hate it when he does that!' Sky exploded, 'He always goes off just when he thinks he's ahead in an argument; never lets you reply!'

Many of the dolphins were now discussing what had just taken place in low tones, the bubble art forgotten. Deneb signalled to Sky and Muddy that they should go, and they swam off towards the shallows, leaving the others behind.

Muddy broke the silence. 'I don't understand how he's still here with the clan with the things he says. Not only that, but he even has a place on the Council!'

'Well,' Deneb observed, 'if you listen to him carefully, he never actually endorses the hardline stuff the Guardians propose.'

Sky looked doubtful. 'Surely he must have spent time with them though, he sounds just like one.'

'How do you know Sky?' asked Deneb archly, 'I hope you haven't been visiting them during your little expedition with Muddy?'

'No, I didn't! But if Rain Ending doesn't come with news about my father at the Gathering...'

'You'll what?'

Sky shook his head and sped ahead, leaving Muddy and Deneb behind him.

CHAPTER 18

"Ah, decisions in love
If it eases your spirit
Believe that you think with your mind
But your body dictates what you think about
And your heart decides what you do"
- *The poet Jupiter by Regulas (9,467-9,491 post Great Alluvium)*

Twenty-eight days later, just before the next full moon, Dusk was once again swimming through the night towards the familiar rock arch. This time Storm Before Darkness was waiting for her, but in the distance she could just make out the shapes of two more dolphins by the moonlight. They were still hovering in the background after she and Storm had made their greetings and, according to their habit, had begun to swim together along the steep, sandy slope.

'Do you have to have those big lugs following you around all the time?'

Storm glanced back at the hulking forms of the two followers, 'Rock and Nightfall? They just want to protect me.'

'Protect you from what? I hate having them follow us around all the time.'

'Look, little one, there are many who fear what the Guardians represent and they might want to harm me — you too if they knew how important you are to me. And besides, they like doing this job; they think it's an honour.'

'You could at least have someone interesting hanging around that I could talk to when you are busy,' Dusk complained, 'those two have the intellect of a sea cucumber — and that's if you combine both their minds.'

Storm laughed. 'Well they don't get the job for being great conversationalists, but they are good fighters! Stay here a moment, and I'll tell them to wait by the arch for us.'

She watched him go back to talk to them. Rock On Sand seemed to be objecting at first but they left after a few words. As they moved away into the darkness she thought she saw Sorrow After Nightfall give her a hard look. She found herself wondering how Storm knew they were such good fighters and why that mattered so much.

Storm approached her from behind and, dropping his pectoral fins, swam above her back, caressing her from tail to head, then turned in slow circles around her head, nuzzling her face with his.

'I missed you so much,' he murmured, 'you don't know how much.'

'Well perhaps I missed you too,' she said tartly, and swam quickly away into the shallows, leaving a stream of flickering phosphorescence in her wake. Storm followed her and easily caught up. He slipped above her and pushed her down with his body until they were almost swimming on the sand.

'Storm, get off!' she said, trying to sound angry, but the feeling of his physical power over her gave her the same confusing mix of emotions.

'Stop swimming and I will!'

She stopped, but looked away from him. He swam again from her tail to her head, this time spiralling around her body, caressing her with his pectoral fins. It felt delicious but she tried to stay unmoved.

'You're driving me crazy,' Storm whispered to her, and this time her eyes smiled. 'Ha!' he cried, 'she isn't made of ice!' He quickly somersaulted backwards over her head and disappeared behind her. In a moment though, he was under her, pressing his belly against hers.

She felt his need for her and a shock of hot desire ran through her body, but she peeled away from him and moved off a little way.

'Storm, no!' she gasped, 'you know my situation as a Novice! This is so unfair of you!'

'Who would know if you are celibate or not?' he growled, 'and anyway that finishes in just three moons!'

'No, and that's it! Now let's talk about something else.'

Storm was terse for a while, but started asking her about the Gathering which was to start the next evening. She answered distractedly, fighting with her own inner desires. Although she did want him in moments of passion, she had to admit to herself that it was a relief to have the excuse of being a final year Novice. Without it, would she take their relationship further? There was something that troubled her about Storm, but she could not say what.

She told him about the planned celebrations and who would be there. He was quite shocked to hear the news about Cloud Passing and also seemed very interested to hear about the ambassador who was coming to represent the clans of common dolphins.

'A Xenthos appearing at a Gathering?' he said, 'Has that ever happened before?'

'Yes, once, in 12,231,' she said. 'I had to unlock some data at dusk yesterday for the Council and that was one of the things I remember.'

'Over a thousand years ago!' Storm exclaimed, 'You Starwriters are amazing. Just how much have they stuffed in that pretty head of yours?'

'It feels like far too much, but maybe that is to do with all the studying at the Academy! I'm hoping it will get easier soon when I graduate, then at least I'll only be using my subconscious for all this stuff.'

'And you really can't recall any of it without an unlocking song?'

'No, I've told you this a hundred times! Just accept that you can't imagine what it is like — you couldn't do it as a male anyway. We can't access any of it without the right unlocking song and the right cosmic arrangement. Can we talk about something else please?'

They carried on talking and swimming in the pale light for hours. Eventually they made their way back to the arch where the two bodyguards were waiting restlessly. The sky was becoming lighter so they quickly said their farewells and Dusk left.

Storm watched Dusk's slim form disappear into the now blue-grey water.

'Kark-Du Storm Before Darkness?' Rock On Sand said respectfully.

'Yes,' said Storm distractedly.

'She is one of those Academy types isn't she, Kark-Du? Must be clever I suppose.'

'Very. And a Starwriter too.'

'A Starwriter?' Rock echoed dully, 'Wasn't that female who joined us a few moons back a Starwriter?'

'That's right,' Storm murmured, half to himself, 'the first one to join us. And a Dreamweaver too.'

Rock began again, encouraged by his leader's softer mood, 'Kark-Du...,' but Storm was back in the moment.

'Come on,' he said brusquely, 'we have a lot to do.'

He led them back the short distance to the region of coral heads that the Guardians were basing themselves from for the present. The sun was half above the horizon now and the shallowest water had a pinkish tinge.

As they neared the mass of dolphins, Storm's second in command, Sharp Beak, made his signature call and approached them. His small wiry body looked odd in contrast to his over-large head. This was tipped with an unusually long rostrum that immediately revealed the source of his name.

'Greetings, Kark-Du, how was your rendezvous?'

'Pleasant enough,' Storm replied. Then, to his bodyguards: 'Rock, Nightfall, go and find something to eat. Meet me back here at half post-noon and bring the rest of the Inner Guard — I have something important to explain to them.'

As they left, Sharp Beak looked interested.

'Well, Kark-Du, you have lost a lot of sleep with your night-time meetings, I hope it has proven worthwhile.'

Storm's eyes flicked towards him, betraying his annoyance. 'She amuses me. And I think she is close to being converted to our beliefs. You know the value I place on her joining us.'

The smaller dolphin nodded, and picked his next words more carefully, cautious of angering his master. 'Did she tell you anything new about the Gathering?'

'The only news to me was that Cloud Passing is to make a Darkening Dive at the Gathering.'

'I've heard of Cloud Passing.'

'He's reputedly a zeta of high integrity who has reached the first level of consciousness — I wish I'd met him. Too bad for him, but good for us. He was a senior Aligner, and this gets him out of the way quicker than we could hope. Everything else she said was confirmation of what our source has already told me.'

'We are lucky to have such a well placed spy Kark-Du.'

Storm grunted. 'It nearly all went wrong. That silly little female that followed him — she might have identified him and then we would have had to redo much of our work.'

'How did you find out who she was in the end?'

'Later, she had a chance meeting with our friend and hinted at what she thought she had seen. It seems it was too much for her conscience to accuse another without telling them first!'

'Ahh. So that's why he led her to us.'

'Typical of his hypocrisy! He doesn't want any zeta blood in his jaws, but he's happy for us to do it for him.'

'Still, he has been very useful. Your plan seems to be going well, Kark-Du'

'I am encouraged. But everything must go perfectly if we are to accomplish our goals. The time is right to finally raise the Ka-Tse from lethargy. So many are growing frustrated with the old, soft interpretations of the Way. They are beginning to open their eyes to the hard facts. The Way is meant for the Ka-Tse alone, not these lesser zetii. They only need waking up to see that they have the power to dominate them. There is already plenty of mistrust; if we can just give them enough reason to hate them, the events we need to happen will take place naturally.'

'And we can move forward now, Kark Du?'

Storm narrowed his eyes. 'Yes. We'll soon have a chance to right the wrongs against our clan. I think one or two good zetii may have to make the ultimate sacrifice, but they will be remembered well for it in time. Thanks in part to their gift, the other Ka-Tse will soon learn that they are the rightful masters of Ocean and their children no longer need to go hungry. They will finally see why they have to stop these lesser creatures taking what is rightfully theirs.'

CHAPTER 19

"Give your family and lovers the respect you give a stranger and you will always be loved."
- Traditional

Dusk approached the headland at the east end of the clan's bay as the day was just beginning. She leapt from the water from time to time and could now see signs of activity. The other bottlenose dolphin clans had begun to arrive in the last two days and the bay was getting crowded with them. Against the first rays of the new sun, there was evidence of their multitude in the distance, with many of the younger ones jumping from the golden water in their excitement. She stopped surfacing and held her breath for the final part of the approach to the headland so as not to arouse suspicion.

Suddenly she was aware of the faint sound of another dolphin's echolocation. It was the deep pulses used to search though the seabed, or to scan another dolphin's internal organs for illness or injury. She was about to change direction when she noticed the sound had abruptly stopped. She realised that the other dolphin must have heard her own echolocation and it would seem strange to turn around. Then, a call, close by:

'It is I, Touches The Sky!'

'And it is I, Fades Into Dusk,' she responded, partially relieved it was him, but also concerned at what he might think.

Sky appeared ahead of her. She decided to bluff it out by putting him on the defensive.

'What are you doing all the way out here on your own?' she asked.

'I was going crazy in the bay, already it's like every Ka-Tse in Ocean is there, and another four clans are still expected. And you? Where've you been?'

'I…just needed some time to think too. Went for an early swim.'

'I was looking for you yesterday evening: no one knew where you were. Dusk, I was worried about you.'

Dusk could see from his eyes that he meant it; he was genuinely concerned and she was touched. She felt guilty, not just for lying now, but because she had treated him badly in the last year. Since she had met Storm she had found it hard to be close to Sky as they had once been, as she was afraid she might give away her secret.

'Well…thanks. But I'm fine, don't worry. Any news of the world from the latest arrivals?'

Sky looked as though he had more questions in his mind but he answered her.

'Same old story. The shortage of prey isn't just around here, it's everywhere. Some of the older and weaker ones look seriously under fed.'

'They have to come up with something drastic at the Gathering. We can't go on like this.'

'It's the same for the other zetii species,' he said, 'they've the same problems we have. That's why it's good that the Xenthos are sending someone this time. If we can get all the zetii to work together, we can get through this.'

She marvelled at the complete contrast between his attitude and that of Storm. Storm would have said that this was weakness, that the other zetii species were inferior to the Ka-Tse and that they couldn't be trusted. Who was right? She looked into Sky's eyes and saw his earnest look: he really believed that this was the right thing to do.

'What if it doesn't work? What if we find that they *are* ignoring the quotas and tricking us? How can we force them to stop taking our food then?'

Sky shook his head, 'What's the alternative? To try and force them to? To attack or even kill them?'

'Sky,' she pleaded, 'what if there's no other choice? Do you want to see the clan's children starve and die?'

'No, but still, the Way is clear, we can't kill another being except for food. No exceptions.'

'But some say that it's acceptable in self-defence, and we *are* under attack.'

'I've heard that too and I know where it comes from, it's a quote from Stone Eyes, that prophet of theirs who lived a hundred years ago. The Guardians follow his teachings you know. Think about what you're saying Dusk! Don't you remember Born? Or Wakes? What killed them? I know what these Guardians are capable of!'

'How do you know, Sky?'

Sky looked at her intently as though trying to read her mind. She felt intensely nervous.

'Never mind,' he said at last. 'Look, tonight Cloud Passing is going to tell the Creation Legend during the opening ceremonies. Come with me and listen to it.'

'Well...yes, let's do that. Thanks — it's a lovely idea.'

As they swam back, she trailed slightly behind him, suddenly seeing him differently. She had known him since they were very small and she realised that she had missed something in the last few years. He was no child any more but a confident adult, with clear ideas about the world. Not just an adult in mind either, he had a strong, powerful body; not massive power like Storm but a natural, lithe strength that let him move with a natural grace.

She followed him back to the clan in a state of confusion.

CHAPTER 20

"And Senx said, 'I have'."

- From the Creation Legend

Fifty-seven clans of bottlenose dolphins had arrived in the bay, most of which had ten to thirty members. A few were larger, like Sky and Dusk's clan, and there were also some smaller, all male groups. In all, over a thousand dolphins were there.

Silent Waters addressed them that evening as the sun settled into the horizon, formally opening the Gathering. In a clearing in the coral the visitors formed a dense, milling circle around her. She held herself upright, with her tail just off the sandy bottom, speaking with a clear, confident voice. 'You honour our clan by joining us this year. There will be much here for you to enjoy; there will be exhibitions of strength and elegance, dance, song, and recitals. Of course, you will meet old friends again; some of you will find new ones, maybe even new lovers.'

She smiled as she said this: for the young adult dolphins, a Gathering was a wonderful opportunity to find a mate from another clan and many of them had become highly excited at the prospect over the last few weeks.

She continued: 'But, of course, there is a serious side to a Gathering, this one perhaps more than any in our history. We live in strange times. Ocean is sicker than our forbearers would have believed possible just one hundred years ago. Many fish populations are at critical levels, and the water temperatures are rising unnaturally quickly. I do not have to remind you of the long memory of our race. Our histories, kept safe over millennia by the Starwriters, allow us to estimate what may come as a result. Eventually, the great conveyor currents will change course or stop, and then the whole Cycle of Life will be disrupted. The Starwriters tell us such things have happened before, but we have never known it to happen so fast, or to such degree. All Ocean's life forms will be affected. Some will adapt, some will perish, but it will be hard for all. Who knows what the end result will be. Therefore, at this Gathering, the Grand Council will meet as usual but this will be their prime mission: to find a way forward for us all. At this stage, we do not expect to regain our old style of life again. Instead we must find a way for the Ka-Tse, for all zetii, and perhaps indeed for Ocean herself, to simply survive.'

Those dolphins that had initially been restless as she spoke had by now grown still and silent. The crowd was unnaturally quiet; just the occasional movement as one drifted gently to the surface to breathe.

She paused, a sad smile in her eyes, then continued, 'I apologise for opening this Gathering with such thoughts, but we must face these facts. However, we should remember the teachings of the Way: the purpose of life is to take joy in life. So we will take as much joy as we can from these five days. Now please join me at the surface to witness the rising of the full moon!'

They all rose to the surface and, on that cue, a chorus began, a song without words, a melody so old that no one knew its origin. One by one others joined in; the music gently rose and fell like an ocean swell. First with deeper notes, then, as the top edge of the pale disc appeared, rising in pitch and pace; gently at first, then as more and more of the bright, white circle appeared, increasing to a joyous crescendo of sound — and finally, as the bottom of the moon peeled away from its reflected image in the sea, just as it seemed the music must implode upon itself with its own crashing power, they stopped. As one.

The silence rang loud for a long time. Then, at last, Silent Waters said, 'Cloud Passing, a dear friend to many here, will now recite the Creation Legend.'

The dolphins settled down once more into the circle at the bottom. A few mothers hushed distracted young ones and then there was silence again.

Cloud Passing moved slowly, stiffly, into the centre and once there slowly turned around. Although the light was failing, every dolphin there felt that just for a moment, he looked directly into their eyes.

When he began, in a clear, measured voice, it seemed too as though his words were meant just for each one of them.

'At first there was only infinite space. Unimaginably cold and dark like the deepest reaches of the sea. Yet empty. No living creature, no plants, no rock, no water. The void waited an eternity of time until the darkness exploded into a million stars, flung outwards like shining sand grains to light the endless night. These stars passed through the icy nothingness, each one bearing its message of light and the promise of life. One such star was Senx. He burned and raged, swelling with fire then subsiding as he learnt to control his power. A number of great, cold stones drifted towards him, drawn by his magnificence and blinding light. Yet they were soon repelled by his great heat and so chose instead to circle him endlessly and to bathe in his light, each in their own path, at their own chosen distance from him.

The third of these stones twisted in agony for countless centuries. Great mountains were thrown up upon it and destroyed again. Rivers of fire scoured its surface. Slowly its torments subsided and the stone began to cool. With the cooling came the first drop of rain; and that most precious substance in the universe: water. The rain fell without rest while the stone spun around and around Senx, countless, countless times. The water fell into the deep cracks of the stone and cooled its fire. As the rain fell, the water rose and gradually great seas filled and their shorelines edged up across the lifeless ground.

The third stone changed. Senx saw the clouds slowly part to reveal that one of his attendants had put aside the drab mantle of its fellows and was now a shining, liquid blue orb. The stone had become Ocean and Senx delighted in her beauty. Ocean continued her slow dance around Senx and he was entranced by her radiance. Dancing together so for an eternity they could do nothing but become lovers. Across the coldness of space he planted light, his seed, into the sea, her womb.

Mother Ocean spilled forth life. The first of her children were tiny, simple things but they grew and changed. Because they were the first and dearest to her they followed her teachings closely and adapted themselves to enjoy her gifts. Ocean's children were small and slow at first but they learnt to swim and to hunt and to think. The fruits of Ocean's coupling with Senx were so bountiful that they filled the sea and spilled onto the land so that it too began to flower and became green with life.

After a long time and many changes came a new creature; smooth skinned, warm blooded, sharp of eye and mind. The first two were T'ret, a sleek, fast, female, and her strong and proud brother Den-tew-ron. They were as bright with life as stars and Ocean saw them and was glad. They spoke to each other, swam, sang, leapt to the sky and revelled in the beauty of the Universal.

As they became more independent, the siblings spent much of their time playing in the shallow waters. They were fascinated with the newly fertile land which held so much promise. When they reached the Age of Decision, they chose to leave their birthing place and to climb from the waters. At first this was hard, as they had to accept the great burden of gravity against which land dwellers must struggle their whole lives.

For many millennia they were enthralled with the exploration of the land, which, although small compared to the vastness of Ocean's waters, held many secrets. They saw the multitude of forms from the simple to the complex, but still they were the most quick minded of all that was there. Over time they became proud and vain and believed themselves to be superior to nature's other forms. One day, Den-tew-ron said, "We are so much above these simple things, sister; let us bend this world to our needs."

They spent an age on their plans, saying this valley shall be filled with water, this lake will be emptied, this plant will be made stronger, this creature will perish. Then, just before they were about to begin their scheme, T'ret was sleeping alone at the edge of the sea and had a dream.

T'ret dreamt that Senx came to her, terrible in his power, and spoke. "Are you so intoxicated with your power that you have lost sight of the Universal? Observe!"

And T'ret dreamt that Senx lifted her up high and changed the flow of the river of time so that she could see the world that she and Den-tew-ron had envisioned come into being: slowly at first, then, gradually faster and faster. The first scenes were happy enough; as they had imagined, the less pleasing creatures, or those they saw no purpose for, soon faded from the face of Ocean. New lakes grew, flooding areas of the land. Those things that they discarded were flushed into the sea and swallowed from sight, that land which they had decreed must be cleared of vegetation was burned and the essence of those things on it were carried as black smoke into the air and seemed to vanish.

But the time-river flowed more swiftly, and, as rivers do when they must flow swiftly, time lost its calmness and became violent and turbulent. T'ret watched in horror as their fine plans became undone; those creatures they had thought of as beautiful soon had nothing to eat and must tear each other apart. Black, acid rain fell from the skies and the great forests began to decay. As they failed to turn the light of Senx into life-giving oxygen, other creatures began to suffer. Birds fell from the sky; other animals dug holes into the ground where they could live out their last days in anguish and watch their young die before their eyes. And all this time all the debris of the land's destruction washed into the sea and those that dwelt there choked upon the filth.

The time-river flowed faster still and T'ret watched the images of she and her brother becoming mad with their power. They destroyed the remaining forests, raped the seas of life and covered the green earth with a cold, grey, liquid stone which hardened and sealed out life. Their descendants multiplied like a mould across the face of Ocean, out of all control. Soon there was not enough food, not enough water, not enough air. In the last scenes, barely visible in a blur, they made weapons of stupendous power that let them destroy the remaining living; millions at a time.

At last, T'ret could bear no more, "Enough!" she cried, "Please, Senx, I will not see any more. We are wrong to be here — let my brother and I go back into the sea and we will forgo these plans!"

Senx said, "You may go back to the sea, but Den-tew-ron wishes to stay and continue with your plans."

"No, he will not!" cried T'ret, "show him what you have shown me and he will not!"

And Senx said, "I have."'

Cloud Passing paused for a long time, his eyes closed, his head bent down. In the silver moonlight, no one moved.

Slowly, he raised his head and half opened his eyes.

'So it came to be. T'ret left the land and returned to the sea forever. From her sprang the zetii, and they chose to live in harmony with Ocean and to keep the balance of the Cycle of Life.

Soon Den-tew-ron and his new kin forgot the zetii; they forgot everything under the sea. They believed themselves masters of all Ocean, and they wielded their power with the carelessness of a child.

It was left to the zetii to live in harmony with Ocean. They shall inherit what remains when the sons and daughters of Den-tew-ron have done their worst. They must keep Ocean safe and their path shall be the Way.'

CHAPTER 21

"Life is too short: live it to the full!
Our lives' values are but the sum of our experiences."
- Saturn Over Antares (12,415-12,438 post Great Alluvium)

Sky and Muddy made their way across the north-eastern curve of the bay towards one of the children's races. Some of Muddy's students were taking part and he wanted to be there to support them. They swam between the large coral heads that protruded from the sand, each surrounded by a swarm of brightly coloured fish. Of these, the small, golden Anthias shone especially brilliantly in the morning light. As they approached each head, the fish simultaneously dived into the crevices of the coral, each swarm of colour vanishing almost instantly — like a flame blown out.

Suddenly, the two friends became aware of a commotion approaching them; at first the sound of male voices, obviously swimming fast:

'Come on Venus, choose me — you don't want those two, look: they can barely keep up!'

'Don't listen to him! He is almost finished now — see how often he has to breathe, he can barely dive he's so fat!'

Then four young adults shot into view from the blue. Three males were in amorous pursuit of a beautiful female. Sky did not recognise her; she must be from one of the other clans. He noticed that she seemed to be keeping her distance from her would be suitors for now at least. She moved quickly but with an easy grace. She had an almost metallic blue-grey skin and unusually dark, intelligent eyes which suddenly locked with his own. He stared back, trying to think of something clever to say.

She came to a sudden stop beside Sky and Muddy and turned on her pursuers. They rushed up, the third of them, who had not yet spoken, blurting out:

'Darling, choose me, I am more worthy of your beauty than these bottom-dwellers. I may not sprint quite as fast as them, but watch me jump! Many call me Lightning because of my great leaps!'

She turned and spoke to the three of them for the first time.

'Alright: let's see you all jump then.'

The three males preened themselves excitedly, at last getting some attention from this lovely creature.

'Shall we jump in turn, or all at once so that you can see who's highest?'

'All at once please. And make it high: I expect to see you vanish from view.'

The three lined up excitedly, then, after a count, they shot towards the surface and leapt high into the air. As they flew upwards through the surface, she moved quickly over to Sky and stared hard at him.

'I went that way,' she said intently, tilting her head. Then she darted in the opposite direction behind the nearest coral head.

Just then, the three heroes came crashing back through the surface in a chaos of bubbles, each making whoops of victory. They milled about as the bubbles cleared and then stopped in confusion, with only Muddy and Sky in view.

Muddy glanced behind the coral head where the exotic female could only be seen by Sky and him. She was still staring meaningfully at Sky who seemed mesmerised.

'Where'd she go?' Lightning demanded.

Sky stammered, 'Well, she...'

Muddy rolled his eyes. 'She went that way!' he cried. 'Quick follow me, and we'll catch her!' To Sky he muttered, 'What I do for you...' and shot off, the three jumpers in hot pursuit.

The female slowly emerged from the coral and peered after them.

'Shame,' she said, 'plenty of muscles, short on brains'.

She turned. 'I liked your chubby friend though. And you are...'

'Touches The Sky,' he replied at last. 'My clan is hosting the Gathering.'

She still stared at him with those disconcerting dark eyes. 'And I am Venus In Mist, of the Western Red Mountains Clan.'

'So your clan call you Venus?'

'Only those who don't know me well. Those I really like call me Mist.'

'Well,' Sky began formally, 'it's my pleasure to meet you here, Venus In Mist...'

Her eyes gave a small smile. 'You can call me Mist.'

They spoke for some time. She told him about her clan, which, like Sky's, was one of the few large enough to have an Academy. She had recently finished her training as a Starwriter and was to take part in some of the Starwriters' songs at the Gathering.

She was clearly very intelligent but Sky noticed that even when they were speaking about serious things, her eyes often seemed to be smiling — was she mocking him? She was very self-confident and had a direct way of coming to the point that was both alarming and disarming at the same time. He was fascinated by her and realised that he had only once before found a female so interesting and — yes, he suddenly recognised the feeling for what it was now — attractive. It suddenly came to him what his feelings for Dusk must be; he wanted her physically — was it love? He had repressed the emotion because Dusk had been so cool to him this last year; he had to protect his heart. And he had only come to recognise it because some of those feelings were now coming to him again; because of this girl, Venus In Mist, with the direct way of talking and those extraordinary dark eyes.

'Sky, you haven't heard a word I just said, have you?'

'Sorry, I was thinking about something else for a moment — tell me again — please?'

'I was saying that I've promised to help one of our clan's females give birth today. It will be my first time to act as a birthing partner on my own,' she added proudly.

'Does the mother think that the baby is coming?' Sky asked.

'She was pretty sure it was this morning. I scanned her and it's in the right position, so yes — we're fairly certain.' She fixed him again with one of those deep eyes. 'I know — come with me.'

'Me? At a birth? I don't think that would be...'

'Nonsense! What is it with you males about babies? You're all so squeamish! You won't be able to be close to the mother in any case. But you can watch from a distance if you like.'

She tilted her head and watched him with a quizzical expression and an amused look that was barely suppressed.

Sky had the uneasy feeling that she was testing him somehow, and found himself agreeing.

'Good! Follow me then.' And off she went, Sky following, wondering what in Ocean he was doing.

They soon came to where the mother was waiting with others of their clan. She was in pain already; the first waves of labour were passing through her body.

Venus In Mist took the mother to a quiet spot in the shallows, Sky followed reluctantly at a distance. Then Mist came over to him and said,

'Wait here and keep quiet. I have told her you are my friend and she is quite happy for you to watch; just don't interfere.'

She left him before he could reply. Mist moved close to the mother and pointed her head at the side of her belly, then directed it along her body. Sky could hear the distinctive frequency of the sonar that she was directing to see inside the mother, using the reflected sound to identify the position of the baby.

'Is he alright?' the mother gasped.

'He... he's in the right position; he is going to come out tail first, which is good of course. You can start pushing soon now.'

'Hurts so much already, can't bear it.'

'Remember your pain control exercises. I'll help you. Now: take your pain and enclose it, keep it inside yourself but separate from yourself. You don't need to rush; your baby has waited a year to come out, he can wait a few more hours. I'll talk you through the pain.'

Mist continued on, her voice dropping to a rhythmic murmur that Sky could barely hear, but he recognised much of it from the pain containment exercises he had learned at the Academy.

'Feel your pain, see your pain. Look and see what colour it is and where it's living in your body. Wrap it up in liquid crystal. Let the crystal harden into a container to hold your pain. See the pain you feel through the crystal walls.

Now separate the pain from your mind. It's still there in your body, you can still see it, it still hurts, but it hurts alone, it does not hurt you. Watch it burn in a crystal of ice — the pain is still there but you don't have to feel it. Leave it to burn out its fire in your belly, safe in its crystal, but don't let the hurt reach your mind. Keep it locked in its crystal, watch the pain, it won't hurt you as it's far away now, and so deep in that cool crystal.'

The mother had it under control now and had a tranquil expression on her face although strong contractions rippled along her belly more and more frequently.

'Leave me to swim for a while my dear,' she said to Mist, I'm fine for the moment. She swam with slow, rhythmic beats of her tail; back and forth; back and forth; taking regular breaths at the surface; a distant look in her eyes.

Mist left her and swam to Sky's side.

'What happens next?' he asked.

'Soon she will give birth, and then she will have to snap the umbilical cord with a sharp twist of her body. In case she can't, I will bite through it for her. Then her baby will usually try to swim up to take his first breath, but if he is too weak the mother or I will help him up, until he can do it alone.'

Sky saw Mist watching the mother intently, a look of concern in her eyes.

'Is something wrong?' he asked.

'Sky, I don't know. When I scanned her I couldn't see any sign of life from it — should be moving a bit by now — probably just my inexperience.'

'I'm sure it'll be fine, you're doing such a great job helping her. Go back to her now, she needs you.'

Her eyes gave a little smile and she went back to the mother, who was taking breaths more frequently now, and spending more time near the surface.

Sky watched them for hours like this. Mist was constantly at the mother's side, offering encouragement or soothing her, helping her with the pain control litany. He marvelled at Mist's patience and strength and at the endurance of the mother who was clearly having a difficult birth. It was not until almost sunset that the baby, a male calf, was finally born.

CHAPTER 22

"The young squander their youth, the old their wisdom."
- Clouds Reveal Menkar (8,633 - ? post Great Alluvium)

'These are perverse times.' Silent Waters looked around the elders who had come to the Grand Council meeting. Nearly eighty of them had come here on this third day of the Gathering. They were almost exclusively dolphins in the later part of their lives, one or two chosen from each clan because of their experience and wisdom. Only the Dune Coast Clan had its full Council present, as was the custom for the host clan. All the dolphins were arranged in a loose circle, mostly upright with their tails occasionally gently stirring the sandy bottom. The sea surface was slightly ruffled by an onshore breeze and sunlight dappled the delegates with dancing rays of light. Sky held his place in the circle, uncomfortably aware that he was the youngest and most inexperienced by far.

Silent Waters went on, 'We have a lot to discuss today. Amongst the more important; the environmental changes we are measuring in Ocean, the actions of the Walkers, and our relationship with the other zetii, particularly regarding the hunting quotas. As you know, exceptionally for this meeting, it has been decided to invite an ambassador from the Xenthos to join us later today, and our Voice of the Others has arranged it.' She gestured towards Cloud Passing with her head as she spoke, but most of those present knew him. At fifty-two, he was the oldest present and his judgement was highly respected.

She went on, 'Let us begin by hearing from one of the Ka-Tse's best known Seekers: Always Counting'. An angular dolphin moved to the circle centre, his eyes darting about slightly nervously. Sky knew him mainly by reputation, and knew that from an early age Always Counting had preferred the sciences to social events. He was known as being uncomfortable speaking to large groups, especially non-Seekers as they used too much emotion and not enough logic for his taste.

'Ahh, thank you Prime Mother Silent Waters,' he began in a thin voice, 'This zeta gives thanks to the Council for their consideration and reports that, ahh, our measurements of the environment show that the seasonally-adjusted mean thermal values for the representative sea-mass continue to increase in a non-linear fashion'.

Sky was quietly horrified — this was just as he feared. He did not understand anything and he was going to look completely stupid. However, Silent Waters interrupted Always Counting gently: 'And what does that actually mean?'

'Ah. That...that the seas are still getting warmer. And faster.'

'Thank you, and can you explain — in simple terms — what this may mean for the zetii?'

'Ahh. Well. Sea temperature changes are not new, they have happened over the millennia from period to period. But this time it is occurring much faster. Faster than ever before since our ancestors began keeping records. The ice caps are melting. We have reports from the northern clans of the glaciers breaking up at an unprecedented rate. There is a, ahh, huge amount of water in those ice caps and the sea will rise as they melt. Now this will cause major changes. For example, a coral reef that currently exists at a certain depth will not be able to exist in its current form if the water depth increases significantly.' He looked about at his audience vaguely. 'Large areas of the land will become submerged and, perhaps most seriously for us, the great ocean conveyor currents will become disrupted. We know this, as it has happened gradually in the past when the climate changed. These currents transport nutrients from one part of Ocean to another. Many species may not survive a major change in their flow. This will have a dramatic effect.'

'Have the Seekers concluded why it is happening?' Silent Waters asked.

'Ahh. Yes, yes. We *may* be in the phase of a natural cycle where temperatures would naturally increase, but the evidence is that the Walkers are exacerbating the problem dramatically, if not actually causing it. We think that the fumes they have been releasing into the air for the past two hundred years are causing the unnatural heating of Ocean.'

One of the elders gestured for permission to speak and Silent Waters nodded.

'It is obvious that the Walkers cannot realise the damage they are causing or they would surely get their foul machines to stop belching out their poisons at once.'

Always Counting looked doubtful. 'I would have thought they must know. Their society seems so dependant on manipulating their environment, I would be very surprised if they have not felt the temperature rise and know what it must signify.'

The elder shook his head, 'Then it must be as many believe. That the Walkers are not in control of their machines. They serve the machines, and the machines simply do not care.'

No one had an answer to that.

Silent Waters acknowledged another dolphin requesting to speak. North Wind moved forward, 'We know that the Walkers are creating this catastrophe with their chemicals and devices. We can be sure that they must know it. They have so much power with their technology that they must be able to stop it if they want to — but they don't. The reason is obvious: this is their plan; they want to disrupt Ocean and to wipe out competitive species!'

Another spoke, 'This zeta finds it hard to believe that any species is that callous. The Walkers can't be aware of the consequences of what they are doing. If they did they would do something about it.'

Always Counting spoke again. 'That just does not fit what we know of their abilities. The Walkers obviously have Seekers and they must be measuring the temperature rise. Perhaps they know what is going wrong but they currently get such a value from their machines that they are prepared to sacrifice the future for whatever benefits they receive now.'

North Wind scoffed, 'That is preposterous! That any truly intelligent being would squander the future for some petty short-term benefit!'

There was a lot of murmuring of agreement at this. It seemed inconceivable.

Silent Waters moved to the centre to restore order. 'Let us move on with our agenda; we can discuss this further where time permits. It leads naturally to another subject that can be dealt with quickly I think. Several of you asked for a review of the guidance we have given concerning contact with the Walkers. In some cases there is occasional social contact and we have agreed in the past that this can happen at each Ka-Tse's own risk and at their own choice. However, we also must allow for the situation where occasionally

Walkers have captured Ka-Tse or other zetii. In some cases they have been treated well, in other cases...well, you have all heard the stories. The proposal is that the protocols for these situations remain the same: any zetii making contact with the Walkers may be friendly and respond to them but shall not allow the Walkers to become aware of the level of communication and intelligence zetii possess. Obviously, it also goes without saying that, in accordance to the Way, they shall not harm them, regardless of provocation.'

Green Wave Falling asked for permission to speak. Pointedly, he resumed the formal style of council address which had been rather ignored by some of the less aged dolphins. 'This zeta gives thanks to the Council for their consideration and supports this motion. It is in the Walkers' nature to exploit their environment. We should not forget that where they have suspected zetii abilities before they have apparently tried to exploit them. There are stories that they have even tried to use zetii to kill other Walkers. There is no reason to believe that this has changed.'

Sky continued to remain silent but listened closely. He had heard these stories before and thought they must be exaggerations. But here they were taking them seriously at the Grand Council! Why would the Walkers behave in such a way?

Cloud Passing came forward.

'This zeta also believes that it is right and proper to keep the existing protocols. I would remind you though of the ancient legend that says that amongst the Walkers there are a few who will understand the Way. It says that one day the Ka-Tse will find those few and we will work together to respect and conserve Ocean, as it is said we did tens of thousands of years ago. Perhaps it is a myth, but we should not forget it. One day we may meet these Walkers, and if so we must be ready to recognise them.'

A few more opinions were expressed, but none were in favour of changing the guidance. Silent Waters asked if any objected to keeping the contact protocol unchanged. None did, so they moved on with their debate.

At almost midday, Silent Waters announced a break. 'We thank the Grand Council for their efforts so far and will now pause so that you may refresh yourself. Green Wave Falling has information for you in this regard.'

He gestured thanks to her. 'As you leave here you will find twelve members of our clan waiting to greet you. Please divide yourself amongst these guides and they will lead you to good foraging. They will take you to separate areas. The hunting is varied so you will have some choice in what you may eat; each guide can tell you what type of prey they will try to lead you to. Do not go far to the south-west. I have been informed that the Walkers have lost one of their hunting devices in a gully there and it could be a deadly hazard for the unwary. We thank Senx for the bounty he may provide you with now; please return when he is at his zenith.'

CHAPTER 23

"Eat the young fish today and your young will eat no fish tomorrow"
- Traditional

Sky and his fellow Novices were among the guides assigned to take the Grand Council members foraging so he had to quickly change roles. He soon found Deneb and Muddy, who took delight in teasing him that it was improper for a Grand Council member to be acting as a lowly guide. Muddy dipped his head deeply as he passed.

'It is truly noble of you to come amongst us common zetii, and share our simple lives for a day, oh great Touches The Sky-Jeii!'

Sky playfully snapped his jaws at him and took his own station. Soon nine of the elders assembled around him. After some inconsequential talk, one of them addressed Sky: 'Tell me, young fellow, there are rumours that one of your females was found dead in strange circumstances in the last few days. What do you know of this?'

'Her name was Wakes Softly. It happened just before the Gathering.'

Several of the elders gathered around in interest at this.

'Some are saying that she had been attacked by other zetii! Can this be true?'

But before Sky could answer Green Wave Falling arrived.

'That incident is being investigated. We are still gathering facts, but it is likely that there will be a simple explanation for what happened. None of you need be alarmed.'

He turned to Sky. 'You are foraging towards the south west are you not?'

'That is right, Jeii, earlier there were squid to be had in that direction.'

'Then I shall join you. I wish to inspect this Walker's artefact we have had reports of.'

The eleven dolphins set off, following the coast. As they exited the bay and left the crowds, a large shape fell into formation behind them, swimming just under the surface, but never surfacing to breathe as they did.

Green Wave Falling glanced at it briefly.

'I see one of the Cleaners believes we shall do well.'

Sky said nothing; this was normal. Three or four sharks, this one a powerful oceanic white tip, had followed some of the clans in as they arrived. They often followed the dolphins at sea, as they led them to easy meals. They would gather up the remnants from the dolphins' feeding and seldom bothered them. They would, however, be most interested in a lost calf or an adult that became too sick to keep up.

At a particular coral outcrop, Sky led them directly away from the shore, out to the deeper water. He used his sonar to judge the depth. When it was right, he turned the group parallel to the shore again. He read the Shades to himself; the Tonella *Xhosii* was dominant; meaning *birth* or *fulfilment* and the water clarity and quality suggested *soon* or *nearby*. That seemed as good an omen for the hunt as one could wish for; he was sure most of the elders with him would read it too.

He called out to them:

'Honoured guests, the squid were at this point on the bank below us at this time yesterday, making their way deeper. May I suggest that you make a line abreast of me and we sweep the seabed nearer the bottom?'

They did as he suggested, diving down to within fifteen meters of the bottom and swam along line abreast, using their sonar to scan the seabed below them. Soon, one of the inshore dolphins cried out:

'Here, below me now, lots of them! Thanks be to Senx for sacrificing these creatures to meet our needs!'

And they dived down, encircling the mass of small squid. As the squid became aware of the dolphins, they shot off in various directions. Many of them squirted clouds of ink to try and distract their predators. Although this did create a confusing picture, the dolphins' sonar still gave them deadly accuracy. Some used more powerful blasts on the smaller squids, temporarily stunning them so they could be snapped up.

Sky ate a few squid, then watched the hunt in progress. Judging the moment, he called out:

'Enough, please, honoured guests! We must leave the rest to breed and feed us another day.'

The remaining squid, about twenty individuals by Sky's estimation and some quarter of the original group, shot into the safer darkness of the great depths. The feeding had taken less than two minutes, but the hunters were satisfied.

Green Wave Falling suggested that the other elders go back to the bay while he and Sky investigated the reported net. They happily did so after thanking Sky for their meal.

The two dolphins went further along the coastline and eventually came to a point where a small islet just off the shore created an underwater gully between it and the land. Sure enough, a fine net was draped across this opening, lost by fishermen weeks before.

They approached it cautiously. The net was torn in places, but its upper edge was still held up by a row of floats, which kept it just below the surface. Its lower edges were entangled in the coral at the bottom.

'Have you seen one of these before, Touches The Sky?'

'I have seen such Walker's devices from a distance in the open sea, Jeii, but never this close.'

'The Walkers use them to gather prey from the sea. They take some of what is caught and discard what they do not care for, dead into the sea again.'

'Why would they kill what they will not eat?'

'Who knows? They do not seem to care.'

'When will they take this?'

'I would guess that they will not. This seems to be abandoned to me, I have seen this before.'

As they closed on the net, Sky saw that it was still doing its deadly work. A number of reef fish were entangled in it, having swum into its nearly invisible fibres. In one upper corner a young turtle hung. Unable to reach the surface to breathe, it had drowned.

'We will warn the Gathering,' Green Wave Falling said. 'Although most zetii would probably detect it, if one were not paying attention they could miss it and become entangled; with fatal consequences. Come, let us go.'

They swam back. As they arrived back in the bay, a group of females, all Starwriters, passed them. As they swam by he recognised Venus In Mist amongst them. Sky would have liked to stop and talk to her and tried to catch her eye, but she looked away at that moment, and the group moved on, talking to each other about the coming evening's events. As he escorted

Green Wave Falling back to the Grand Council's meeting place, he felt disappointed and hurt, and hoped that perhaps she had just not seen him. He comforted himself with the thought that he should see her that evening when the Starwriters would be massing for an unlocking song. He would try to speak to her then and find out what was wrong.

Chapter 24

"We mistrust the strange."

- The 'Seer' Stone Eyes (13,222 -13,264 post Great Alluvium)

The Grand Council came to the last points of discussion that day as the sun met the horizon. The onshore breeze had been strengthened by the heating of the land and a sharp surface chop diffused the light and created eddies of sand on the bottom. The dolphins swayed gently back and forth in the swell without noticing it and kept station in their circle. Sky still had not spoken but was feeling less uncomfortable than before. His attention had begun to wander while a senior Healer from one of the southern clans had given a long and detailed report. He had been thinking about Rain Ending and hoping he would come soon with news of his father. Suddenly he realised that the Healer was coming to a conclusion and that he must have missed something important.

'...and until this warm season the algae was fairly plentiful but now it is almost non-existent. Something is getting into the river and killing it; we think it may be coming from a big Walker settlement that is on the riverside upstream. You have all traditionally sent your clan members to our bay when they fell ill, but I have to tell you that in the next year the supply may stop completely.'

Sky suddenly realised what she must be referring to. For thousands of years the dolphins had gone to this bay to treat many forms of cancer. The unique species of brown algae had remarkable powers and nearly always resulted in a complete cure. Now it seemed that the only known source of it was almost gone.

Silent Waters spoke, 'This could indeed have dire consequences. We have grown used to thinking of these diseases as unimportant as we had a ready and effective treatment for them. If that cure is now destroyed many lives will be lost needlessly. We must hope that other sources of the algae still exist that we have not yet found. This zeta suggests that the Healers meet separately and arrange a systematic search amongst the clans in the coming year. Please treat this as a priority.'

There was a general agreement to this, and Silent Waters thanked the Healer for her report. Then she addressed the meeting again.

'And now to the final item for discussion today. You have heard much in the last days concerning the issue of the hunting quotas. As you know, normally we would have the perspective of other species represented by the Voice of the Others. At this Gathering, however, we have a unique chance to hear from an envoy of the Xenthos who has kindly agreed to represent his kind and explain their position concerning the prey shortages we are all experiencing.'

At her gesture, Cloud Passing politely indicated to a stranger to enter the circle. Smaller than the assembled bottlenose dolphins, the lone common dolphin looked quite unique. He was smaller than they, with a slender build. The grey of their backs gradually became lighter on their undersides, but his back, and indeed most of his body was a very dark grey, closer to black. In stark contrast, his flanks were yellow while his belly was white, and this colour extended up the sides of his body at the fore part. It also continued in a narrow band in front of his eyes, giving the appearance of a white mask. When he spoke, it was clear that he knew their language quite well, although his accent was strange. He bowed to them.

'The Xenthos thank the Ka-Tse for your hospitality and wish that the waves always follow you and that Senx smiles upon you. This zeta's name in your language is Trevally Outpaced.'

Cloud Passing moved into the circle and bowed in return. 'We thank the Xenthos for allowing you to join us. You honour our clans with your journey, which was long, even for the renownedly fleet Xenthos.'

Trevally Outpaced smiled at the compliment and bowed again. Cloud Passing continued, 'Forgive me for being direct, but you and I have spoken of this at some length. You know of the concerns that we have about the shortage of prey. For many centuries we have agreed quotas for hunting with the Xenthos, the Xa-Hana and others. In spite of these quotas we are seeing a dramatic fall in key species. Many clans are going hungry and do not understand why the fish stocks do not replenish as they once did.'

The envoy nodded gravely. 'The Xenthos have the same concerns, and I have spoken to clans of the Xa-Hana and other zetii; they all say the stocks are diminishing.'

Suddenly North Wind pushed forward and interrupted: 'Then tell them to stop breaking the quotas so the prey can breed and replenish!'

There was a shocked silence then Silent Waters spoke, her voice icy. 'Councillor North Wind will leave this meeting. Now.'

He stared at her defiantly for a moment and looked about to speak, but then suddenly turned and swam rapidly off, his awkward swimming style jerking his body up and down.

Silent Waters turned to the envoy whose body was stiff with anger. 'Please accept the apologies of the Grand Council for that outburst.'

Trevally Outpaced's posture softened slightly and he nodded. 'I can yet understand the emotion of that zeta,' he said at last, 'I have to tell you that some of my kind have had similar thoughts of the other zetii species, but I am here to tell you that the Xenthos do uphold the quotas, even though our children go hungry at times!'

Old Cloud Passing spoke again now, his voice calming and reasoned. 'These are sad times when zeta mistrusts zeta. Most of us know the likely true reason for the shortages, and it is not due to the excesses of any of the zeta kinds. We must build trust again between us. Trevally Outpaced and I have discussed this and he has suggested that we send one of our own to spend two moons with his clan as a gesture of good faith. Our emissary can then return with one of the Xenthos who can spend time with the Ka-Tse. Both sides will see for themselves if the quotas are being followed. Later, perhaps we can make a similar offer to the Xa-Hana and others.'

Green Wave Falling sought permission to speak and it was granted. 'This zeta gives thanks to the Council for their consideration and fully supports this wise motion. Our envoy to the Xenthos should be one of the elders who can represent our interests properly and follow proper protocols in this key mission. This zeta should be honoured if the Grand Council would consider him for this purpose.' He bowed backwards into the circle again.

There were some murmurs of assent from the elders, but Trevally Outpaced spoke again, apparently choosing his words carefully.

'The Xenthos would indeed be highly honoured to have such a wise zeta amongst them, but I would make one observation that may be important. As you know, we Xenthos do not love the nearness of the land as do the Ka-Tse.

Our home is the deep waters of the open sea. We swim hard and fast and we dive deep; it is our way. These sixty days may be…taxing for a Ka-Tse and youth may be a more…' he searched for the words, 'pressing attribute for your ambassador than wisdom.'

Green Wave Falling spoke again, his expression stony, 'This zeta understands the concerns Trevally Outpaced outlines and suggests that in the circumstances we choose another, younger zeta.'

Sky nervously signalled that he wished to speak. Silent Waters gave permission, saying: 'The Grand Council recognises this clan's Voice of Youth.'

Sky began speaking in a normal tone, concentrating on following the proper protocol. He soon realised that some of the elders were struggling to hear him though, and raised his voice. 'This zeta gives thanks to the Council for their consideration and suggests that a good candidate for this mission would be Silent Waters' own son, Deneb Rising. I know that he even speaks some of the Xenthos tongue.'

Silent Waters looked surprised, but it was clear that the suggestion was well received by the elders so she assented. 'When shall this take place then?' she asked.

Trevally Outpaced answered, 'My clan is due to be passing near here soon. I should try to rendezvous with them now, and I could return to collect your son in three days time.'

'Then perhaps this zeta can assist in a lesser capacity.' Green Wave Falling said. 'Our clan may not still be in this bay in three days time. However, I know of a rock arch to the east of this bay that makes a good meeting point. I could escort Trevally Outpaced to it when he leaves us today and then take Deneb Rising to it for the meeting in three days time. I can then also at least ensure that our own ambassador has some coaching on proper protocols before he departs.'

Silent Waters nodded seeing that this was well received by the assembled elders. 'The Grand Council asks the respected Councillor Green Wave Falling to make it so. Let us thank the good Trevally Outpaced for his time here today. It is to be hoped that in two moons time, when my son and he return again, a new period of trust and cooperation between the zetii will begin. We should also thank Passing Cloud for his efforts in negotiating this arrangement.'

Trevally Outpaced indicated his desire to speak, and at Silent Waters gestured invitation, spoke to them all, but with his eyes mainly on the old male dolphin.

'We Xenthos have had little contact with your kind of late, but we have been honoured to have had these dealings with Passing Cloud. His wisdom and sensitivity have been an inspiration to us and I think I speak for many when I say that I was saddened to learn that this is his last Grand Council meeting. The Ka-Tse will be the poorer for it. For myself, from the brief time I have spent in his company, I feel privileged to say thank you, Passing Cloud-Jeii.'

Passing Cloud looked pleased but very embarrassed at the compliment. Silent Waters moved to help her old friend by closing the meeting. 'These are words well spoken and they will resonate in many hearts here. There are many here who feel honoured to call this fine zeta Jeii. Tomorrow is the last day of the Gathering, and as you know we close it with a very special ceremony at noon. I am sure you will all wish to make your personal farewells with him before then. Thank you all again for coming so far to be with us here.'

CHAPTER 25

"I see my lover approach
Her sweet face
Graceful movements
Senx sprinkles her back
With dancing light
She comes to me
My heart leaps
Her mouth opens to speak
I await her words' caress
But she pours forth venom!
Who committed such wickedness
Whilst I slept
That looked so like me?"
- Three Standing Shells (13,282 -13,325 post Great Alluvium)

Taking advantage of the last of the light, Sky made his way along the shore line looking for something to eat. He had passed several others in twos and threes when he heard up ahead another dolphin probing the sand with sound. With a thrill he recognised it as Dusk. He called out his signature call: 'It is I, Touches The Sky!'

Dusk responded and appeared out of the blue up ahead. He smiled, 'What are you doing, Dusk?'

'Just trying to find something to eat. I don't have much time, we've a big meeting of Starwriters from all the clans this evening — we are decoding a complicated song with lots of harmonic layers. It's the kind of thing we can only do at a Gathering. What're you doing?'

'Hunting too — haven't found anything though.'

She shook her head in frustration.

'Nor have I, and I am so hungry. What's worse is that the visitors are having problems finding enough to eat. They're too polite to say anything, but it's really embarrassing as we're the host clan this time.'

'Well, I don't think anyone would blame us. Everyone knows that most of the prey stocks are at record low levels. That's what they were talking about at the Grand Council meeting today.'

'Really!' she exclaimed, 'And what good will that do I? All this talking and nothing ever happens!'

Suddenly she shot up through the surface and flew high in the air, spinning rapidly as she flew. Sky smiled to himself and waited for her to reappear. She was prone to make these explosive leaps when she was very happy or very angry. He loved her passion but knew she was working herself up to a rant about something. She crashed back into the water with a blizzard of bubbles and swam back to him.

'Ooh, I needed that! So tell me, now that you're suddenly a Grand Council member; what's going on? Those elders talk and talk and nothing changes. I heard that you even had a Xenthos at the meeting. I hope you all gave him a hard time! Those Xenthos are taking food that is rightfully ours.'

'Dusk, you can't believe that stuff. There is no proof that they're taking more than their share of the quotas. The Xenthos zeta seemed genuine enough to me, I think they've got the same problems as us — he said that some of the Xenthos are thinking the same things about the Ka-Tse.'

'You can't believe what he says — they're trying to trick us. They must be eating more than their share — look at them swimming around in those huge clans; sometimes a thousand at a time; when they go through an area they strip it bare of all living things. And I've heard that they are breeding out of control, they are just increasing in numbers so that they can dominate the other zetii — we'll be unable to compete with them.'

'That's nonsense. Who told you all this stuff?'

'I don't remember! A friend! Someone who knows we need to actually do something instead of just talking about it!'

'Dusk, you need to change your friends then, they are filling your head with poison. Think about what you're saying for a moment — think about the Way.'

'Sky, you idiot, you sound like these old fools who can't see that everything is different now. Ocean has changed, the Way was written for some lost romantic age. The Ka-Tse must *act* to survive! How can you be so weak!'

She stared at him for a moment, her expression pleading. He was nonplussed at her anger and did not know what to say. With a hard shake of her head, she was gone, swimming back in the direction of the clan. Sky was shocked and confused. Meeting her again he had been filled with happiness, he had dared to think to himself for a moment, that maybe it was true, maybe he was in love with this crazy, passionate creature. But then she had crushed him again — seemed to despise him even, and the things she believed now! Something or someone was changing her. He resolved to find out exactly what or who it was. He would start by going along to the Starwriters' song. Maybe he would see something there, or perhaps find out where Dusk went when she vanished late in the evenings. Then he remembered that Venus In Mist should be at the song too. He shook his head. Perhaps he might even find out what he had done to offend her too! He was about to go when he noticed a movement. On the edge of visibility he faintly saw the shape of something big moving. He sent a stream of sonar in that direction. There were four large dolphins out there. They were spreading apart to either side of him, but not using their own echolocation.

'It is I, Touches The Sky, of the Dune Coast Clan!'

No reply. Now the two outer ones started to move towards the shore, still staying at the edge of visibility, still not using their sonar.

Sky started to feel a coldness inside him, and remembered Cloud Passing's warning that he should not leave the clan alone.

'It is I, Touches The Sky, of the Dune Coast Clan! Are you our guests?'

This time there was a short, harsh laugh in reply.

Sky turned and started to swim back towards the clan. At once the four dolphins started to move in towards him rapidly, so he swam at full speed. The four matched his pace, two behind him, one each side and closing. His tail pumped furiously up and down, his heartbeat hammered in his head, but still his pursuers kept pace. Now they were using their echolocation freely, and he could tell by the sound that the two flanking dolphins were closing in on him, narrowing the gap between them. He knew it was still a long swim to the clan, and he did not see how he could make it. Now the two dolphins were each only a body length away from him, and he heard a grunted command from behind him.

'Get ready...'

Suddenly, appearing from the blue ahead of him there was a group of ten or more dolphins coming towards him! At first he thought it was more of the Guardians, but then he realised it must be a hunting party from one of the visiting clans. Without a word his pursuers turned and sped off back the way they had come, vanishing in a moment.

The leading dolphins from the hunting party shouted cheerful greetings to Sky and asked if he had seen any prey. Clearly they had not realised anything strange had been happening. Probably just thought the other four dolphins were hunters too. And they were right, he reflected grimly.

CHAPTER 26

"Keep this flicker of light in your heart for me.
I cannot keep it longer in mine."
- Ankaa Ascendant (11,688 – 11,731 post Great Alluvium)

Sky was threading his way through the bustle of visiting dolphins towards the west end of the bay when he saw ahead of him a group of the visiting elders from the other clans gathered together. As he was about to swim past them, a dolphin excused himself from the group. Sky recognised his old teacher, Passing Cloud.

He moved alongside him, saying, 'It is I, Touches The Sky.'

The old dolphin looked pleased. 'Ah, Sky. How is everything?'

Sky explained what had just happened; his mentor listened quietly, a concerned look in his misty eyes.

'Jeii, you told me not to leave the clan alone. I am sorry.'

'Well, never mind, you are safe, and I have some news — I have made arrangements that a senior Aligner will come here to our clan to take over your training in a few days. That was the last thing I needed to organise, so I can relax now. I am very glad you are here, I was hoping to have a few words with you before I go. Swim with me for a while.'

Sky fell alongside him. Although he knew what tomorrow would bring, hearing the old one say "before I go" in such a matter-of-fact way suddenly brought home that this was the last time he would speak to him alone. Of all his teachers, Passing Cloud had impressed him the most. Every word he said was carefully considered, every thought in tune with the spirit of the Way, but not with the oppressive, axiomatic style of Green Wave Falling. Instead he would explain the whys of each question, or, more commonly, he allowed his students to discover them for themselves. For a long time Sky had not even realised that he was doing it, and then one day he had made the passing comment, "a lesson learned may be lost, a lesson discovered lasts forever." Sky realised then this was part of his art. He did not drag his students wearily behind him to new knowledge; he set them in a good direction and let them discover it for themselves; providing guidance and interpretation where they needed it.

Sky summoned up the courage to ask what had been on his mind in the last days: 'Jeii, tomorrow you'll make your Darkening Dive. Why are you leaving us? You're so loved here.'

The old dolphin looked touched but pretended to speak in a scolding way. Still, his smiling eyes showed he was not serious. 'Now, now; we have discussed this before Sky. You know that every zeta has the right to choose the manner of their own passing. It is an elemental part of the Way: Right to Life, Right to Death. I hope you are not trying to change my mind.'

'No, Jeii, of course not, but if you could tell me why this is a good thing it would help me be at peace with it. We'll miss you so.'

'And I shall miss all of you. Especially you, young Sky. You were one of my finest students. You have an instinctive understanding of many refined concepts that other Novices have to learn by rote, which is why I have selected you for a special path. In a way that, in part, is an answer to your question. I am so very old now. I made plenty of foolish mistakes when I was younger, but as I aged I gradually found the inner meanings of the Way and at last learned who I was, what I might be, and how to become at one with Ocean. In the last part of my life I have enjoyed knowing at last what was important. I also learned what I might be able to change for the better and promised myself that whatever I could do, I would. I have lived by that rule for some time now and admit that I am quite proud of my success in keeping to it. But now it becomes hard. My mind knows what I should do, but my body tires of following its orders. I carry a companion with me all the time now: my pain. I control him, but it is a long struggle, and while I seem to tire more easily these days, he never does. I think I would like a rest now. I have done all I set out to do. If I stayed now, my life would become too much of a compromise.'

Sky could not think of anything to say. Cloud Passing continued on, 'Some make the Darkening Dive as an easy way out; some because they dread the thought of a long illness; the painful struggle at the back of the clan on a migration; the shadowing Cleaner waiting patiently behind. But many reach a point in their lives when they have accomplished all that they wished; have fulfilled their responsibilities, seen their young grow up, and want to say goodbye with a clear mind. They want to be remembered as they always were in their own mind's eye: full of life and love; not some sickly creature that burdened those it loved. I have had a good life and I now would like to have a good death. I want to meet her at a time and place of my choice. Tomorrow I shall be surrounded by friends this one last time and I shall enjoy it. Beside, I am sure they will feel obliged to say some nice things in the circumstances!' He laughed at Sky's discomfort at his joke.

'Come now, Sky, I have been lucky enough to have had a life that I can feel proud of. Help me celebrate it tomorrow.'

Sky gave a sad smile, 'Certainly Jeii, and I'll try to remember what you've taught me. I only hope to have some of your wisdom one day.'

Cloud Passing looked pleased. 'Well, that is the finest compliment a teacher can have. Now I must go, I have promised to call on many clans tonight. Farewell, Sky.'

'Farewell, Jeii. You'll live on in my heart'.

'Ah. And *that* is the very best that *any* of us can hope for.'

CHAPTER 27

"Would that we might scratch our histories upon some rock, ever there to remain. But the zetii know that nothing in Ocean lasts forever and nothing stays the same in her waters. Therefore honour the Dreamweaver and the Starwriter. Without their art we are simple creatures living the moment. All the joy and suffering of our ancestors was for nothing. The wisdom of the millennia is nothing."
- *Denebola's Daughter (10,006 – 10,045 post Great Alluvium)*

There were twenty-four Starwriters and three Dreamweavers involved in the song; as always, all of them were females. Sky had only a rudimentary knowledge of how the process worked, but knew that this must be a complex song to involve so many of them. He knew that the timing of the Gatherings was in part dictated by the astronomical events that could only be accessed by large numbers of Starwriters at once. He also knew that the Calculators used a similar technique; they would be taking advantage of the Gathering to gather together in a form of shared consciousness to process the complex data gathered by the Seekers since the last Gathering.

The Starwriters were gathering into three groups, all facing towards the setting sun. The onshore breeze had gone now and the sea was mellowing. As the sun approached the horizon Sky watched the Tonellas change to the Shade of *Ndria* against a background Kruma of *Vraxia*. A confusing reading: *death* overtaking *youth or change?* He forgot the thought as he made out

Dusk amongst the Starwriters, but she was already dropping into the lower levels of consciousness and was oblivious to him. He also saw Mist, who did seem to look back in his direction, but she had a far away look in her eyes and he could not tell if she was still aware of her surroundings or deliberately ignoring him.

'Don't worry my dear, it's not you that's upset her.' He turned to see an elderly female near him. He recognised her as being from Mist's clan.

'I am Touches The Sky from the Dune Coast Clan,' he said.

'Yes, I know. And I am Fading Current from the Western Red Mountains Clan. You do know what's wrong with little Mist, don't you?'

'Well, I know about the other day of course. But I think I've upset her in some way, I don't know why exactly…'

She shook her head, 'No, you've done nothing wrong. What did you see at that birth?'

'It was hard to watch. After so much work, when the baby came out and didn't move, the mother was heartbroken. She just kept lifting it to the surface to breathe, calling to it, singing to it, but it never took one breath. She wouldn't let it go. At dusk two Cleaners came and circled: waiting. Mist and I drove them off but they kept coming back. Eventually, late in the evening the mother told us to go; she wanted to be alone with her baby to say goodbye to it.'

The three Dreamweavers moved into position facing the three groups of Starwriters. They began a slow rhythmic chanting. The Starwriters lay on the sandy bottom in the very shallow water. The sea was calm now, and they easily lifted their bodies slightly to breathe when they needed to.

Fading Current spoke again, quietly now so as not to disturb the Dreamweavers, who were taking the Starwriters deeper into their trance-like state. 'Yes, eventually the mother came back at dawn, after she had said her farewells.'

'But poor Mist, she blamed herself for the baby's death. I talked to her about it — tried to reason with her — there was nothing else that could be done and…'

'Look my dear, when a female is upset, the last thing she needs is some male trying to "reason" with her. She just wants you to listen to her and to be supportive. Learn that simple truth and you will save yourself much heartache in life.'

The chant was growing deeper and slower now. One of the Dreamweavers started a new chant now in counterpoint to the primary song. Sky could not make out any words.

'But why did it die?'

'Nothing could be done. Half of the babies born these days do not survive, it seems to have become worse in my memory, something in the fish we eat I think, or some decay in the moon's influence perhaps. But that baby had no chance. I'd scanned the mother myself a few days ago and said as much but little Mist wanted to try. And that's what's upset her; she thinks she failed. Maybe she's acting strangely to you now because you saw it. Now you must just approach her and support her in her grief. She will thank you for it later.'

'Thank you,' said Sky, rather embarrassed. Then to change the subject he whispered, 'Do you understand what they're doing?'

The Starwriters were now at the surface with their eyes just above the water, their tails resting on the bottom. The sun had fallen below the horizon leaving the Moon and the planet Venus the only objects visible so far in the gradually darkening sky.

'Yes, I know this, I used to be a Starwriter myself. They are descending through the levels of consciousness. They will spend a little time now in the fourth level: in the unconscious mind but with conscious control. Then the Dreamweavers will quickly take them through the fifth level — dreaming — and the sixth, a dreamless, deep unconsciousness. Then they will move them down into the last level, where they are unconscious but can receive thoughts at a subconscious level.'

'Thank you for that, but I am at least familiar with the seven levels, I study at the Academy.'

'Ah, then yes, you will be familiar. You may even leave the rest of us behind in our everyday second level and move to the first level one day.'

He wondered if she was mocking him for being pompous but she seemed genuine enough and he murmured something about hoping to achieve that one day.

Now all three of the Dreamweavers were adding different layers to the chant, merging and diverging again in strange harmonies.

'This is a special song,' Fading Current whispered, 'having three Dreamweavers singing allows them to use tertian trichords to create invariance. That, and the special alignment of Saturn tonight will let them open some ancient, complex data that we can rarely access. See, the stars are becoming visible. Look by Regulus, next to the moon.'

Sky wished he had not seemed so clever about the seven levels of consciousness. She had then completely lost him in her description of the music. He focused on the great white orb of the moon. As the sky became darker he saw a bright light appear close behind it.

'I can make out something close to the moon, but it's hard to see yet.'

'It's Saturn, and the alignment is unique for this song. The moon will cover Saturn before long, and the juxtaposition of these elements is what the Dreamweavers are timing their songs for. They always have to perfectly match the delivery of the unlocking song to the movement of the stars and planets.'

The pace of the song was increasing now with a steady, pulsing beat like the heartbeat of some great beast just under the seabed. Some of the Starwriters started to make small sounds in time with the song; gradually more picked this up until they were all faintly chanting to the rhythm of the song, with their eyes all fixed on Saturn. The planet marched westwards across the sky, its pace mirrored by the following Regulas. But the huge moon followed behind Saturn at a faster pace, gradually gaining on the planet.

Slowly the bright light of Saturn was subsumed into the much larger moon. As their lights merged, the combined chanting of the Dreamweavers and Starwriters reached a crescendo and at the moment the planet finally vanished, the song abruptly stopped. Three more dolphins slowly emerged from the darkness, one going to each of the three groups. They too were in a form of trance.

'Calculators,' Fading Current explained, 'they have come for the data from the song.'

Each group of Starwriters now clustered around its Calculator and they began murmuring in unison to them a low, constant chant of information.

'What are they saying?' asked Sky.

'The song was something to do with records of the ice caps and glaciers over time. The Seekers asked for it. This song contained information dating right back to 9,500 I'm told. Look, they're finishing.'

The Calculators were withdrawing now, still in their dream-like state, but the Starwriters were gradually coming back to full consciousness and drifting off in ones and twos. Sky looked for Dusk but she was already gone. He swam towards her group, and she alone was missing, vanished into the darkness again. Where did she *go* at night? He stopped in indecision, looking around, when Mist passed, her eyes slowly coming back into focus.

He called softly, 'It is I, Touches The Sky!'

She woke a little more and turned to him, still clearly confused. 'Sky?'

'Yes, it's me. If you can, I'd like to talk to you about the birth of that baby. I've been thinking about it a lot and I need to know how you felt about it.'

'Really?' She looked at him hard, focussed now at last. 'Alright, let's swim together awhile. It would probably be good for me to talk about it.'

Her eyes smiled. 'You *are* sweet after all. I've already had my unconscious mind drained tonight; now perhaps you can help me empty some of these dark thoughts in my conscious mind.'

CHAPTER 28

"Rejoice now in a life well spent
Each day lived out to full extent
Death he easily transcends
Surrounded here by these old friends"
- *Second Rainbow (8,127 -8,159 post Great Alluvium)*

The Whispering Caves had been used and revered by the Ka-Tse for longer than even their histories recorded. This place had been used during spring rituals for millennia, and it was on calm days like this one that the event was most dramatic. Close to the south-facing shoreline, the seabed fell away quickly to an almost sheer wall. The steep rock face was almost totally covered in hard and soft corals except for a vertical gash in its face. Here the water shimmered in an unearthly way, looking almost oily; distorting anything that passed through it. No coral grew near the opening, as a fresh water spring issued forth from the cave. This was critical to the cave's status, as it was the precise alignment of its opening and the inner caverns that gave it such value to the dolphins. If coral growth occluded the opening, the equinoctial sun would not be visible from the Sun Chamber within; further, the distorting qualities of the halocline — the mixing boundary between salt and fresh water — made this place famous for interpreting the Shades.

The crowd of dolphins gathered quietly in the sandy shallows, facing out towards the deeper water. In front of them was a small group of elders, one from each clan, floating at the surface above the uppermost of the cave's three openings.

The group of elders faced the shore, all very still, many with their eyes closed as they slowed their heartbeats in readiness for the ceremony.

Silent Waters represented the Dune Coast Clan among the elders, and as they were hosting the Gathering, she was leading the ceremony. She moved towards the mass of dolphins slightly, her voice seeming tranquil, somehow made slightly remote by the mental distance she was placing between herself and her immediate surroundings.

'Today is always a day of celebration, as Senx passes once more into this hemisphere, marking the start of his season of strength: the season of contradictions, when we traditionally find abundance and the great storms. On this day we also say goodbye to an old friend. One who has lived the Way in his every thought. And in recognition of his special place amongst the Ka-Tse, the elders wish to invite him, and any companions he would have for his Darkening Dive, to enter the Sun Chamber and see Senx pass over the equator, once more to dwell in our skies.'

There was a murmur of approval from the assembled dolphins at the announcement of this rare honour; normally only the leader of each clan would be allowed into the cave on this day.

Cloud Passing moved slowly forward, clearly moved by the gesture. 'Thank you Prime Mother. I would be honoured to witness Senx's passage. As for companions, I should ask for two: yourself, to represent all my old friends and all that was wonderful in my past. For the other, to represent all my hopes for the future, I would ask for one of the many here that I have tried to guide in the Way. If I have been able to influence them in some small manner for the better; if, at some time in the future they are faced with a hard choice and they think, for just a moment: "what would he have said?" then my life was worthwhile. For my second companion I choose Touches The Sky.'

Sky was stunned to be called, but, with everyone watching him, he swam forward to Cloud Passing's side.

'Jeii, you honour me.' He whispered.

'Nonsense,' muttered the old teacher, smiling, 'it's just that with my old eyes I might miss the critical moment — I need you to nudge me when Senx plays his part.'

They both swam out slowly towards the group of elders. Someone called a gentle farewell to Cloud Passing; it was followed by another, then another. Soon a rising murmur of softly spoken wishes for an easy descent filled the water with sound.

He stopped and turned. He faced them all in silence for a very long moment, then bowed deeply.

'Farewell, my very good friends. Keep to the Way. Do not think of discarding it now when our need for moral guidance is greatest. And think of me sometimes.'

He turned and Sky followed him to the group of elders.

The sun was approaching its zenith now and the group of dolphins, still at the surface, began to breathe slower and deeper, in preparation for a long submersion. Sky was stunned to find himself in such auspicious company at such a time, then suddenly realised that he was about to hold his breath for the longest time in his life. He felt panic rising and his heart beat start to race, in fear that he could ruin the ceremony.

The familiar sound of Cloud Passing's barely audible voice came to him. 'Now young Sky, is this what you learned in all those lessons? Count your breaths, one...two.....three.......four.........five; that's better. Now listen to your heart; slow it down, I can hear it too; yes...yes.....better. Don't show me up now, I have always said you were my star pupil. Focus your being in your mind and your chest; you don't need the rest of your body, shut it down for me now.'

Sky did as he was told, slipping back into the habits of his training. Starting from a state of total consciousness, aware of every part of his body, he began to withdraw into his mind. He imagined his body filled with a red light, then saw that light receding from the tip of his tail, from his fin tips, up his body, slowly gathering in his mind and heart. The light dimmed but concentrated, soon it was just there in the core of his being. He was barely aware of his body any more, just the slow, so very slow thud of his heart.

At a signal from Silent Waters, the group took a final breath and silently dived down the short distance to the upper opening of the cave. This was at the top of the steep slope and it opened towards the surface. The dolphins entered one by one, Sky last. As he dropped into the darkness his eyes became accustomed and he realised the small opening led to a vast cavern with a shelving sandy floor. This sloped downwards in the direction of the open sea, and there were two more openings in the cavern wall on that side. Opposite where the dolphins now lay on the sand was a vertical slit in the rock, the primary exit point for the spring, with the bright surface behind. But below it, pointing down to the depths, was another smaller opening, with dark blue water just visible.

Sky was beside Cloud Passing. All of the dolphins lay motionless on their bellies on the sand, their eyes fixed on the vertical slit.

Sky watched the Shades, fascinated. The dark blue water was *Ndria-chon* or perhaps just *Ndria: bad intentions? Obscure?* No: *death*, he supposed. The still surface of the sea meant that the shafts of light coming through the upper opening of the cavern hardly moved, so the overall Shade was *Tsim*, meaning *little*, or *of no consequence*. How could that be, he wondered, this was of the greatest consequence!

He slowly became aware that the others were humming a barely audible chant; rising and falling like wavelets striking a beach, slowly increasing in pace and volume. He realised that the light was increasing at the narrow opening, the light at the surface becoming brighter and brighter, soon swallowing the feeble light rays from the upper opening.

The song lifted its pitch further, rising to a climax. Sky saw that a shaft of light from the opening before them now cast a narrow beam on the wall to their right. As he watched mesmerised, that beam eased around the wall behind them until both song and star reached their zenith together, and the dolphins were flooded by light. This was the moment they had waited for; the sun had now passed over the equator into the northern hemisphere for the first time that year.

The chant slowed and stopped. There was a faint murmur of appreciation from the dolphins in the cave. Then Cloud Passing roused himself and swam forward a short way. Silent Waters and Sky took station on each side of him. He turned back to the elders, the sunlight streaming past him in rays onto their faces. He bowed once more.

Then Sky noticed a curious thing. Although the sea surface was still calm, the sun's rays were now coming directly through the narrow opening into the Sun Chamber as it only did in this way for the first day of spring. Now that the rays passed through the swirling waters of the halocline the rays were no longer static, they danced behind the silhouette of the old dolphin in an unearthly way. The Shades obediently changed and their meaning was totally altered: *a great matter; of high import*.

Passing Cloud turned away and led his two companions down the long sandy slope, through the equivocal shafts of light, away from the beckoning surface and towards the dark blue of the lower cave opening.

They followed him out through the opening and emerged outside the reef wall. Sky realised suddenly that they were very deep, and wondered how long they had been without a breath. A small but insistent voice started to nag in the back of his mind. He silenced it. They now swam directly away from the wall, out into the blue. Soon there was nothing to be seen, just the faint light of the surface. Below them, the deepest indigo.

Passing Cloud stopped and turned.

'And now I must go.'

He gently pressed his head against each of theirs in turn as a kiss; they said nothing.

He smiled at Sky.

'Remember you promised me a song.'

And then he turned and swam slowly straight down towards the depths.

Sky started to sing; an old song, each word heavy with loss.

'When the wind continues to blow
When you waken a little too slow
When there's a voice in your head you still don't know
Well, that's just mine my love

If that wave fell a little too fast
If the rainbow now has passed
If the moment you treasured didn't quite last
Well, that's me there my love

See the child grow up that used to play
See the moment you treasured and wished would stay
See those you love still taken away
Well, that's just time my love

Darkness comes, you feel the night
Darkness we need, to see the light
Darkness reminds us of the joy of sight
Well, that's me there my love

I'm sorry now for the odd angry day
I'm sorry now for my foolish ways
I'm sorry now for being taken away
Well, that's our loss, my love

Keep the days that made us glad
Keep the good ones, not the bad
Keep the memory of the joy we had
Well, that was mine my love

Know the west wind in your head
Know the meaning of the things I said
Know the last thoughts of the dead
Well, that's all we ask my love'

Sky's voice trailed away as he watched him dropping into the cold darkness. Passing Cloud had stopped swimming now; the air in his lungs was so compressed by the pressing depth that he fell easily. He just let himself be taken: his tail tilted slightly to one side so that he gently turned as he descended serenely into the abyss; now, more than ever, at one with Ocean.

CHAPTER 29

"The troubled mind
Starved of truth
Cannot bear the hunger
Cannot wait still longer
For the knowledge it craves
Without proper sustenance
In time, in despair
It feeds itself
With imaginings. "
Third Wave Breaks - (3,001 – 3,043 post Great Alluvium)

Sky came across Muddy in the shallows late that afternoon. They swam together for a while, through occasional groups of dolphins. The bay was still busy, with some of the clans leaving immediately, but most planned to wait at least until the next morning to depart. They passed many individuals and groups exchanging farewells and making plans to meet again at the next Gathering.

They talked about their old teacher, exchanging fond memories and anecdotes. Sky's friend gently probed him about what had happened in the cave and on the last dive, but it was hard for him to talk much about it and Muddy respected his privacy. Sky just said the old dolphin had been happy to the end and that was enough for now.

Suddenly they saw Deneb approaching them quickly. 'Sky, come quickly — Rain Ending is here! He doesn't want to come into the crowds so he's waiting alone for you.'

Sky and Muddy followed Deneb to one end of the bay where Rain was waiting. He greeted them warmly. Sky had to ask the question in his mind straight away.

'Have you any news about my father?'

'Yes. But I warn you, it may not be what you would wish to hear.'

'Tell me anyway. Knowing whatever it is must be better than this uncertainty.'

'Very well, I'll tell you all I know. After you left me I started moving in the direction of where the Guardian clan had been when last I had seen them. It took me some time to get there and then I discovered they had moved on. But I followed the coast along and eventually got lucky; I heard one of their returning hunting parties and followed them back. In fact their clan is only a day's swim to the east of here now but I get the impression they may be moving on soon.'

'Have you been with their clan then?' Deneb asked.

'No, I wouldn't dare to do that. Once I realised where they were staying, I kept near the shore where I knew that foraging parties must pass from time to time. I hid and waited, and over a few days I saw several groups and individuals go by. I was waiting for one of them that I had met before — I don't want to tell you his name — I'd met him years before; before he became a Guardian, and we were friends of a sort.'

'Is he the one who told you about my father before?'

'That's right. He didn't know him that well back then. Eventually, I heard his voice; he was in a small hunting party. I trailed them, and at last there was a moment when he fell behind the rest. I talked to him and asked him to meet me later. It took some persuading but at last he agreed.'

'So,' Muddy prompted him impatiently, 'what did he say?'

'When I met him again he really did not want to talk at all. He seemed frightened of what might happen to him; terrified, more like. I had to remind him of an old favour he owes me. At last he agreed to talk and tell me about your father.' He paused, looking at Sky apprehensively.

'Go on,' Sky told him. 'You can tell me.'

'Well, it seems that you father *did* rise to the position of Kark-Du — that's what they call their leaders. He was a pretty popular leader from what I can gather too. But not with everyone. It seems that some of the young males didn't like the way he ran things. They thought he was too easy going, too close to what they call the 'Old Way'. They wanted him to adopt the really hardline version of the Way — the most extreme interpretation of that seer of theirs, Stone Eyes.'

'So what happened?'

Eventually there was a kind of a rebellion. One of the young males challenged your father's leadership. It ended up as a fight between the two of them — a vicious fight by the sound of it. For a while it looked like your father might win but then the younger zeta got the advantage and hurt him pretty badly. It seems he was driven off and never seen again.'

Sky spoke quietly: 'Didn't your contact know where he is now?'

'I knew you would want to know that so I asked him. Eventually he agreed to go back to his clan and ask around discreetly, but I really had to pressurise him. I had to agree that this would be the last thing I ever ask of him and that I would only ever try to see him this one more time.'

'So you haven't seen him yet?'

'No, but I am going to meet him now. I need to leave right away or I'll miss him. I'll be back at first light tomorrow and I can tell you what I've learned then.'

Deneb looked at Sky who was staring at the sand, lost in thought. He turned to Rain Ending. 'You had better go then. Thanks so much for doing this for him.'

Rain nodded once and then left.

Deneb and Muddy turned back to Sky and were about to comfort him when a lone messenger appeared, one of the Dune Coast Clan. She announced herself officiously adding, 'Touches The Sky is to report to the Council. You must follow me.'

'Can't this wait a little?' Deneb asked. 'He's just had some bad news.'

'No. My instructions are that he is to come at once.'

Sky followed the messenger, his head still spinning with the knowledge that his father had been driven out of the Guardian clan and been hurt badly by someone. He tried to think what the Council might want him for now. Something to do with the Gathering? The Grand Council?

He did not have to wonder for long. The messenger brought him to a small sandy patch surrounded by low coral reefs. There, four of the Dune Coast Clan Council waited, upright over the sand, their tails just above it. Silent Waters addressed him as the messenger departed. 'Touches The Sky, you have been summoned here before Council because an allegation has been made against you; a very serious allegation.'

Sky stopped in front of them, confused. He said nothing.

Silent Waters stared hard at him for a long moment then nodded to Green Wave Falling who was beside her. He also looked at Sky, but with a cold, dispassionate look in his eyes. 'Bring forth the accuser!' he called.

From behind the Council the shape of a large dolphin emerged from the blue. Sky recognised it and his heart sank.

'It is I, Last To Speak!'

CHAPTER 30

"Punishment never falls lightly on the guilty
But its weight is felt tenfold by the innocent"
Unasked Questions - (4,429 – 4,471 post Great Alluvium)

'And because I exposed his secret he tried to kill my little daughter!'

Last To Speak flung out the words as he completed his story. He remained defiantly in front of the half circle of the Council and turned to stare at Sky who was behind him. His gaze seemed full of hate. Sky shook his head imperceptibly but knew he must not speak yet.

Silent Waters nodded to Green Wave Falling, who, as Voice of Truth, was acting as the inquisitor for the Council. He raised himself off the seabed on his tail to his full height. 'The Council would learn why Last To Speak states that he "revealed the accused's secret".'

'When the strange zeta, Rain Ending, first came to our clan, I was present when he told some of us of his suspicions about Touches The Sky. I was the first one to reveal to Sky that the clan knew of his foul past, so as a result his anger focused on me and he looked for revenge.'

'And you believe that he tried to exact that revenge on you through your daughter?'

'There can be no question of it! There was a large class of students under his control, but only my little Bellatrix Unseen nearly died! It was just luck that she survived!'

'Very well, Last To Speak may move aside for the present. The Council will question the accused. Touches The Sky, do you admit that you were in sole control of the class on that day?'

'I can confirm that fact to the Council. I had intended...'

'Enough! You will answer our questions with a simple yes or no unless we clearly ask for a more detailed explanation. Do you understand?'

'Yes.'

'The Academy gives clear guidance as to the maximum depth that students should be exposed to. Do you claim to have maintained those limits? Bear in mind that we can call upon other witnesses to confirm your story.'

'I think I may have gone deeper than the guidelines.'

'You think! You *think*? These children were placed in your care! They addressed you as Jeii! Do you not *know*?

'I...I did go deeper than the guidelines. I had intended to keep to them but I...'

'Enough! The Council notes that the accused admits to exceeding the depth limits for his class. Was the student, Bellatrix Unseen, beyond those limits when she became unconscious?'

'Yes, she was, but not for long; I didn't notice only because I had lost concentration for a moment and...'

'The Council further notes that the accused admits that he was not monitoring his students while they were beyond their accepted limits. Did you, as her supervisor, notice that she had become unconscious?'

'Well, no, one of the other students told me, but I would have soon I am sure.'

'And what did you do then?'

'As soon as they told me I started lifting Bellatrix to the surface — to try and save her.'

Green Wave Falling nodded soberly. 'The Council notes that the accused admits that he *only* attempted to save the student in his care when the other students had made it clear that they had seen her plight.'

'No, it wasn't like that — I would have reacted immediately anyway!'

'Be quiet! You were not asked a question! If it pleases the Council, the Voice of Truth has concluded the inquisition.'

Sky waited with a numb feeling in his stomach as the Council members exchanged a muffled conversation. To one side of them Last To Speak stared at Sky, his eyes malevolent. At last, Silent Waters spoke. 'The Council is deeply disturbed by this matter. It is clear that students' lives were recklessly endangered by the accused on the day discussed. What is less clear is whether this was due to simple foolishness on his part or if it was a malicious act as the accuser claims. Given the upheavals of recent days, we will postpone our judgement for three days. This will give time to conclude the final details of the Gathering and allow us to meditate fully on the facts of this matter.

Sky was dismissed and he left to search for his friends. He found Deneb and Muddy where he had left them. They listened to his story sympathetically. At the end Deneb spoke first. 'I was afraid of something like this. Last To Speak is out to get you for some reason. I just hope the Council sees that it was an accident.'

They talked into the evening but finally decided to get some rest and meet again at dawn when Rain Ending should return.

Dawn came and went the next day with no sign of him. Sky grew more and more agitated. 'Has he changed his mind? Left without telling me?'

'No,' Muddy reassured him. 'He was so grateful for you saving him that day. Something must have happened.'

'Then let's go and look for him. I can't stand this waiting anymore. He said they were east of here — let's just follow the coast that way and maybe we'll find him coming this way.'

They set off, spread out abreast just in sonar range of one another so that they could search the widest area. Sky was in the centre and could hear the other two's ranging echolocation intermittently as they followed the shoreline. As the sun approached noon there was an urgent call from Muddy to shorewards. 'Sky, I've found him! Come quickly!' Sky passed the message onto Deneb who was further out to sea then quickly swam to Muddy. He found him hovering beside the inert form of Rain Ending, whose body was gently rolling back and forth in the swell on the shallow sand. Sky looked at him in horror, he was covered in bites and bruises, one eye was swollen shut, his jaw looked broken or dislocated. Deneb joined them a moment later, saying quietly, 'Is he...dead?'

Muddy shook his head. 'No, but he's really badly hurt, with several broken ribs. I just helped him take a breath. Help me again.'

They lifted the injured dolphin to the surface where he did seem to take a small gasping breath. Sky looked into his uninjured eye and saw a flash of recognition there. His voice came very faintly, it was obviously painful for him to talk. 'Sky, I met my friend, but we had just...had just started to talk when we were ambushed...must have followed him.'

'Who followed him?'

'Them. Guardians. Attacked me — us. Don't know what happened to him.' He stopped, with a wheeze of air and they held him at the surface to breath. He was obviously fading fast. Deneb gave Sky a meaningful glance.

Sky spoke soothingly close to Rain's face. 'Don't try and speak now. We need to get the Healers to help you.'

Rain shook his head imperceptibly. He spoke slowly, in obvious pain.

'No news about...where your father...now. But...told me the name of... new leader...one who hurt your father so badly.'

Sky, shook his head slightly. 'Rain, you don't need to...'

Rain looked at him as though from a great distance and spoke very faintly, pronouncing the words with great effort. As his life slipped away, he whispered: 'Storm...Before...Darkness.'

CHAPTER 31

"Love is a darting, silver thing
Shining, tempting, frightening
It teases, ensnares, repels
Easily caught; easily lost
Kept a lifetime
Or mourned for one"
Mountain Fires - (3,668 – 3,717 post Great Alluvium)

'I've got to try and find him!'

Deneb shook his head. 'You'd be crazy. You've no idea where he is or even if he's still alive. And you've got a punitive Council decision hanging over you in Senx's name!'

Muddy nodded in agreement. 'Forget it, Sky, at least for now. It's too dangerous, far too dangerous.'

They were swimming back to the clan, having committed Rain's body to the abyss with as much reverence as they could. It was not much of a ceremony but they did not know of any friends that Rain had who would have wanted to come. They had said what they could and let him go.

Deneb closed his eyes tightly as he swam for a while, then opened them, his expression pained. 'These Guardians are prepared to kill other zetii! I wouldn't have believed this before but now we've seen it ourselves. And not for the first time! You know where else!"

Muddy looked across at Deneb sympathetically. 'You mean Wakes Softly, don't you?'

'Well it makes sense doesn't it? The injuries she suffered — that was an attack by other zetii — the Guardians must have killed her too.'

'But why?'

'I don't know for sure, but something to do with what she told us — remember — she thought it was a Councillor that was spying on a Starwriter ceremony, and then meeting a stranger secretly — it must have been a Guardian.'

'Who in the Council would do that?'

'Well the obvious one,' Muddy said, 'is North Wind. Should we tell someone? Won't it be dangerous for us if he suspects we know?'

Deneb looked hard at them, his face grim. 'I don't care if it's dangerous. I want to stop this killing somehow. Let's not tell anyone yet, we don't have any real proof. We'll just keep a close eye on North Wind and see if we can find out more. Sky, you are keeping quiet — can't you see that the Guardians are causing these deaths?'

'Yes. You don't have to convince me. There's more that I know — I'm not allowed to say — but they are very dangerous.'

Muddy and Deneb exchanged glances but said nothing. Sky regretted saying anything and hoped that they would assume he meant something that came out of the Grand Council meetings.

Now they were approaching the clan and they could hear other voices as the seabed shelved up towards the beach. Muddy made an effort to change the subject, saying:

'Deneb, what about your special mission? How's your Xenthos coming along?'

'Poorly,' he grimaced, 'I've been trying but there hasn't been much time yet to practice.'

'When do you go?'

'Trevally Outpaced was originally coming back the day after tomorrow but then Green Wave came to see me last evening and said that the envoy later told him that they might actually be back a day earlier than that. So he'll take me to meet him at this rendezvous point he knows tomorrow. He wants to cram in some extra diplomacy lessons on the way I think! Then he's going to leave me there and the Xenthos will pick me up in the next day or two.'

'You looking forward to it?' Muddy asked.

'Well, it's certainly an honour to be chosen, but I find the responsibility a bit daunting. I'm supposed to be building confidence between them and the Ka-Tse. What if I make some mistake and offend them in some way?'

'You'll be fine,' Sky assured him, 'you're the perfect diplomat, you've inherited your mother's skill.'

'In any case,' Muddy added, 'from what I hear of the Xenthos, you'll probably be left behind in an exhausted heap in a day or two. They're always moving and don't like it near the shore. Don't expect to see the seabed in the next sixty days. And the depths they dive to! By the time you come back...'

Muddy trailed off and Sky saw that he and Deneb were staring at something behind him.

'Who's she?' murmured Deneb, looking at the slim shape of the approaching female.

'*That's* Sky's new friend,' Muddy whispered, 'and I don't suppose we'll be needed around here now.'

Sky was about to protest when Venus In Mist arrived beside them, looking them over with those disconcerting dark eyes. She spoke to Muddy and Deneb.

'I'm terribly sorry to interrupt you like this, but I'd like to speak to your friend for a short while. Alone. Do you mind?' Her eyes gave them the sweetest of smiles as she tilted her head in a disarming way.

Deneb Rising replied.

'Not at all, please take your time. Sky, we will be hunting over by the reef at the north east headland if you want us later.'

As they swam behind Mist, Deneb looked at Sky and, out of her sight, opened his eyes wide in compliment to him. Then they were gone.

Mist turned her attention to Sky.

'You know my clan leaves tomorrow don't you?'

'Yes, I did, I'd just forgotten...I've had a lot on my mind lately.'

'Well, I suppose that's understandable. I know you must have loved Cloud Passing. Was it hard for you yesterday?'

'I...I'm not sure I can talk about it yet.'

'Look,' she said, looking at him intently, 'last night you helped me a lot. I'd kept in all my thoughts about that baby dying — I was blaming myself for it and holding it all in. You spent all that time listening to me and I started to realise that there probably wasn't anything I could have done differently, and I started to deal with the pain. I haven't had that kind of communication with anyone before. Maybe I can help you too.'

Sky watched her as she spoke. She had an intensity about her that was unique; when she talked to him it felt like there was no-one else in Ocean for her. He thought she was also probably the most beautiful female he had ever seen. Then he thought about Dusk and felt guilty. But why, when Dusk seemed so disinterested in him? He spoke at last.

'Look, Mist, I'm really glad that I could help you. And I think it would help me to talk about yesterday, in fact a lot of things, I just need a little time to get things straight in my own head. But when I'm ready, I *would* like to talk to you. You're…special.'

'Sky, when my clan leaves tomorrow, you know I probably won't see you again. Maybe at another Gathering, but that won't be for at least three years.'

'When do you go?'

'Early tomorrow post-noon,' she moved closer to him, and spoke more urgently. 'Listen Sky, I like this coastline. I like the zetii here. If I said I wanted to join your clan for a while, maybe forever, what would you think?'

He was shocked by the possibilities. It was not unusual for dolphins to move from one clan to another, but this was something to do with him. Was she expecting something of him? Wasn't that what he wanted? He had to find out what was happening with Dusk, once and for all.

'I'm sure my clan would welcome you…' he started.

'No doubt, they seem very polite. But what would *you* think?'

'Mist, can you give me one night to think about things please? Let me meet you here at noon tomorrow and I will know what I want.'

He could not read her expression as she nodded back to him.

'Alright. Think hard then. And remember, after noon tomorrow my clan leaves. I need to know if I follow them or my heart.'

And she was gone, leaving Sky alone, the dropping sun sending dancing shafts of light through the shallow water onto the sand ripples around him. Vraxia overlaid with Lasa-ka: *a change or decision — great, of high import.* He set off to find Fades Into Dusk.

CHAPTER 32

"Never assume that the merit of an argument is proportional to the
emotion or volume applied during its delivery."

- *Saturn Over Antares (12,415-12,438 post Great Alluvium)*

Dusk was with some dolphins from one of the visiting clans she had
befriended. She had just spent some time babysitting one of the young ones
so that his mother could go and hunt. As the mother returned, Dusk led the
calf towards her. As soon as he recognised her signature call he chirped with
joy, swimming over to her and took station just beside her dorsal fin; riding
the pressure wave as she swam.

'You are a darling Dusk,' the mother said, 'that was so helpful.'

'You're welcome, he is a delight. He must be approaching his naming
ceremony soon, have you any names in mind?'

'Yes, he will be a year old just after the next new moon. He loves starfish,
so I thought perhaps something including that would be nice; perhaps just
"Plays With Starfish"'.

Dusk smiled, but thought that when the youngster was a sexually mature
young male he may not care for the name so much.

'Yes, that's a cute name, but you know what they say: name the child on
the child's naming day.'

'Oh, I will of course. I'll get his Shades read on the morning of the
ceremony to see if I get any inspiration there.'

'Do the other family members have any ideas?'

'His grandmother would probably like to have something including "Alphecca" after her, but no one else has any strong opinions. We're not sure who his father was, so that's not a consideration.'

Dusk nodded. It was fairly common for dolphins to be polygamous so it was not unusual for the exact father of a child to be unknown.

The baby sidled down below his mother and nuzzled at her side. She tilted her body so that he could suckle briefly at her nipple. She turned back to Dusk who still swam alongside her.

'What about you my dear, any fine young males that catch your eye? You would make a wonderful mother.'

'Well, I'm a final year Novice,' Dusk said evasively, 'so I couldn't for another couple of months anyway.'

'Still, all these handsome creatures at the Gathering! I don't know that I would be so restrained in your place! And you have some fine young males in your own clan. What about that good looking fellow who was picked out to go into the Sun Chamber? Don't you fancy him?'

'That's Touches The Sky. I've known him a long time, but just as friends. I don't know, it just never went beyond that.'

'He looked like a zeta who will go far to me. A fine hunter too I dare say. Snatch him up my dear! Ones like that are few and far between.'

Just as Dusk was about to reply, Sky appeared ahead of them, making his signature call and heading towards them.

'Well, that must be fate!' exclaimed the mother, 'I'll leave you to it; remember what I said!' She swam off, leaving Dusk alone and embarrassed.

Sky arrived and they swam together alongside one another parallel to the shore. The sun was setting and the night-time creatures were slowly starting to emerge from the coral heads they passed.

'What was she saying?' he asked, 'What was that about fate?'

She thought quickly. 'Oh, we were just talking about finding a name for her son; she has some strange ideas and is looking for inspiration. Anyway, what are you doing here?'

'I...I was just thinking of you and wanted to talk to you. To ask you something.'

'Well, that sounds pretty serious. What is it?'

'What do you want out of life Dusk? How do you imagine your future here with the clan?'

'Wow, serious stuff! I don't know, I haven't thought about it too much I suppose. Anyway why would you assume I would stay with the clan? I mean. I might, but who knows? Lots of zetii move from one clan to another.'

'Do you think you might then?'

'I don't know. Maybe. I guess it depends on what there is for me here or if it seems better somewhere else. So, you tell me, what are you going to do with your life?'

Sky paused for a moment.

'I'd like to be happy. To do nothing I would regret. To follow the Way.'

'To "do nothing you would regret"? What kind of an ambition is that Sky? And to follow the Way? Can't you come up with anything of your own? It's like you're always quoting from a lesson.'

'What's wrong with that? So, they are the kind of things our teacher would have said — old wisdom — but why should that make them wrong?'

Dusk was exasperated. This was exactly what drove her crazy about him.

'Because times have changed! You just don't see it Sky! Ocean is coming to pieces and our place in it has been turned inside out. You've been spending too much time with those ancients on the Council — you sound just like them!'

'Dusk, there's no real alternative. You want us to just take what we need and ignore the consequences? Then what makes us any better than every other species in Ocean?'

'Because...because we have no choice, that's why! If we keep to the old ways we're going to just die out. Probably that's going to happen anyway, but at least we can keep going as long as we can.'

'No, Dusk! We think of the zetii as the most culturally sophisticated creatures on the planet — what would your logic make us?'

He was angry now but arguing from principles. Dusk was frustrated more than angry; Sky was so stubborn. But she realised for the first time that he was not just quoting from the Way. He was not weak, he just followed a doctrine that she now doubted after all she had heard from the Guardians. But he had clearly thought about it all and believed it. She recognised that he had the same passion in his beliefs that she found so attractive in Storm. But who was right? Then she realised how dark it was becoming: she had to go; she would be late for her meeting with Storm. She was hoping to see him before the ceremony started that evening.

'Sky, we are getting nowhere here. Look, let's talk about this more some other time. I'm sorry but I have to go now; I just need to spend some time alone.'

Her eyes gave a little forced smile and she swam off along the shoreline to the east, leaving him there in the shallows. As she swam she tried to replay their conversation in her mind. She had to respect Sky's position, he had spoken with a confidence and conviction that showed he believed what he said, but was it just naïvety? She knew what Storm's opinions would be, and although she loved his certainty, she wondered yet again if he could be wrong. She was sure that tonight's events would be significant. She had not wanted to see the ceremony but Storm had insisted; he wanted her to join the Guardians and wanted her to see every part of their ways. But the ceremony had sounded repulsive to her — nothing like it would be permitted by the Way.

She resolved that this should be a test of her commitment: she would try to view the ceremony objectively, but if it did prove to be as bad as it sounded she would have to think seriously about breaking off her relationship with Storm. As she learned more and more of their ways it was starting to just feel too wrong somehow.

She was deep in thought as she swam along the coastline and did not notice the distant form shadowing her in the twilight.

CHAPTER 33

"Judge them by how they judge"
- Traditional

Sky trailed Dusk in the darkness. As the sunlight disappeared it became very dark and he was afraid that he might lose her. He could hear her navigational sonar up ahead from time to time and he followed that. He did not dare to use his own in case she heard him, and as the water became black, he had twice collided painfully with an unseen coral head. He also occasionally saw a faint stream of light particles in her wake as she disturbed the phosphorescence. Then, after a while, the half moon rose and he began to see better, especially when she swam over the sandy areas between the coral outcrops. He continued following her for over an hour, taking care not to surface for a breath at the same time as her in case she might hear his exhalations.

Eventually, she slowed and stopped near an isolated rocky arch. This protruded from an area of rock and coral that jutted out from the shelving sandy sea bed. She made her signature call: 'It is I, Fades Into Dusk!'

Sky felt a nervous tremor pass through him: she was meeting someone here! There was no reply so they were not here yet and she settled down as though to wait. He realised that they might come from any direction and he could be seen there on the sand. So he worked his way back to the shallows in a big circle and then swam carefully out on top of the rocky area with the arch. Soon he was well placed in a good vantage point up there where she could not see him. The rock rose close enough to the surface so that he could even make short trips up to breathe without being seen, and the upper surface of the rock was convoluted enough that he could hide himself in it when Dusk would surface to breathe.

After some time Sky thought he heard a dolphin's sonar in the distance. Dusk must have heard it too as she roused herself and gave her signature call again. Then he saw the large form of a male dolphin appear in the dim light.

The newcomer approached Dusk and they caressed. They swam in gentle circles below Sky, pectoral fins brushing against each other. Sky hated the sight of the stranger's large body up against her slender one. So this was where she went. This was obviously her lover. This answered all his questions and he felt cold inside watching them together. But why the secrecy? Where was his clan?

Sky could see that they were talking but he could not make out what they were saying. He decided to go, there was nothing else for him here; he knew now, Dusk had a lover. He had known this was a possibility but knowing it for certain hurt. He quietly turned and was about to leave when he heard more sonar approaching: other dolphins — a lot of dolphins. The pair below him turned expectantly towards the sound. Sky stopped, curious to know what this meant.

The moon was higher now and against the white sand below him, Sky saw a column of dolphins file into the sandy area. He thought there must be around sixty of them at least. They formed a wide semi-circle facing the large male who Sky sensed was their leader. At the centre of the crescent there was a knot of dolphins, with one individual flanked by four large males. They seemed to be protecting or controlling him; in the dim light Sky could not be sure.

The leader moved forward slightly into the centre of the half-ring facing the newcomers, Dusk edged around to join one end of the line of dolphins. He had moved to where all could see him; she seemed to want to seek anonymity.

The large dolphin addressed them in a clear voice: 'My brothers and sisters, you are the chosen ones. You are among the select few zetii who have accepted their duty as the Guardians.'

Up in his hiding place, Sky was shocked. The Guardians! Dusk was here with the Guardians! The male continued on below him.

'It is no easy task, and many of you had hard journeys to endure before you could join this select band. Some of you saw that ours is the true way for the Ka-Tse and sought out our family. Others were banished from other clans, usually because you despised their soft attitudes and sensed that the version of the 'Way' that they pathetically cling to is an anachronism; incapable of saving our kind from a new and dangerous future. One thousand years ago, the Seer Stone Eyes warned the Ka-Tse what would happen, but only a few enlightened zetii heeded his words. He saw the changes taking place in Ocean; the dwindling food supplies, the rapacious Walkers competing for our food as they learned to take everything from Ocean — even killing the Great Wanderers by the thousand. He foretold that a time would come when there would not be enough for all zetii to eat and that only the most noble of the zetii — the Ka-Tse — might be saved. He told his followers that in order to survive, the Ka-Tse must take their proper place as the dominant species in Ocean. He did not say that other zetii should not eat; only that they should not eat until every one of the chosen Ka-Tse, the Guardians, have eaten their rightful share.'

The leader paused, and swam up the short distance to the surface to breathe. He gestured with his head to the others and they all did likewise. Sky pressed himself back into a depression in the rock as this happened. When they had all descended again he surfaced briefly himself, still just out of sight of the crowd below him.

The leader continued his monologue: 'We now carry on the duty that Stone Eyes prescribed. You will all survive the great upheaval that Ocean is enduring because you follow the true teachings set down by the Seer. Now, more than ever before, it is vital that we remain true to our beliefs. In the next few moons great changes are coming. The Ka-Tse will have an opportunity to prove their dominance over lesser zetii!'

Sky listened, confused. What was he talking about? He felt that somehow he should warn the Council about this, but how, without revealing he had been in contact with the Guardians? The voice went remorselessly on, 'But our survival is fragile and reliant on our remaining steadfast and loyal. Each one of you depends on the strength and loyalty of the others. If one of you is weak, all suffer.'

He paused, staring at them each in turn. Many of them flinched under his stern gaze. Finally, he continued, a hint of sadness in his voice. 'And so, it grieves me to tell you that in the last days, two amongst you have transgressed, have broken their vows of loyalty to the clan and has put our security at risk. One was found yesterday and dealt with promptly at the place where his wrongdoing took place. But now we find another needs to learn the importance of obedience.'

He fixed his gaze now on the dolphin surrounded by the four guards. The prisoner seemed to shrink under his gaze. The leader approached him. 'You know the laws of the Guardians. Once you join the clan and take the vows of fealty to the Seer, no contact with non-believers is permitted without permission! What do you have to say?'

The prisoner, a young male, spoke in a fast, frightened voice: 'Please, Kark-Du, it was just for a moment, my old clan was passing and I just wanted news about my sister and mother, I only spoke to one of their hunting scouts for a moment.'

'Silence! So you admit your crime. You know the law, I can sentence you to death for what you have done.'

The leader paused, and looked around him at the hushed crowd. On top of the rock, Sky was listening, shocked. Shocked at the aggression of their beliefs. And shocked that this Kark-Du was Dusk's lover!

The Kark-Du turned again to the terrified prisoner and focussed on him. 'However, I am told that your story is probably true, and you have at least showed the courage to admit your crime. Given that, and your youth, I will pardon your life.'

The prisoner looked pathetically grateful, but his expression changed to horror as the leader continued on: 'Instead, you will swim the tunnel of retribution. He raised his voice to address them all: 'The clan will gather to witness the punishment!'

Sky was about to go up for air when the dolphins below him suddenly started moving. They all surfaced for a breath, then a group of males formed two lines up the sandy slope beside the arch. They then turned to face each other. The rest of the clan moved up to one side of the lines of males, and arranged themselves so that they were facing towards the rock on which Sky lay, with the two rows of males in front of them. They settled on the bottom there expectantly. The moon was much higher now and they stood out clearly against the pale, rippled sand.

With a feeling of cold dismay, Sky realised that his situation had changed. If he left his hiding place amongst the rock and coral on top of the arch he would be bound to be seen by the crowd below him. The half moon would be behind him and he would stand out in silhouette against the silver of the surface. He had already wanted to take a breath before the Guardians had started to move; now the feeling took on a nagging urgency. He started the exercises to reduce his body's oxygen needs: slowing his heart, focusing on his core, reducing the blood circulation to his extremities. He wanted to remain fully conscious though, he needed to know what was going to happen below him.

The two rows of males now raised themselves on the sand, their tails just off the sand, their backs arched slightly forward so that they formed a corridor up the gently shelving bottom. The guards escorted the prisoner to the lower end of this tunnel. He looked terrified. The leader spoke once more. 'You all know the words of the Seer Stone Eyes: "This is the testing time for the chosen ones and only the strong deserve to survive. The desires of the individual are subservient to the needs of the clan."' He turned and stared pitilessly at the young dolphin, then continued his address to the crowd, 'This zeta betrayed your trust and jeopardised the clan. Show your wrath. If he deserves to live he will be made stronger this day. If he is proved weak, the clan is better rid of him now.' He turned back to the prisoner, 'You know what to say I think.'

The young dolphin looked ready to faint, his eyes darting around the crowd, pleading for help, but none was offered. Eventually, in a small voice he said, 'I give thanks to the Guardians for the lesson I am about to receive. I ask my brothers to teach me well.'

Then, he was off, swimming as fast as he could up the slope of the tunnel.

Sky watched in fascinated horror as the young dolphin entered the tunnel, swimming as fast as he could. As he drew level with each pair of dolphins they attacked him viciously, driving their rostrums into his side and raking his body with their teeth. The leader swam alongside the tunnel, encouraging the attackers to be more brutal, but also — bizarrely to Sky's mind — encouraging the tormented youth to keep swimming, to make it to the end. Eight pairs of males savaged him in this way, and although the punishment was over quite quickly, as the young dolphin came to the last pair he was finished. One of his attackers drove into his side with a particularly powerful blow and the air emptied from his lungs through his blowhole. He sank to the bottom unconscious, still just inside the corridor. The last pair of dolphins continued to attack his lifeless body until, after a while, the Kark-Du shouted a command and they stopped. The two lines of attackers withdrew a short distance and the leader made a gesture. What seemed to be his lieutenant, a slight dolphin with an unusually long rostrum, moved forward and examined the fallen youth, moving his oddly large head back and forth as he scanned him with sonar.

Sky watched still, but with growing distraction: he really needed air badly now. The lieutenant spoke dispassionately: 'He has several broken ribs, his tail is badly mauled and he has probably lost one eye. Water is starting to enter his lungs but he is not dead yet.' He looked quizzically at his master.

The Kark-Du considered for a moment, then said, 'Sharp Beak — see if he can be saved. Don't waste long on it though, either he is strong enough or he feeds the Cleaner. The meeting is over.'

He started to move away, Sharp Beak motioned to two other dolphins who moved forward and between them lifted the body to the surface where they pressed his sides encouraging him to breathe. Soon he took a few choked breaths and then continued in a rattling, laboured way. Maybe he would survive. In spite of the agony he was clearly in, Sky almost envied him; he was so desperate for air now, darkness was starting to creep into the edges of his vision. If he did not give his body oxygen soon he would die here. Sky saw that the dolphins were starting to break up and move off. He saw Dusk approach the leader. She seemed to be very agitated and was addressing him passionately. He could not hear what she was saying though and the pair of them swam off into the night, followed by many of the clan. A few remained around the injured youth.

As Sky watched Dusk go, a sudden realisation crept into his confused mind. Her companion was not just a Guardian Kark-Du; this must be Storm Before Darkness, the zeta who had driven out his father! But he could not think about it now, a numb feeling was spreading through him. What was the point of it all? He was empty, disappointed, he felt like there was nothing left to live for, the world seemed far away and unimportant. He was fading, he was almost losing consciousness. The darkness beckoned.

CHAPTER 34

"Beware death's cool embrace
About the melancholic heart
Darkness creeps into the mind
The joys of days past now distant
Be not seduced!"

Miaplacidus Obscured
(13,093 – 13,146 post Great Alluvium)

Sky was almost gone; fading into unconsciousness, when he became aware of a shape approaching him: he concentrated hard, then realised that it was the injured dolphin who was now swimming in feeble circles at the surface, watched from a distance by his guards. He was swimming almost directly towards Sky; he must see him. Suddenly he stopped just in front of Sky, staring at him with his uninjured eye. 'Who are you?' he hissed weakly.

Sky roused himself a little. 'A friend,' he whispered, 'I saw what they did to you and I want to help. Just pretend to ignore me now and I will come and get you later. What's your name?'

The youth stopped, wincing in pain.

'I am Catches In Air of the…of the…' He stared at Sky who looked back at him pleadingly. He turned to look back towards the guards, then back at Sky again. Sky smiled encouragingly, his head spinning. If they would just go now, he could breathe again and leave this awful place.

The youth looked at him once more, his gaze full of pain. Then he shouted hoarsely, 'A spy! There's a spy here! An enemy of the Guardians!' He turned back and smiled weakly at Sky, who suddenly burst into life. With his last reserves of energy he shot the short distance to the surface, his mind filling with blackness — then — bliss! He left the water and took a deep lungful of beautiful, cool, clean air. He turned and fell back to the water, his vision clearing rapidly, although he had an oppressive, throbbing pain behind his eyes. As the bubbles cleared, he saw that three of the four guards were heading towards him at speed. They were all big, powerful, dolphins, each over three metres long. The fourth was beside the injured youth, looking undecided as to what to do.

Sky shot off along the coast to the north west towards his own clan, the three guards in pursuit. His head still hurt from the lack of air and, swimming as fast as he was, his body was struggling to meet his oxygen needs. He had little doubt as to what his fate would be if he was caught, so he swam as hard as he could, trying to ignore the pain. He fled up into the shallows, hoping to lose his pursuers in the darkness. He weaved in and out of coral heads, hearing sharp bursts of sonar behind him as they tried to track him. He gauged that they were not together, they seemed to be spread out abreast of each other, trying to encircle him. He knew what was coming.

Sky was following the short, vertical, coral wall that now fringed the shore. It weaved in and out in a series of miniature bays and headlands ahead of him. From time to time he shot from the water, taking a breath and looking at the scenery ahead of him, hoping to find somewhere to hide. He could hear one of the guards close behind him now — he must be gaining on him! On his next jump he was dismayed to see the other two guards jump at the same time as him, off to his left — trapping him against the fringing reef. He heard one of them laugh before he fell back into the water. Sky's tail drove up and down through the water but it was no use, they were gaining on him. He had started this sprint with his blood almost empty of oxygen, his pounding head was proof that he had never caught up with his body's needs again. On his next leap he realised what their plan was. Up ahead, a narrow headland of sharp rock extended far out into the sea, creating a small bay ahead of him. The two flanking guards blocked any chance of him swimming around it; he was being driven into the bay where he would be trapped. It was just the kind of tactic he, Muddy and Deneb had used in the past when hunting their favourite fish. But this time he was the one who would die, and no one was thanking Senx for his passing.

Now Sky could detect the headland up ahead with sonar. He could hear his pursuers too, they were close behind but spread out to make escape impossible. Then Sky could see it. The night was lifting with the sun about to rise and he found himself against the vertical wall of the headland. The coral encrusted rock continued up, through the surface as a low cliff above him. He turned to face them. They stopped in front of him, blocking the way completely. One of them spoke.

'How do you want to do him, Rock?'

Rock answered, a smile in his voice: 'We'll rush him all at once — don't want to take any chances. This won't take long; he's not going to vanish on us this time.'

Sky thought desperately. What did he mean, "This time"? Then he realised this brute must have been one of the hunters that had trapped him in the bay one night; when he had leapt onto a rocky ledge and evaded them. He looked around desperately. There was no ledge this time. But the rock of the headland was not so high…and might not be too wide…but then it could be very wide. In sudden desperation he did something very hard for a dolphin: he leapt into the unknown. With an explosive burst of energy he shot up through the surface and leapt high over the rocky headland. He had no idea how far it was, and he fully expected to crash down onto the sharp rocks where he would flop helplessly till he died — a slow and painful death. But as he shot skywards he saw with a surge of hope that it was not far to the other side of the headland. He realised he might just make it and he flapped his tail futilely in the air as he dropped, the rocks and water rushing up at him. He crashed back into the water just at the edge of the rock on the other side of the headland, and felt a hot ripping pain as his belly scraped along the vicious volcanic rocks of the headland. He had done it! He had leapt over the narrow headland and his pursuers were still on the other side! He realised there was some of his blood in the water around him, but although his injury was beginning to hurt he could still swim. Now he had to move; it would not take them long to round the headland. He knew he was getting close to the bay where his own clan was, so he set off at once. Almost immediately he saw a group of six dolphins heading towards him; a group of his own clan's scouts. The leader, who Sky recognised as Hunts Alone, recognised him.

'Sky! What are you doing out here on your own, and what have you done to yourself?'

Before Sky could answer, the three guards appeared around the headland. When they saw the scouts with Sky they stopped, clearly not liking the odds any more. One called out, 'Come back, little friend, we haven't finished our games yet!'

Hunts Alone called back at them. 'Where are your manners? Do you not give your signature calls when you meet strangers?'

The guard laughed, and then, his voice full of sarcasm, shouted, 'I am so terribly sorry. Allow me to introduce us all. We are the Guardians. And now, we must leave our friend in your care and bid you farewell.' Then they turned and swam back the way they had come, still laughing.

Hunts Alone looked shocked and turned back to Sky. 'Guardians! I'm sorry Sky, but I'm going to have to report this. You are going to have to face the Council. They'll have to decide what to do with you.'

CHAPTER 35

"Test not my love so now
The depth of your love
Is hidden to me
By mirrored surface
Is there place for me to dive?
Seek not yet
To fathom mine"
- From the Arcturus' Love Sonnets

Sky was summoned to a hastily convened Council meeting that same day. Hunts Alone escorted him across the by now strangely quiet bay to the meeting point. As they surfaced Sky saw that a storm was building in the west: great piles of cloud were building into enormous, threatening towers, their upper layers bubbling slowly ever higher then spreading out into the upper layers of the atmosphere in an ominous flat top. Below the clouds the sky was dark slate. One of the last clans from the Gathering was making an early start, moving off away from the clouds; making low leaps as they swam.

Hunts Alone led him to the meeting location which was close to a river mouth in the shallows. As they drew nearer, Sky saw seabirds diving into the water. There must be fish there he thought distractedly, then berated himself for thinking of such trivial things at such a time. As they approached the river mouth the water became cloudier, dirtied with sediments washed from the land. The colour was also different; more of a Shade of brown than blue; Sky recognised the Kruma as *Laxia* now: *new life* or *uncertainty*. And the murkiness of the water made this *Gid-ana*: *imminent* or *very close*. He wondered if the Council had chosen such a setting deliberately or if this was just coincidence.

Then Sky heard low voices up ahead. As he and Hunts Alone approached, the shape of the Council members became more distinct in the turbid water; waiting upright, their tails gently brushing the low sea grass as they swayed back and forth in the light swell. Hunts Alone stopped at a respectful distance, allowing Sky to move alone into the semi-circle. Silent Waters opened the session:

'The Council convenes to consider a reported transgression of the clan's Code — namely the prohibition against any wilful contact with the so-called Guardians.' She looked closely at Sky. 'This is a very serious matter as you must know. The Council will ask you questions now to try and establish the facts. You must answer each question truthfully. Do not expand on your answers; just tell us the exact facts in each case.' She turned to her left. 'The Council recognises the respected Councillor Green Wave Falling. He will make enquiries on the Council's behalf.'

The old dolphin moved forward stiffly, the missing tip of his dorsal fin giving him an odd outline in the dirty water.

'Touches The Sky, we have been told that members of the Guardians have been seen and they seemed to know you. Have you made contact with the Guardians?'

'Well, Jeii not exactly...'

'Do not address your replies to me, you are answering to the Council. And do not try to be evasive! Answer our questions yes or no. I shall ask you again, in simpler terms: have you seen members of the Guardians?'

'I must tell the Council that yes, I have.'

'Did they come across you by accident, or did you go to them?'

'I — I went to them, but I did not...'

'Answer the question! Did you speak to any of them?'

Sky remembered the battered youth, and his brief, plaintive conversation with him, 'Yes, I did, just...'

Green Wave glared at him, 'You test our patience! Any form of contact is forbidden, it makes no difference *what* you spoke about! Did you see the Guardian clan last night?'

'Yes.'

'Under what circumstances?'

'I witnessed a…a Guardian ritual.'

There was a stirring and exchange of glances among the Council members at this.

With a sinking heart, Sky saw how this was going to end. At least he had to try and warn them about what the Guardian leader had said: about something happening in the next few moons that would lead to Ka-Tse dominance.

'May it please the Council, I overheard them say something that may be of great…'

Green Wave's eyes widened in anger, 'Silence! You have said more than enough!'

He shook his head sadly and turned back to the Council. 'This zeta regrets to report that the evidence is unequivocal. The Code has been broken. There can be no excuses for this youth.' He went on, his voice rising with emotion as he spoke. 'In recent days grave doubts have been raised concerning Touches The Sky's integrity. I beg to remind the Council that he is no simple zeta either. He is not only a member of this clan; not only a Novice at the Academy; not only entrusted by this clan to act as the Voice of Youth; he even represented the Ka-Tse at a Grand Council Meeting! He can claim no ignorance of the law or the consequences of transgression!' His voice sank to a more solemn tone: 'There can be only one punishment for him and this zeta commends the Council to enact it immediately.'

Sky spoke in a clear voice. 'This is not fair!'

Green Wave glared at him. 'Must I have you removed?'

Silent Waters spoke, 'With the Council's permission, this zeta would like to ask a question.'

Green Wave spoke quietly, but was clearly agitated, 'Whilst the Council has the highest respect for the Prime Mother's perspicacity, this would be highly irregular. Tradition dictates that the accused has only one inquisitor.'

'Nonetheless, this zeta begs the Council's indulgence on this occasion.'

No one else objected, so she continued, 'Touches The Sky, I sense that there is more that you have not told us. I will ask you but one question. Can you give us a good reason why you did this thing?' Her eyes smiled reassuringly at him.

Sky thought desperately for a moment. There was a good reason — he went to find Dusk. But if he said that then she must suffer exile. Maybe after this she would leave the Guardians alone and come to her senses. This was her only chance. With his heart full of pain he slowly said, 'I am so sorry Prime Mother…there was a good reason, I promise you…but no, I cannot say why.'

She closed her eyes for a long time, then opened them. She spoke slowly, her voice clear and cold. 'The Council hereby banishes you from the Dune Coast Clan. Your office as a Voice is terminated. You will leave immediately. You will speak to no one. Your name is lost to us now. Your deeds are forgotten. You cannot be seen. We have no memory of you. You no longer exist.' She turned and swam away from him; the other Councillors followed.

Sky was left alone in the swirling murk. He felt numb. All his friends were gone. He no longer existed. He had done his best to follow the Way and now he was alone. He surfaced for a moment, then turned and swam off towards the gathering storm.

In the bay a lone dolphin waited. She surfaced regularly, watching the passage of the sun. It was still just visible, not yet quite engulfed by the coming storm. She waited until she was sure that noon had passed. She made a final, high jump. For a brief moment, while she was at the apex of her flight, she thought she could see in the distance a single dolphin making low, travelling leaps from the water, heading towards the lightning on the horizon. She fell back into the water, paused for a moment, then turned and joined her waiting clan. They set off to the east, away from the storm.

CHAPTER 36

"The noblest of gifts is one that is given knowing that it shall be received with no possibility for gratitude."

- The creation anthologies

Fades Into Dusk returned to her clan still angry at what she had seen the previous night. She had been shocked when she had realised what was going to happen, then even more so when she became aware that she knew the dolphin who was to be punished — the young male who had been so flirtatious with her, Catches In Air. Afterwards, she had a terrible argument with Storm. She had said that she thought the punishment was barbaric and unnecessary. He had made his usual arguments about the need for the Ka-Tse to change; that the soft ways of the past were over, they must be strong to survive. He said that if there was one sick fish in the shoal, the shoal did not slow down to wait for it, or they would all die. Likewise, they could not permit one zeta to endanger all of the Guardians just because he was weak. She had ended up shouting at him and he had become very angry; frighteningly angry. He had brought his face close to hers and snapped his jaws in her face — for a moment, she had really thought that he was going to attack her — then he had got himself back under control. He had tried to change the subject, wanted to talk about Starwriters: had she met the Dreamweaver who had joined them? But she could not take any more and had left him there, his eyes once again full of dangerous anger.

She made a long detour on the way back to the clan, to give herself time to think. By the time she arrived there the sun was falling behind the clouds and a steady rain was falling. The wind was increasing too as the storm approached and the surface waves were growing in height. Breakers crashed against the shore, throwing white surf high in the air.

Under the water, in spite of the growing turbulence and the restless sand, the bay seemed strangely still; the last of the visiting clans had gone now. She found the members of her own clan milling about near the north west end. One of the first she recognised was Muddy and she gave her signature call. He replied and came towards her. He looked grave.

'Muddy, what's wrong?'

Muddy replied, his voice low, 'It's Sky, haven't you heard? He's exiled.'

'Exiled! Why? What's he done?'

He shook his head uncomprehendingly, 'They're saying that last night he was with the Guardians. Even witnessed one of their rituals!'

Dusk felt icy cold. It *must* have been the same thing she had seen, but how? Why would Sky be there? Did that mean that the Council knew that she had been with the Guardians?

Muddy moved alongside her comfortingly and stroked her side with his pectoral fin. 'I know, we're all shocked. I can't imagine what made him do it. I won't believe that Sky did this deliberately without some reason. He is just too...too *good* to get involved with those maniacs.'

'Did he give a reason?'

'No, Hunts Alone overheard his inquisition and apparently he wouldn't say. It was quick, Hunts said. They questioned him and he hardly said a word. He said it was like he was trying to deliberately hold back something or protect someone. Now he's gone.'

Dusk was reeling. 'Gone?' she murmured.

'Deneb was just here, he's really upset and angry. He can't believe that Sky would want to visit the Guardians either.'

She nodded, fearful again. 'Where is Deneb?'

'You just missed him. Green Wave Falling has taken him off to the meeting place where Deneb has to wait for the Xenthos. Poor Deneb, he was really shocked by this, he really feels like he's lost his brother.'

'Yes, yes of course. Look, Muddy, I want to be alone to think about this, it's just too much...' she paused, lost for words.

He smiled slightly. 'I understand. We've all been hurt by it, he was such a good friend. And he was especially fond of you of course.'

She looked at him in surprise, 'Me?'

'Oh, yes. Most of the clan thought you two must have gotten it together by now. He really admired you I think. Anyway, I'll leave you alone. Just call me if I can help.'

He left her. She lay still, being rocked back and forth in the growing swell. Clouds of bubbles were driven under the water around her by the breaking waves above, but she did not see them. She just kept saying to herself over and over again, 'What have I done? What have I done?'

CHAPTER 37

"And when you are abandoned
Completely alone
There is one who'll love you still
She waits in the shadows
Shy, patient; always ready
She knows you'll take her as partner
For your last dance
She's not jealous of past lovers
Cares not what wrongs you've done
Demands only total faithfulness
Accept her cold embrace
You'll have no other lover"

- The poet Jupiter by Regulas (9,467-9,491 post Great Alluvium)

Sky rocked at the surface in the big, rolling swells of the deep ocean and stared into the white fiery sun.

Take my sight if you want Senx, I do not want to see any more of this world.

It was becoming an effort for him to stay at the surface; his body seemed heavy, in spite of not having eaten for many days. A distant part of his mind registered that the heaviness seemed right somehow; as it felt as though his insides were turning to stone. It had begun with his heart, knowing that everything he held dear was gone: no clan, no friends, no Mist, no Dusk. Then it had seemed to creep through his insides, as though they were turning to — no, not stone — to hard, stony coral. But not vibrant living coral; instead the bleached skeleton of a dead reef. Still, somehow it was able to grow, it had filled his body and now its stony tendrils had begun worming into his mind.

I am ready for the Cleaner.

His eyes burned in pain as he forced himself not to blink. The glare from the surface filled the edges of his vision. He sought to control his mind which wandered constantly. He had laid at the surface for many days now, far from the nearest land. He had lain there day and night; his back and dorsal fin were blistered from the intense sun. He had swum away from the land without any real plan, just wanting the clean purity of the deep sea. No seabed, no other dolphins, just blue. At first it had helped, he had felt stronger, then the loneliness started to gnaw at him. And the realisation that this was how it would be from now on. Always. He knew that it was possible he might find some other clan, but in reality it was unlikely. Most clans were understandably suspicious of exiles, and they usually ended up alone forever. He had heard that the Guardians welcomed exiles but he had seen enough of their ways to know that he could never join them.

But if he did, might he see Dusk again? No, she was lost to him in any case — she had her new Guardian companion. And so was Venus In Mist, beautiful Mist, gone now with her clan, far from here. Would she learn that he had been exiled? She must already hate him for not meeting her that last day as he had promised, now she would despise him too.

His eyes burned painfully into his mind.

Let's end it here.

A sudden larger swell rolled over him and as his eyes submerged he thought he saw a large shape glide below him at the edge of visibility.

The patient one. Waiting for me to finish.

This reminded him of another ending: Passing Cloud, who he had loved so much and whose darkening dive had been a beautiful, dignified ending. The old dolphin had gone to the void peaceful and content with a life well lived. Now he had squandered his.

He blinked and looked again. He could not see properly now and closed his eyes hard for a moment to try to regain his sight, then cursed himself for lack of willpower. I cannot even control my senses now, let alone my mind. What happened to all those grand pretensions of reaching the First Level?

Tiredly he began to pull his mind together.

I suppose I'm ready. I'll make my darkening dive now.

As a reflex he commenced the controlled breathing ritual as he had practised it daily during his time at the Academy, then stopped with a bitter smile. This was not a control exercise; he did not need to extend his breath hold time for anything. He was not coming back.

But it seemed right somehow. After the years of rigid self discipline the concentration needed to retreat to the smallest recess of his mind prior to a long dive had become natural to him. Although he had failed to ever fully reach the first level of consciousness during those dives, he had been given tantalising glimpses of how it must be and it had deeply moved him.

So be it. My darkening dive will follow my teaching and the Way.

He slowed and deepened his breathing. Listened to his pulse and began the deliberate withdrawal down into the lower levels of consciousness, reducing his body's need for oxygen to a minimum. According to his training he visualised his awareness of his whole body, pictured a red glow representing his conscious presence in every part of it. Then, with each slow outward breath, the glow dimmed, at first reducing from the tips of his fins, then passing slowly up from his tail and into his body. He monitored his pulse again and slowed it further; making his heart pause for a little longer between each beat.

He slowed his breathing further still. The red glow was receding further now with every exhalation, now just in the core of his body and his brain. In a few more breaths it retreated into his mind alone. He was dimly aware of the rest of his body and surroundings. All far away now. He was entering the deep diving trance, and the combined effects of hunger and lack of sleep served to distance him further from his outer being than ever before. With each outward breath his eyes slowly closed and the sphere of his awareness diminished. His body was saturated with oxygen but demanding almost none, his circulation was down to near comatose levels.

As in the best dives of his training, he did not really choose when to start the dive. He just felt his body tilt, his tail lift from the water, and the weight of it softly pressed him through the silver membrane and into the gentle caress of the endless blue.

His consciousness was concentrated in a small part of his being, the small yet distinct part of his mind that was his essence. It was the state of mind that he had deliberately trained himself to reach in the past: at the bottom of the fourth level of consciousness; primarily in the unconscious state but still under the distant control of the conscious mind. But this time he had reached it almost without trying.

He swam steadily directly downwards, his body motions seeming very far away. The sunlight pierced the water in gently waving parallel shafts, dappling his body. Sky saw that *Xhosii* was the dominant Tonella, the Shade depicting *birth, fulfilment* or *duty*. The wavering light shafts seemed to further taunt him, with the message *changes* or *choice*. He tried to dismiss it. It made no sense for him. Birth meant nothing. And fulfilment? Of what? And duty? Did he have any duty?

His dive continued and the blues began to darken around him. The shafts of sunlight became feeble and then began to fade. Ahead of him the water looked black as night. *Ndria*, the Shade of Death. He stopped swimming down now; there was no need, his lungs were compressed and he was heavier now; falling freely.

He saw a shimmering horizontal layer in the water just below him; as he fell gently through it he was faintly aware of the abrupt drop in temperature. The light was almost gone. Above the Shades still said *duty*; below only *death*. The shafts of light were gone, the uniformity of the remaining light implying certainty. Certainty of what? Death? Or Duty?

Now he was deeper than he had ever been before.

I am leaving your domain, Senx. I seek Death. She must be near now, please don't let her play with me. Take me quickly.

Suddenly the water below him seemed totally dark: absolute death awaited. He felt relief, soon it would end, and he would be part of Ocean as all things eventually are. He looked once more upwards. The Shade of *Xhosii* was still dominant but very dim now, barely discernable. I am swimming away from Duty. Suddenly he felt doubt. What duty? No one wants me, they wanted me to go.

Then he remembered the last words of his teacher: "If I have been able to influence them in some small manner for the better; if, at some time in the future they are faced with a hard choice and they think, for just a moment: "what would he have said?" then my life was worthwhile."

What would Passing Cloud have said? Probably that we have a greater duty than to the self, or the clan, or even our species. That he had special obligations as an Aligner. We are the keepers of Ocean. *Keepers* of Ocean! Not the *guardians*. Was that his duty? Should he be trying to stop the Guardians corrupting the Way? Should he confront Storm Before Darkness?

Am I the coward now? Choosing this end when I still have a duty to fulfil?

He was sinking faster now. He became aware of a quiet but insistent desire on the edge of his consciousness. He thought of the surface, how very far away it was, how very hard it would be to reach it now. A tendril of fear snaked an icy path across his mind cracking his brittle concentration. He forced it out remembering his training and something Passing Cloud had said once: "In the darkness the pathway to life is dim. If fear clouds your eyes you will certainly lose the way".

To life! And here he was using that training to choose death!

The desire suddenly grew again and panic gripped him for a moment. With a major effort he suppressed it and levelled out his attention in his upper consciousness, ignoring the instinctive need for air. Remembering: *Does your body serve your mind, or control it?* According to his training he probed out to the edges of his mind and noted the areas of encroaching shadow at its limits, closing in on his awareness.

His mind was dimming now but a small thought formed and hardened and filled what was left of his consciousness.

Very well, I'll try to come back. I'll try but I really don't know if I can now. I am very deep in the darkness and the Cleaner is hungry for me.

With a great effort he began to swim upwards. His body seemed terribly slow to respond and his reserves of oxygen were very low. The darkness did not seem to alter and his body's demand grew again, hurling itself against the fragile shell of his self control.

I am not rising. I am too heavy. I am sinking. I will die here.

He kept swimming, his mind on the edge of unconsciousness. He was no longer sure he was swimming at all. But he had tried. He had tried so hard.

It was still dark. He must be sinking. *Must keep swimming.*

He thought that the water was lightening and he felt a momentary glimmer of hope. But the surface was still so far away! He would never make it! Panic began to crack the shell and he started finning hard, wasting valuable oxygen.

Panic and die, panic and die, servant or controller?

He forced himself to swim steadily, to keep his oxygen needs to a minimum, to preserve what remained for his mind. The Shades changed.

Duty.

Choices.

Changes, duty, life.

The water was much lighter now but his consciousness was darkening. He could make out the surface of the water but not tell if he was moving towards it anymore. The shadows in his mind grew closer, tighter, around his flickering core of consciousness. He realised that he had stopped finning but could not force himself to start again. It seemed much less important now anyway. He felt himself losing consciousness and falling back into the depths of his own subconsciousness.

I'll just sleep for a little while...

A tiny, distant spark of awareness awoke him for a moment and he struggled to remember what it meant. A message from his body, something small but seemingly important. He tiredly tried to concentrate for a moment then recognised the sensation — a wave was lapping across his back, his body was rolling gently at the surface. Yes, he thought he recognised it now but it was too hard to do anything about it. He relaxed again and began to sink into the reassuring embrace of unconsciousness once more.

Breathe. Breathe. Breathe now or she will take you down again. Yes, that was it, that was what he was meant to do, he should take some air. It seemed very hard and very far away, but he sent the message to his body. He had no idea if the message arrived, he was left in a tiny glimmer of consciousness for what seemed an incredibly long time. The blackness of the rest of his mind, his body, everything — it spread in all directions forever. Then, shockingly, a white light exploded in his head and he convulsed as his body tried to expel the water he had taken into his lungs. Awareness returned suddenly and painfully as he shook in spasms.

After a long time he regained control but felt weak and nauseous. His lungs hurt. His head hurt terribly.

I'm still alive.

He marvelled at this.

He paused, wondering where to go. He did not want to go back to the coast where his old clan was; he had to avoid them. He had to find a place where there were no other clans. Then he remembered that there were two small islands far off the coast opposite the bay where the Dune Coast Clan had been staying. He had never heard of any other clans being resident there. The sun was still clearly visible so he used that for orientation and started to slowly swim in the right direction. He would begin his new life there.

Chapter 38

"Spend time enough alone and passing jellyfish will appear erudite companions."
- Three Standing Shells (13,282 - 13,325 post Great Alluvium)

The rugged coastline of the more westerly of the two islands appeared first. He had known that they must be in that direction for some time; in an otherwise clear blue sky, there were dense balls of cumulus cloud over the islands, and as he had drawn nearer, seabirds had started to appear. He had even passed a floating coconut that must have fallen from one of the islands' many palm trees.

The wind was light, but there was a large, slow swell running towards the islands. When he surfaced in the valleys between the lazily lifting hills of water there was no horizon, but from the peaks he could make out the land clearly. The middle of the island he was approaching had white sandy beaches fringed with palms, but the headlands were rocky cliffs. Against these, the swells crashed and subsided, causing great plumes of white to rise high in the air as each rolling wave collided with the rock.

As he got closer, he picked up the bottom with his sonar, soon after he could see it; for the first time in many days. Now the bottom shelved upwards and he was once more in the familiar environment of a coastal zone with its many territorial inhabitants. Sky followed the shoreline parallel with the beach. The bottom was fairly level here with infrequent coral heads. The

Shades were ambiguous, somewhere between Sciaa and Sciaa-chon. *Towards the familiar, regressing* or *stasis, middle*. They made no sense so he ignored them. He looked around for something to eat, he had found a few fish in the deep ocean but pickings were lean out there and he was still weak with hunger. Then he rounded a coral head and almost swam into a tight shoal of small Jacks. They panicked when they realised he was hunting and the shoal split in an explosion of silver bodies. He was just faster though and took two of them. They made good, sweet eating. A welcome change: he had not recognised one of the thin fish he had caught out in the deep sea and it had been full of sharp spines and unsatisfying. Now he was back amongst creatures he knew. He could survive here.

He carried on his exploration of the coastline, feeling much better. The water clarity was reasonable but he could still see further with echolocation so he used it frequently. It showed him the continuing scenery of coral heads interspersed with sand patches opening up ahead of him. The hard rock and coral reflected sound much better than the sand and so were quite distinct to him. He could even distinguish the soft bodies of the larger soft corals and sponges against the hard rock. He could make out the larger individual fish, and the shoals of smaller ones. Sometimes he could even guess what species they were — that disciplined shoal of long bodied fish he could make out: probably young barracuda, hunting for small prey.

Then his attention was fixed. He sensed something in the distance that was distinct from its surroundings. The sonar image was of a large creature lying on the bottom. Its bulk meant it must be a dolphin or similarly sized shark, but it was quite still. He drew closer until he could see it. Yes, it was a dolphin. An elderly male, laying on his front on an area that was almost entirely sand, apart from a single small lump of coral just in front of his head. He looked somehow different to the other bottlenose dolphins to Sky. His back was a darker grey, his belly white but had many grey spots. Sky thought he must be dead, but he resisted the temptation to use sonar to scan him for a heart beat in case he was not. It was considered very rude in dolphin society to scan someone internally without permission. Instead, he announced himself: 'It is I, Touches The Sky!' He paused, awkwardly. When meeting a stranger from another clan it would be normal etiquette for him to also add "of the Dune Coast Clan" but he could not do that any more. He had no clan.

He drew closer to the recumbent form's left side. It had not moved. He could see that there was a curious, almost circular scar on the old dolphin's forehead, and then realised that his left eye was missing; the socket a mass of old scar tissue. Growing more certain that this dolphin was dead he went around to its right side and moved in so that his rostrum was almost touching its side. The eye on this side appeared to be uninjured, but it was closed. Sky started an internal scan. The eye snapped open.

'Do you *mind*!'

'I'm so sorry; I thought you must be dead!'

'Not the last time i checked!' He spoke with a gruff voice and had odd, accented speech. The old dolphin roused himself from the sand and shook himself.

'I really am terribly sorry. My name is Touches The Sky, of the...um...' Sky trailed off, hoping the other would now introduce himself quickly and cover his embarrassment.

'Why are you here?' the one-eyed dolphin barked at him.

'I'm just exploring — looking for food.'

'Are you a scout? Is there a clan behind you coming to eat all that's left here?

'No, just me. What were you doing just now?'

The old dolphin stared at him for a long moment, his eye half closed. 'i was watching that coral growing. Goodbye now.'

He started to swim off. Sky noticed something else odd about his manner of speech apart from the accent (and rudeness). He used the diminutive form of "I" which was only normally used by young dolphins prior to their naming ceremony. Sky had never heard an adult do that before. He followed after him, calling, 'I am Touches The Sky, I'm sorry but I did not get your name...'

The old dolphin stopped and turned his good eye towards Sky. 'You still here?'

'Well, yes, and I was wondering what I should call you?'

The old dolphin looked at Sky as though he was demented.

'Call? Name?' He drove his beak into the bottom and flicked up a cloud of sand. 'What do you call that?'

'Um, sand,' Sky replied slowly, unsure of his meaning.

The other waited a moment as the sand fell, then deftly caught one grain on the tip of his rostrum. 'And what do you call that?'

'A grain of sand of course'

'Just that? No special name for this one?'

'No, of course not.'

'What about all the others i just threw up?'

'Grains of sand, that's all.'

'And all these others,' he gestured around him at the sandy bottom, 'up to the beach, around this island, in *all* Ocean, none have their own names?'

'No, you can't give names to every single thing, they are just…just part of Ocean.'

'Have you ever heard of what many like to call the Way?'

'Of course! I am…I was a Novice for years, I studied it every day.'

'A Novice! Ha! Amazing! And *what* did they teach you was the ultimate goal of your studies?'

'To reach the first level of consciousness. To be at one with the Universal. An indistinguishable part of Ocean.'

'Yes, yes, quite. "Become a zeta without a shadow". And how are you going to cope with being an indistinguishable part of everything, when you insist on trying to have a name for each separate part you see?' He swam off again towards the shore. The conversation was apparently over.

Sky watched him disappear into the distance, baffled. It seemed the old dolphin had no name, or none that he would give. And what was he talking about? Sky had once met a dolphin with a parasitic worm infestation in his brain. It had been too late for the Healers to help him and he had gone slowly mad before dying. Was this old one-eyed dolphin mad? Or did he truly have some insight into the first level of consciousness? He was intrigued. Where had he come from? He looked and sounded different from any dolphin Sky had ever met before. Maybe he *was* just mad. Or maybe he could learn something from him. Either way Sky could not think of anything better to do than follow him. Where else could he go?

CHAPTER 39

"That careless selfish deed
Made now at time of need
There's a lifetime to regret
And no means to forget."

- River Now Dry (13,108 – 13,127 post Great Alluvium)

A tropical downpour flattened the slate grey waters of the Dune Coast Clan's bay. From below, the surface danced in the hammering fall and the thin layer of fresh rainwater seemed to mix reluctantly with the sea, as though it tired of this endless cycle. A few of the children made small leaps, but the low clouds and rain seemed to keep even them pressed down into the waters.

Fades Into Dusk too, felt crushed by the dark sky as she made her way into the shallows. She was supposed to be looking after some of the young ones this morning and she was dreading it. Normally she would have enjoyed this task, but they would expect her to be bright and cheerful and she felt nothing like that. In the few days since Sky's exile she had just felt empty. At first, she had been very afraid too; afraid that her secret must be found out and that she would be forced to leave. But now she knew that Sky had told no one; he had saved her. So her fear had ebbed, only to be replaced by a creeping, insidious flood of guilt that seemed to be drowning her.

She greeted the female who had been looking after the five young dolphins. She was pleased to be relieved and ready to go hunting. Dusk approached her charges who were looking morose and bored. Bellatrix Unseen spoke first:

'Fades Into Dusk-Jeii will you tell us a story?'

'Yes,' the others chanted, 'Story! Story! Story!'

'I'm not sure I'm in the best mood for story telling. Why don't you all do that dance again you did at the Gathering? The starfish one — that was so nice.'

Lost In Moonlight looked petulant. 'We've done it so many times we're bored with it. If you won't tell us a story can we go over to the eastern beach? There's supposed to be a Narrator still there.'

Dusk considered this. The Narrators were lone dolphins that moved from clan to clan relaying news and telling stories. Mostly these were traditional tales but the better Narrators could improvise very well. They often appeared at Gatherings.

'Alright then. But we'll have to be back here by half-post noon.'

The children cheered and made leaps of joy. They all adored hearing stories and here was the chance to hear some new ones.

She led them across to the bay. The rain had stopped now and a promise of blue sky appeared on the eastern horizon. In the shallows they found the Narrator, an ageing male with a slightly twisted lower jaw. It looked as though it may have been broken once Dusk thought, and he had several missing teeth there. She exchanged greetings with him and he smiled and made faces at the children.

He spoke to them with a deep, rich voice, opening his eyes dramatically as he did so: 'And what can I do for you then, my little ones?'

'A story please!'

'Of course! Any favourites?'

This led to a heated debate. Some wanted something new, others had firm favourites. The Narrator glanced in amusement at Dusk. She tilted her head as a shrug in reply, so he broke into the children's squabbling.

'Wait, wait, look here!' They gathered around him and he pointed with his rostrum at an isolated rock in the sand. The long black spines of a sea urchin responded to his nearness by waving defensively. Also on the rock, was a small hermit crab, this one living in a discarded whelk shell. It was busy foraging along the edge of the rock but it suddenly realised it was surrounded by the dolphins and froze. It wiped one eye nervously and stared back at them timidly.

'Little Una-Pi,' the Narrator said quietly, looking at it. 'She didn't always have to find discarded shells to live in you know. Not until, that is, she made the mistake of *lying to Senx.*'

He looked back at his audience, a question in his eyes. Without a word they arranged themselves quietly in a circle around him, lying on their bellies on the sandy bottom. The gentle swell rocked them back and forth as the Narrator began.

'Long, long ago, it happened. Long before the massive waters of the Great Alluvium rushed from the land when the great ice walls fell. Even before the Ka-Tse had learned to weave their stories into the stars. Ocean was a different place then. The animals were very different from today. One you might have seen but not recognised was Una-Pi. You see, in those days, Una-Pi, grew her own shell to protect herself like other crabs.'

The Narrator then gestured towards the Sea Urchin. Dusk noticed that the spiny black ball was edging itself around the rock now, apparently uncomfortable with the presence of so much attention. The Narrator continued:

'Ned-Lah were very different then too. At that time they had no spines at all, their bodies were quite smooth and white. But stranger still was Eightarms. Now you all know what he looks like today, his supple body and his clever eyes, hiding in the rocks except when he comes out to hunt at night. In those days he never hid. That's right — in those days, Eightarms lived in a most beautiful shell and he floated gracefully about Ocean's waters in it, swimming free.

Now although Una-Pi had a shell in those times, it was a fairly dull brown sort of crab shell. She would often say to her good friend Ned-Lah, "Look at the beautiful shell that Eightarms has, floating so high above us as though he is better than us. We deserve more than this." In truth, Ned-Lah did not much care; he was quite happy with his smooth white body. But Una-Pi coveted Eightarms' wonderful shell. It was so light and so delicate, with many exquisitely formed chambers. More, all of the colours of the rainbow could be seen in it as Eightarms drifted past.

One day Una-Pi called to Eightarms and said, "You are so beautiful and full of grace, I have composed a song for you."

Of course he was flattered and drew close to her. She began to sing very well, a soft, soothing song that gently rose and fell like a lazy wave on the sea. She sang softer still and he drew nearer to hear. She reached up with her claws and rocked his shell in time with her music and soon his eyes closed. Una-Pi sang and rocked and rocked and sang and soon Eightarms was in the deepest of sleeps. Then that devious crab carefully lifted his sleeping body out of the shell and gently laid him on the ground. Then she cast aside her drab crab armour and slipped her naked body inside that lovely shell. She felt so proud! And off she stalked in her new shell, leaving the poor Eightarms asleep on the sand.

The next day Una-Pi was strutting about in her new shell, when the great, terrible voice of Senx came to her through the waters, calling her name. High above her she could see the bright face of Senx looking down to find her. She guessed at once what Senx must want and desperately sought to hide the lovely shell. She found a hole under a large rock. It was just large enough that she could back the shell into that hole and there she stayed, her head and legs out of the hole, with the shell stuck well inside.

Then Senx spoke directly to her. 'Una-Pi, do you have Eightarms' shell?'

'No, I do not, O Great Senx. Most certainly not.'

'Come out of that hole so I can see you better.'

'I would prefer to stay here if I may.'

'Why do you not come out of that hole, Una-Pi?'

'I merely seek shelter from the great warmth of your face, O Senx.'

'Indeed. And you do not have Eightarms' shell?'

'No, no, but I know who does. It was that Ned-Lah. He took it because he is ashamed of his smooth white skin. He wanted to hide from the world.'

'Are you quite certain of this, Una-Pi?'

'Absolutely certain, O Senx. Now may I be left in peace in my hole?'

'You may stay in that hole as long as you wish, Una-Pi.'

At that, Senx turned his gaze elsewhere. Una-Pi felt so pleased with herself that she had fooled Senx. Pleased that is, until she tried to move. To her horror she found that the great rock had somehow shifted slightly and now it rested heavily on the lovely shell. Try as she might she could not move it. She finally realised the only way she could go to find food would be to come out with her naked soft body exposed into the dangerous world.

Of course that was Senx's punishment for her. And that was not all. Una-Pi never found her old crab armour again. From that day forth she had to always find the empty shells of other creatures to live in. On the very same day Senx made another change. In case Una-Pi might feel spiteful towards Ned-Lah, Senx gave him a fine covering of black spines so that he would never have trouble from the likes of that crab again.'

Bellatrix interrupted with a hushed voice: 'And what about Eightarms?'

'I'm glad you asked me that. Well he was very angry at first that his shell had been stolen. But instead Senx gave him great intelligence and cunning, and a means to squirt out a black disguise if he were threatened. More than that though, he gave him the greatest appetite for Una-Pi and her kind, and from that day onwards he hunted her whenever he could.'

The Narrator swung his rostrum in a curve to the seabed in the traditional gesture indicating the end of a performance. Dusk smiled at him as the children clamoured about him with questions about what happened to various other creatures, but he pulled away.

'No more, no more. I have other clans to visit, other children to tell stories. Be good now and remember what happened to that naughty Una-Pi.'

With a nod to Dusk he was gone, swimming away from the bay alone.

Lost in Moonlight came over to Dusk.

'Fades Into Dusk-Jeii, did you know that story?'

'No, I did not, but it was a good one, wasn't it?'

'That Una-Pi was horrible to her friend Ned-Lah. Why would someone do that?'

'Perhaps she didn't think out what would happen properly.'

'No, Jeii, I think she was just mean. You wouldn't let someone else take the blame for something you'd done wrong would you?'

Dusk looked into the trusting eyes of the young dolphin and wondered what to say. She looked past her into the distance for a moment then answered carefully.

'It would be wrong to do that of course, Moonlight. Only a really selfish zeta would do such a thing.'

CHAPTER 40

"Should I give you knowledge or show you how to find it?"

- Snow On Blue Mountains to the assembled Novices at the 11,617 Gathering

Sky soon caught up with "One Eye" as he had now named the old dolphin to himself. One Eye was hanging vertically, head down, next to a protruding ledge that jutted from one of the larger coral outcrops. Sky was impressed at the way he was able to stay suspended like that with no apparent movement.

Sky drew closer to him, then realised that once again he had approached him from his blind side. He resolved to make an effort not to do that again, it was like sneaking up on someone. In any case, there was little he could do about it this time as the old dolphin had his good eye directed under the ledge, so he would not see him whichever direction he approached from. Perhaps next time he should also make a point of using echolocation as he approached as well.

'What do you want now, boy?'

Sky tried not to show his surprise. The old dolphin had not moved and could not have possibly seen him; he had made no sound and he had not heard One Eye using sonar. How had he known Sky was there?

Sky drew closer. 'I was wondering if you would mind me staying around this island for a day or two?'

'Thank you for asking. Yes, i would.'

'Oh.' Sky peered under the ledge. 'Can I ask what you are looking at?'

'Them.' One Eye did not move but Sky followed his gaze. A brown moray eel, covered in bright yellow spots was under the ledge. Its jaws were held open, revealing rows of sharp, translucent, white teeth. Its gills moved gently back and forth as it breathed. Sky was looking for the rest of "them" when he realised that there was another creature: a tiny, spindly shrimp; white, with orange bands on its legs and body. The shrimp was in the mouth of the moray, stepping neatly between the rows of vicious looking teeth, brushing everything with delicate, long, white antennae. From time to time it would detect some morsel between the teeth and would then deftly remove it with one of its pincers and pass it into its own mouth.

'Now,' One Eye observed, 'that little fellow should taste pretty delicious if he resembles some of his cousins. So why doesn't the big chap eat him?'

'It's a mutually beneficial arrangement of course; they've been doing it for millions of years. The larger creatures get cleaned of debris and parasites; the shrimp gets a meal.'

'So everybody wins.'

'Well, yes. It's a bit like the relationship zetii have with their prey: we take what we need, maintaining the fitness of the shoals, always leaving enough of them so that they can prosper and find enough food.'

'I see. So what happens if one day the morays find that there has been a dramatic reduction in the number of these shrimps?'

'Well, there'd be competition between the morays to get to the remaining shrimps' cleaning stations I suppose. Many of them wouldn't get cleaned, so they'd be more prone to disease. The morays would certainly suffer as a result.'

'Indeed. Perhaps some of the morays might be inclined to band together and give themselves some fine title. Proclaim that they had the right to have first choice to be cleaned say?'

Sky could not imagine creatures as apparently dim-witted as moray eels being so well organised but he went along with it. 'Alright, suppose they did: what would happen to that group of morays?'

One Eye's body fell gently through the water; his head remaining at the same level, his tail swinging gracefully downwards in an arc until he was once again vertical in the water, but this time with his tail flukes just off the sand. It was done effortlessly: Sky did not see how he had initiated the manoeuvre. He noticed that every movement One Eye made had a complete economy of effort and a careless grace. Throughout the turn, his view of the industrious shrimp had been constant, as though he had tilted around an invisible pivot point in the centre of his eye.

'I should imagine that they would do rather well. As an organised group like that, they could easily ensure that they dominated the cleaning stations, excluding the other, individual morays.'

'But that would be wrong, one group forcing the individuals to suffer just because they did not belong.'

Sky saw One Eye turn slightly to look at him, his gaze quizzical, and, Sky thought, perhaps slightly amused. 'Wrong? What does that mean?'

'It would not be right...it would be...against the Way.'

'So you need the Way to tell you what is "right" and "wrong" then?'

Sky shook his head; swam quickly to the surface to take a breath and to think for a moment. What did make something wrong? He rolled his head downwards, tilting his tail into the air; letting the weight of it drive him gently back downwards to join the old dolphin. 'Isn't that what the Way is for; to show us what is right and wrong, the correct way to behave?'

'Why not let everyone just decide for themselves? i decide for myself.'

'It would be too hard for most zetii, they don't want to have to work out if each thing is right or wrong. And anyway, some might decide a particular thing is right, others that it was wrong.'

'Would that be a problem?'

'Well yes...I don't know. Why do we have the Way then, if everyone could just decide for themselves?'

'Ah,' One Eye tilted his head slightly, looking at Sky through his half closed eye, 'Well, you just said that most zetii would not want the bother of working everything out; they like their philosophy ready made. And it would be chaos if everyone had different interpretations of a particular situation; society couldn't function.'

'So you're saying that's all the Way is: a means of making society work?'

'Essentially, yes. There is no special magic to the doctrines of the Way. Perhaps some time in the past a few zetii like you and i were out for a little hunt amongst the seagrass. Then they had a good idea, and over a snack they came up with some guidelines that would work for most clans in most situations.'

Sky screwed up his eyes. Everything he had learned since he could remember said that the Way had been compiled by the wisest of the ancients and that it had almost mystical powers; that its teachings were absolute and all-knowing. The idea that it was thrown together by a few ordinary zetii over their midday meal was impossible. 'No,' he protested, 'it couldn't be that simple.'

'What else then? Do you prefer those stories that in the distant past, creatures came from another star and gave the zetii all their knowledge? Couldn't our ancestors have just worked it out for themselves?'

'But zetii society is based on everyone following the Way; we say that someone is a "good" zeta if they follow it. And yet you're saying anyone could make it up themselves.'

'I did not actually say that at all. But let's say there are two zetii. They both are separately faced with identical difficult moral decisions in their lives. One follows the Way absolutely, he makes each choice based on its teachings. The other one has somehow never heard of the Way. She makes each choice based on her own evaluation of each situation. It so happens they both make the same decisions in every case. Which is the better zeta?'

'Most would say the one that followed the teachings of the Way.'

One Eye shook his head slowly. 'But the second zeta not only made the same choices each time, she agonised over each dilemma herself. She made her choices based on her own beliefs, not because she felt the need to comply with society's demands.'

Sky considered this, confused by such radical thinking. He took a moment to surface for air. One Eye remained on the bottom. Did he ever breathe? Sky returned to his side. 'Yes, I suppose I can see what you mean. She would've had to have actually thought everything through for herself. But most clans wouldn't be very tolerant of her, even though she was making the same choices each time.'

'Ha!' One Eye exclaimed, 'The boy's not such a fool after all. Now tell me: you've been through some hard times of late haven't you?'

'Well, yes…I was…exiled from my clan for…'

'Don't bother — it doesn't matter to me. And you have a certain look that is familiar to me. You've looked the Cold One in the eye recently, I think.'

With a shock Sky remembered his dive out in the deep sea; how close he had been to dying that day.

'Yes. I went looking for Her.'

'But you decided not to stay down there.'

'No.'

'Why? What made you come back into the light?'

'The Shades hinted at something. Something about duty. I felt I might have things to do.'

'Duty eh? Well, that's just possible.'

One Eye was very still for a while. He seemed to Sky to be looking inside himself; in some other place. Then he was back, focusing slowly on Sky again. 'You remind me of someone. Perhaps this needs more thought. You *can* stay for a day or two. Welcome to Forlorn Island!'

CHAPTER 41

"With my first love I flew the skies
With my next love I saw Senx rise
My third, made me a little wise
My fourth, more so with all his lies."

- Children's jumping song

Fades Into Dusk swam away from her clan, following the direction of the strong westerly wind which had kicked up steep, breaking waves. On another day she might have enjoyed launching herself from the wave faces but now she just made low leaps as needed to take air or look ahead. This was a familiar route for her but she had not swum it in the many days since Sky's exile. It seemed very different this time though; in part because she was making the journey in daylight. Her classes had finished early as one of the teachers had been unwell; some kind of stomach upset. The clan Healer had prescribed regular, small quantities of a particular red algae, otherwise fasting and a day of rest. The Novices were therefore unexpectedly free and she had managed to slip away. The other reason the journey seemed strange was that this time she had a different purpose for making it.

Sky's exile, and the way in which it happened, had deeply affected her and her mind was in turmoil. At first she had been excited by the Guardians and their new ideas, but her last experience with them had been shocking, and she had begun to realise that she had only really wanted to believe in them because of her attraction to Storm Before Darkness. Now she could not help comparing Storm and Sky, and Storm fared badly in the comparison. She found herself respecting Sky more and more. Yes, he wanted to keep to the old ways, but when she thought back, he never argued compliance out of simple obedience to the Way. He always seemed to have thought about the issues and he had genuine compassion for others. 'Storm was passionate about his beliefs too — very passionate, but he did not care if others were hurt in achieving them. He had often talked about "necessary sacrifices". She had assumed that this was partly rhetoric but the punishment ceremony she had witnessed had opened her eyes to the reality of just how serious he was. She had always believed that it was what you did that mattered, not what you said you would do. And Storm acted violently. And Sky...well, Sky had followed her to the Guardian ceremony. Why? Not to betray her — he had his chance to do that. More than that, he had sacrificed himself for her. She had thought about it so many times now and there was no other explanation. He could have used her as an excuse for being with the Guardians and he might have been let off such severe punishment. She, however, would have been exiled, and deservedly so — she had to admit that now. Sky must have followed her that night because he cared about her. And to accept exile instead of her — she could not have imagined anyone doing that before.

She considered confessing what had happened but she admitted to herself that she was too afraid. She did not think she could survive the loneliness of exile; it was the worse form of punishment for any dolphin: social contact and the clan was everything. She could not bring Sky back now, but she could do something to atone for what she had done: she would end her relationship with Storm. At first she had intended to simply never go there again but she needed some kind of closure. And out of respect to Sky she wanted to tell Storm that what the Guardians believed was wrong and that she wanted no part of it. That would feel good at least, and then she would never see him again.

She swam along the section of shallow, fringing reef. Something large swam by just on the edge of visibility, going the opposite way. It paid her no heed and she in turn ignored it. Probably a big Cleaner of some kind she supposed. No threat to a healthy adult like her, but if it carried on towards the clan it might be a concern for the young or sick. She would mention it to the scouts later; she would just have to pretend she had seen it nearer the bay. Suddenly there was a voice ahead of her: 'It is I, Venus in Mist, of the Western Red Mountains Clan!'

Dusk responded instinctively as the other appeared out of the blue ahead of her. It was a young female with an unusual metallic blue-grey skin and dark, deep eyes. She spoke confidently to Dusk: 'I'm glad to finally meet you, Fades Into Dusk.'

'How do you know me?'

'I've heard about you from your clan. I came to know Touches The Sky, and when zetii talk about him, your name is often mentioned.'

'I can't think why, we're just friends.'

'Really? Are you sure? Listen, I met Sky and I like him. I mean, *like* him. I was supposed to meet him after the Gathering but something happened — he didn't show up and I thought that was it. I thought it might be something to do with you in fact. I left with my clan. But later we came across a hunting party from your clan and they told us a story of how he had been exiled for contact with the Guardians. Then I realised why he'd missed our meeting. Then I came back here to look for you.'

'Why do you want to see me?'

'It's simple. Do you want him? Have you got some kind of hold over him?'

Dusk was shocked at this female's directness but tried to think. Did she want Sky? 'I don't really know, I haven't thought about it that way. There's nothing between us now, but could there be sometime? I don't know.'

'Well that's enough, I suppose.' She stared at Dusk with those odd dark eyes. 'Listen, if you see him again and decide that he's not for you, just tell him that Venus In Mist wants to see him again. Tell him to find the Western Red Mountains Clan. Alright?'

'Alright, I'll remember.'

Venus In Mist looked at her hard for a long moment, then nodded once and vanished off into the blue.

Dusk paused for a while trying to work this out. Did she want Sky? She did not know. Should she help this strange female who obviously did? Her instincts told her no. No, she would keep this meeting to herself. She would think about it more later, but for the moment she needed to continue with her plan.

She soon arrived at the familiar arch where she had always met Storm. He was not there of course, he was not expecting her. No one was around, so she followed the shore further on. The Guardian clan was normally along that stretch of coast.

Past the arch the shoreline consisted of fringing reef again. At the water's edge, a wall dropped down a few meters to meet an almost flat, white sandy sea bed. The restless waves were deepening the sand ripples that paralleled the shoreline, picking up particles of sand and tossing them about. As each wave broke on the shore, a cloud of white bubbles was driven down in to the shallower depths. Purple surgeonfish darted agilely through these clouds, searching for food dislodged by the violence.

Dusk heard voices up ahead and slowed down. She recognised two of Storm's bodyguards: Sorrow After Nightfall and Rock On Sand. She could not make out what they were saying at first, then she heard Nightfall saying, 'We'll have to get some more, he won't last long on that. You know what Kark-Du told us.'

Dusk saw them now through the swirling water, and announced herself, 'It is I, Fades Into Dusk!'

The two big dolphins stopped talking at once and turned towards her. She saw that they were hovering around an opening in the reef wall, the entrance to a cave.

'Greetings, Fades Into Dusk,' Rock said politely.

Dusk was about to say that they could call her Dusk, but then stopped herself. She would not see them again after today anyway.

'Would you be looking for Kark-Du?' Nightfall asked, with what she suspected was a faint smirk.

'Yes. Can you take me to him?'

'Oh no, we have to guard the...this cave. Important mission, it is. But you just follow the shore for a bit and you'll see the clan. He should be around, we're expecting him soon.'

She looked at the cave more closely now. It was not large, but would just about admit a dolphin to enter. It must have another opening inside; perhaps going up to the surface, as when each large wave broke, an eddy of small bubbles emerged from the entrance. She had no idea why they would want to guard such a thing.

'Well, I'll leave you to your important work. Do make sure no one steals it.'

She had just moved a short distance away when she thought she heard a faint voice, it sounded as though it came from the cave. She turned to look. Rock and Nightfall must have heard it too; they exchanged glances, then Rock shot into the cave. She heard some muffled sounds from within: they sounded violent. She was about to speak to them when Storm appeared from behind her. He looked at the cave and then at her. 'Come here now!' he commanded and led her out of sight of the cave. 'What did you see?' he demanded.

'Nothing! Just those two hulks hanging around a cave.'

He snapped his jaws twice angrily in front of her. She was really frightened, he looked like he was about to attack her. She decided not to mention the voice she had heard. He stared at her as though trying to decide whether to believe her. He moved closer until he was almost touching her face with his and spoke coldly: 'I forbid you to go anywhere near that cave. Do you understand?'

She seethed inside. Dusk hated being told what to do. She would enjoy telling him that she was never going to see him again now. But then she was struck by a strange series of thoughts. *Why* couldn't she go near that cave? What was in there? And what was Storm talking about at the ceremony about the Ka-Tse coming to dominance in the next few moons? Why was he so interested in her being a Starwriter? She made a sudden decision to try and find out more, to learn what was going on. She tried to look meek and submissive, 'Alright, I'm sorry, I didn't know it was important, Kark-Du.'

He softened, 'Alright, little one, you don't need to call me that. Just stay away from it. Now, why haven't I seen you for so long? Are you still upset about the punishment ceremony?'

'I was, but now I've thought about it and I see that…it must be necessary sometimes.'

'Yes, exactly.' He seemed calm now, reflective even. 'I don't like to have to inflict suffering on one of our own you know, but sometimes it must be done. And to kill a zeta — well I hate having to do it. Yet sometimes the individual must suffer for the good of the many, even make the ultimate sacrifice. I don't like to see a good Ka-Tse die, but sometimes it is the only way.'

Dusk somehow sensed that he was not talking about the punishment ceremony any more. This talk of killing Ka-Tse — killing any zeta — was repellent to her, and more than ever she wanted to tell him she was leaving. As though he had read her mind, he went on, 'You had me worried when you were gone for so long. I even thought for a moment that you may have decided not to see me again.' He focussed on her again. Once again she felt a chill of fear. 'I can't let you leave me you know, I need you. And besides, you know so much about us. No, we couldn't let you leave.' She looked at him, feeling cold inside. How could she have ever loved him?

'Come on,' he said, 'let's swim in the shallows like we always did. And did I mention? That Dreamweaver has been telling me about unlocking songs, it's really fascinating. I'd love to see how it works. Why don't we talk to her, and find out if there's anything interesting in that lovely head of yours that she could sing out?'

Dusk followed him, determined that he was not getting at any of the information she carried. She would make some excuses about the position of the planets or something and arrange to come back another day. She felt she had to do it; if only so that Sky's sacrifice was not without purpose. The Guardians were planning something, now she was going to find out what it was.

CHAPTER 42

"If you want a more fulfilled life, lower your expectations."
- Loss Consoled (13,317 - ? post Great Alluvion)

Sky's mind slowly edged into normal consciousness. He awoke slowly, disorientated at first. He was alone in a small bay, with a near vertical rock wall beside him. The bottom was soft silt here, mostly devoid of life. A couple of small hermit crabs trudged across it, leaving their distinctive tracks on the surface. The silt was pocked with many small holes. From these, a number of delicate eels were half protruding, their bodies swaying gently in the slight swell as they awaited passing morsels of food. At his first movement, the nearer ones retreated backwards down their holes, waiting for this potential threat to pass before daring to cautiously re-emerge.

Now he knew where he was. Yesterday, as night fell, One Eye had led him into the lee of this headland to spend the hours of darkness. The old dolphin had explained that they could expect a slight west-going current given the recent winds and the present new moon. Behind the headland they could relax in still water. He had taken some time to fall into the sleeping state, but gradually his conscious mind had receded. Of course, part of his mind remained at a level of low activity, telling him when to breathe. Much of the time he had one eye open, sometimes after surfacing to take air he would continue swimming in gentle, aimless circles for a while. He had no recollection of One Eye actually sleeping though. He had been there at the start of the evening at least; moving around the little bay, investigating with his sonar. Now, there was no sign of him.

Sky set off around the headland to look for something to eat. He managed to surprise a small flatfish and soon afterwards a passing cuttlefish helped satisfy his immediate needs. As he went a little further, the silt turned to a wide area of seagrass. There, in the shallows, he came across One Eye who was poking at something on the bottom. Sky moved alongside him, taking care to approach him on the side of his good eye. One Eye was carefully picking up a flimsy white plastic cup with his jaws. As he lifted his head into the light, Sky once again noticed the curious, near perfect circular scar on his forehead. One Eye turned the cup over in mid water then dropped it. It slowly sank again, carried gently sideways in the current.

'A Walker artefact,' Sky said, 'but what do they use them for?'

'They drink out of these.'

Sky spent a few moments digesting this information. The idea of drinking was rather foreign to him as dolphins never drink, getting all the water they need from the bodies of the creatures they eat. However, he had heard of the concept and knew what it meant. Looking at the thing, he could just about imagine how it might work. The Walker would be holding it in the air of course; and it would be somehow filled with water, so gravity should hold the water inside the container as long as it was kept with the opening uppermost. Then the Walker would somehow suck it out. They probably had some kind of siphon or specialised tongue to enable them to do this, and they would have to keep the bottom of the thing pointing downwards all the time or the liquid would fall out. It seemed extremely complicated. Then the oddest thing of all struck him. One Eye had named the thing's purpose without any hesitation or ambiguity. He had never met a zeta before who knew much about the Walkers and he was immediately intrigued. 'How do you know that?' he asked.

'I've seen them do it. Look, here are more of their things.' He gestured towards the surface where two clear plastic bags drifted to and fro in the slight surface waves.

Sky looked at them curiously. 'If these things are useful to them, why do they discard them so often?'

'They seem to make more of them than they need. Or perhaps an item has served its purpose or no longer functions properly, so the Walkers just drop them into the sea. Some of them rot away, but these things seem to last for ever.'

'I don't like the drinking thing, but these are quite beautiful,' Sky said, looking at the plastic bags. The sun was shining through them now as they rocked back and forth. 'They look a bit like big jellyfish.'

'Yes, some of the old hardbacks think that too. Then they eat them and choke to death.'

'Do all the Walkers have these sorts of things?'

'Most, in my experience. Some seem to own more things than others.'

'What do you mean, "own"?'

'Ah! A rarely used expression; i'm not surprised you're unfamiliar with it. But it is quite important to the Walkers. Look, say one day you have a son, you could say that he was your "own" son, no one else's, he *belonged* to you.'

'But one zeta cannot "belong" to another.'

'No, alright; that was a bad example. Very well, look here, you see this rock? i am going to say that this is *my* rock, it belongs to me. I *own* it.'

Sky looked at him, mystified.

One Eye continued, 'Now you go over there to that sponge by the sandy patch, yes, that one. Now let's say that that is *your* sponge, and you also *own* that whole sandy patch. It's *yours* alright?'

Sky was reconsidering his original impression that the old dolphin was mad. 'But what happens to the sponge when I go hunting? It's still here, it grows by itself; how can it be mine? And the sandy patch? Why would I want to call it mine? There're lots of sandy patches in Ocean and anyone can swim over any of them; why should I claim that I...*own* this one?'

'Well, we would have to have some kind of understanding between us that this is my rock and that was your sponge. i would not touch your sponge and you would not touch my rock.'

'Why would I want to?'

'It's only an example! It could be anything! The Walkers like to stay in one place and they like to gather things around them. It seems to be their purpose in life, to collect as many things as possible.'

'What do they do with them all?'

'Who knows! Now enough of these questions about Walkers. i need something to eat. Go and look after your sponge! i'll come back here in the post-noon.'

Sky watched him leave. He swam back to the sponge and circled it twice, trying to fathom what this all meant. Then he swam over to the rock. He looked around. One Eye was gone. He cautiously prodded the rock with his snout and waited.

Nothing happened.

CHAPTER 43

"The foolish prefer a scandalous lie to a dull truth."
- Unnamed Shade (3,055 - 3,084 post Great Alluvion)

Dusk was swimming towards the Guardians again. No one expected her there, and she hoped that the Guardian clan were still in the area beyond the mysterious cave. She was going to try to find out what was going on in there. She had no desire to see Storm again; in fact it was important for her plan to work that she did *not* see him. She was also relying on his natural secretiveness and lack of communication with his guards. If she had misjudged that she could be in serious trouble; maybe even real danger. He had said some frightening things the last time she had seen him, and she knew that he was capable of real violence.

It seemed to her to take longer than usual to reach the rocky arch, but soon after it, she came close to the cave. She stopped using her sonar and swam more slowly. Soon she heard voices. She stopped listening: three, no, four of them. She could not hear the words but it sounded like calls of farewell, then there were just two in lower tones. She guessed this might have been a changing of the guards for the cave. She hoped the new guards would know her, if not, her plan had no chance. She moved a little closer and recognised the voices of Rock On Sand and Sorrow After Nightfall. She felt some relief. They not only knew her but were fairly stupid too. This might work. She swam away from the shore so that she was out of sonar and visual range, then circled around and swam back in towards the land. Now she could approach the cave as though she was coming from the direction of the Guardian clan.

As she drew closer she consciously changed her swimming style, from being slow and cautious to rapid and purposeful, using bursts of echolocation to make it clear she was coming. As her eyes made out their forms up ahead she announced, 'It is I, Fades Into Dusk!'

The two large dolphins looked at each other doubtfully then replied in unison, 'Greetings, Fades Into Dusk.'

'Greetings to you. I come on a mission from Kark-Du. Who's in charge?'

Rock looked suspicious but replied, 'I have that honour. But we thought Kark-Du was coming here himself this post-noon.'

Dusk heart sank; that would spoil everything. She had to work fast. 'Yes, he'll still come later, but he sent me ahead with a special mission.' She lowered her voice conspiratorially. 'Kark-Du wants me to speak with the prisoner.'

Rock glanced at Nightfall and composed his features into an innocent expression. 'What prisoner would that be?'

She fought to keep her nerve. If her hunch was wrong she could be in big trouble now. 'Don't waste my time! Don't you know that I have been spying on the other Ka-Tse clans for months now! You have seen me with Kark-Du often enough — don't you see I am in his confidence!'

Rock looked shaken but remained defiant, 'But we have strict orders not to let anyone see him.'

Dusk spirits rose: *him*! There *was* a prisoner, and a male at that. She kept the pressure up: 'Keep your voice down or he'll hear us! Look, Kark-Du believes that prisoner may trust me and give useful information. I am to speak with him privately and try to gain his confidence.'

'Maybe we should wait for Kark-Du...'

'If you want to see how angry he can be, go ahead! He's expecting me to present him with a full report when he gets here. I'll just wait here in that case. When he arrives you can explain to him why you felt it wise to countermand his orders.' She moved away to one side and started sending little bursts of sonar into the sand as though searching for food.

The two guards exchanged a brief but heated whispered debate. Then Rock turned to her again and in a loud whisper announced, 'Alright then: go in.'

She brushed past them defiantly and entered the darkness. In spite of her bravado her heart was pounding. Now, maybe she would find out what this conspiracy was about. She just hoped that whoever was in here would not give her away.

Chapter 44

"Fear may be your enemy or your ally.
It depends which of you is in charge."
- Attributed to Second Dawn Passing or Fallen Palm (c.9,998 post Great Alluvium)

High above them, the bright forms of the shallow-water fish were just visible against the silver surface. The wall here fell almost straight down far below them, here and there gorgonias — fan corals — spread their myriad branches across the prevailing currents, capturing minuscule creatures to feed their thousand tiny mouths.

Sky followed the older dolphin along the cliff wall. They paused for a moment as two Eagle Rays swam past them; their spotted wings rising and falling slowly, their long, thin tails trailing behind.

'They're beautiful,' Sky commented to One Eye.

'What makes them beautiful to you?'

'The way they move I suppose. They are so graceful; they seem completely at ease in the water.'

The dolphins swam on for a while, then One Eye stopped above a ledge in the cliff wall. He looked down at something there and Sky came to his side to see what it was.

Among the rocks a large fish lay on its side, its eye staring blankly, its mouth agape. It was dead or very nearly so and there were large white patches on its side suggesting disease had caused its end. Two fireworms were arriving at the scene: long, red, segmented worms with countless legs, their sides covered with white, stinging bristles. At their heads, formidable jaws were working in anticipation.

As Sky watched the first fireworm reached the fish. It moved up its body until it found the opening of its gill. It pushed its head into the opening to gain access to the tender membranes there. Its companion moved up to one of the sores on the side of the fish. As they began to devour its flesh the fish shuddered slightly.

One Eye looked at Sky quizzically. 'Are they beautiful to you?'

'No, how could they be; look what they are doing!'

'If you saw one moving alone across the seabed would it be beautiful?'

'Well, perhaps, yes. I suppose they are beautiful to look at, but seeing them like this makes you forget that.'

'Then a beautiful thing becomes ugly if it performs an ugly act?'

'I suppose so. Surely you can't find them attractive when they are doing this?'

'What would happen if they didn't do this?'

'Well...the fish would rot. If they, and creatures like them, did not eat the dying things the seabed would soon be choked with rotting material.'

'i don't think i would find that beautiful.'

'And this is, then?'

'Yes. If you can accept that beauty means fulfilling nature's purpose, then these worms are beautiful. If something contributes to the wholeness of Ocean and does not disturb the balances we call it beautiful.'

Sky wondered who "we" were, but had to excuse himself to surface. When he returned, One Eye had moved on from the now dead fish. Sky picked up their conversation, 'So, acts that harm another can be beautiful?'

'That's not what i said. And it is often not the case, especially where malice is involved. i doubt those worms have much malice but the more intelligent a creature is the more it should be accountable for such things.'

'Especially zetii then.'

'For example. And they are not always. i had a visitor here not long ago who knew that well.'

'Who was that?'

'He had been badly treated by those so-called Guardians. They have strange ways and seem capable of almost anything.'

Sky shuddered. 'I have seen what they are capable of.'

Sky surfaced again to breathe, then realised that One Eye was still down there, and tried to remember the last time he had surfaced for air. He did go up sometimes but it seemed there were impossibly long intervals between his breaths. He came back alongside the old dolphin. 'Will you teach me how you make each breath last so long?'

One Eye looked at him with a slightly surprised expression. 'Do i? Well, yes, i suppose it must seem so to you.' He looked slightly perplexed and murmured to himself, 'How do i do it now?' He turned again to Sky. 'We'll try then. Follow me.'

He led Sky up to the surface and along the wall edge until they came to an area of shallow water on top of the wall. One Eye gestured to the expanse of white coral sand. 'Go lay on that and relax. Don't mind me.'

Sky did as he was bidden, and lay on his front on the flat sand. The light was very bright there in the shallows and the water was noticeably warmer. His body was rocked slightly by the slight swell just above him. He relaxed as much as he could, wondering what One Eye could do to help him. The old dolphin moved alongside him. Sky suddenly jumped in surprise. One Eye had scanned his side with penetrating sonar, he was looking inside him!

'i *said* don't mind me. Forget your silly inhibitions; i am trying to help you here.'

Sky tried again to relax. He supposed it was foolish in a way; after all, if he was ill he would let a Healer do this to him.

One Eye gave several more bursts of sound along his body then grunted. 'It's no surprise you are burning up oxygen, several of your muscle groups are still working here.'

'But I don't feel like they are; I feel quite relaxed.'

'Feel this.'

Sky felt One Eye direct bursts of sound into his abdomen. It felt as though his muscles were shaking inside him, as though they were being massaged from within. He realised that the muscles around his diaphragm were under tension. And he consciously willed it away, deliberately releasing it slowly, completely. One Eye moved along his body, using the invisible force to identify other parts of his body that were tense, directing Sky to release them. Finally the old dolphin was content with the result.

'Good. Now your body is optimised for diving. Remember exactly how this feels, boy: use no part of your body unnecessarily. It's a waste and Ocean hates waste. Now! Let's optimise your mind. Go and take a breath, come back here and relax just as you are now.'

As Sky returned to the sand he released his body once more, using the techniques he had learned in the Academy, but now going further, feeling himself relax more than ever before. His body felt light, displaced from him.

'How do you feel now?'

'I feel good. Very relaxed. Ready to dive.'

'No you are not. How does my voice sound to you?'

'Like it always does, I suppose.'

'Well it shouldn't. It should sound as though i am far away, speaking to you from another place. You are far too high in your conscious mind. You should be at the bottom of the fourth level of consciousness; almost unconscious but still with conscious control. You need to be in the state of waking dreaming.'

One Eye spent much of the rest of the day coaching Sky. Making him let go; stopping all unnecessary effort, reducing the blood flow to his extremities, slowing his heart. He showed him how to withdraw in his mind to a small place deep inside his head, where, with the slightest effort, he could still be aware of the world and his body, but distantly, like the faint light of a falling star at dusk on the far horizon.

Eventually One Eye seemed content. 'Let's see if this has worked. Follow me.'

He led Sky back to the cliff and then down. At last they came to a cave in the wall where he stopped.

'What is it?' Sky asked.

'A tunnel. It goes under the island and comes out in the shallows on the other side of the headland. You are going to swim through it.'

'But the other side is so far from here! It isn't possible!'

'If you believe that something is impossible then you will be proved right. But i tell you that if you do as i have shown you and *believe* that you can do it you *will* do it.'

Sky looked at him, a feeling of coldness rising in his belly. 'I will die.'

'Yes, of course. But it need not be on this day.'

'You really believe I can?'

'Yes. Come up and take a last breath.'

One Eye brought him to the surface. Sky looked out of the water, fearful that it was for the last time. Close by, on the rocks, a pelican was perched. It eyed him warily. Sky remembered when, seemingly a lifetime ago, Cloud Passing had taught him a question and answer, so that he might be recognised by another Aligner. On impulse now, he said to One Eye, 'Can the hunted trust the hunter?'

One Eye snorted. 'You will have a hunter chasing you through that tunnel if you don't focus now! A hunter made up of your own terrors and imaginings. Now concentrate!'

Sky tried to prepare himself; slowing his breathing, trying to relax his body, but the thought of the tunnel kept forcing itself to the front of his mind. It would be long, oh, so long, and nowhere to breathe. It might be narrow, there could be false passages and it would be black, totally dark. If he ran out of air there would be nothing to do. He would die struggling against the cold hardness of the uncaring rock.

Then he felt One Eye press his head against his own. He spoke soothingly, quietly. 'Remember that dying fish we saw boy? Remember the worm that crawled into his head and ate into his brain? You have a worm in your head now and its name is Fear. Get it out or it will eat into *your* brain. Leave your fears aside. They may be true, they may not, but it won't help you to drag them with you through that long tunnel. Leave them here at the surface. Purify your mind and trust in yourself. You *can* do this thing. Just swim.'

As he listened to the words, Sky felt his fear fading. He withdrew into the back reaches of his mind, picturing the dull red glow representing his awareness of himself concentrate into that one point. He felt alone and content in that place. The rest of his body, the rest of Ocean was still there, but very far away. He felt his head tilt down, his tail lift for a moment into the air, and he had started his dive.

He entered the tunnel mouth and swam into its depths. Very soon it was totally dark. No light means no life, so soon the creatures of the outside were behind him; he was penned in by the sterile limestone walls. As the light failed he started to use short bursts of sonar to see ahead. He closed his eyes; there was nothing to see and it made it easier to stay in the diving trance.

Just swim.

From his far vantage point at the very back of his mind he was aware that he was swimming. Probably it was for a long time, but maybe it was just for an instant. He felt far removed from what his body was doing, and far from the possible consequences. He wondered for a moment if he had ever experienced this before. No, never. Yes, always. It was hard to separate the present from the past.

Just swim.

Time probably passed. Probably a lot of it. And then more. An eternity of swimming in darkness. He became aware of a message coming from his body, a call for something.

Just swim.

The floor of the tunnel seemed to rise slightly, then dropped. Like a mouth opening. Then the sound picture drew teeth in his mind, immensely long, sharp teeth hanging down menacingly from the ceiling, more vicious replicas rising from the floor to meet them. He was swimming into the jaws of a monster.

His heart rate started to increase, his eye snapped open, he suddenly realised how badly he needed to breathe. It was still totally dark. He could not see the monster's jaws but they were there and he realised that they actually seemed less frightening than dying here with no air. This was the end.

A voice came from somewhere. A steady voice. Calm. 'It's that worm again boy. Get rid of it and swim.'

With a huge effort he did so. He slowed his heart again and forced his body back under control.

I am going to die anyway; at least I will die with me in control, not the worm.

He carried on swimming, into the jaws, his back gently brushing the stalactites as he passed. He felt himself fading again. The bright red light of his consciousness was small, smaller, the tiniest dot of light, now fading, fading, almost gone. His mind seemed to slowly fill with a pure, white light. He supposed this was death. He opened his eyes to see what death looked like.

Beside him, his back dappled in the brilliant light was One Eye. Just above him, the surface danced. He tilted his head at Sky, his eye smiling. 'Take a breath boy — you deserve it.'

Sky surfaced and realised just how sweet air could taste. 'You followed me through,' he gasped.

'i thought i should keep that worm from your head and the hunter from your tail.'

'The hunter?'

'Yes, the hunter made up of all your terrors that were ready to chase and devour you.'

'I see. Yes, I think I would have been hunted and caught if you had not.'

One Eye gave Sky a long, hard stare. 'And the hunted can trust that the hunter will kill.'

CHAPTER 45

"Extraordinary times demand extraordinary compromises."
- *The 'Seer' Stone Eyes (13,222-13,264)*

Dusk cautiously moved further into the gloom of the little cave. The entrance was narrow and led to a tunnel of similar size. As she moved into it the light from the entrance dimmed so she used echolocation for guidance. This allowed her to visualise where she was going: the tunnel curved to the left and started widening a little; the ceiling rose somewhat too. It was quite dark now, but as she rounded the curve she saw a dim light ahead, coming from the ceiling. The tunnel widened into a small chamber, about three times her body length across and just as high. There was a little opening in the ceiling letting in the light and a very small air space: probably just big enough to get a breath, she thought. The sky was visible through the hole; it must come up through the ground on the shore.

For a moment she thought there was no one there, then a cracked voice came from the shadows: 'What is it you want now?'

She knew that voice! She whispered: 'It is I, Fades Into Dusk.'

The owner of the voice moved slowly into the shaft of light from the hole. 'Dusk? Can it really be you?'

She could not believe it. His body was covered in wounds, some partly healed but many not. He looked haggard and hungry, his eyes seemed empty, but as he looked at her some hope appeared in them. She went to him, pressing her head gently to his. 'Deneb, what's happened to you?'

He leant against her, his eyes closed in pain. 'Wait a moment.' He lifted himself to the small air space, positioning himself so that his blowhole could reach the surface and took air. He had to press himself against the sharp rocks of the cave ceiling to do it. She could not imagine how it must be in here when the sea was rough outside; how had he breathed then, when the water was being driven in and out of that hole with huge force?

As he sank again she caught a glimpse of the skin of his back and she had her answer.

'How are you here?' he asked, 'Does anyone else know about me?'

'No, and I can't explain now. I've tricked my way in but Storm could come at any time, I have to go before then. But I'll get help for you, I promise!' She started to go.

'Wait, don't go yet, there is something I have to tell you! The Guardians have me here for a reason. They are planning on using me. When I was waiting to meet the Xenthos, a group of the Guardians ambushed me and attacked me. They hurt me pretty badly. They forced me to come here, and I have been here...fifty-two or fifty-three days I think, nearly two moons anyway. So the Xenthos must think we didn't turn up for the goodwill exchange.'

'Don't worry about that, saving you is more important — I've got to go now!'

'No, you don't understand — I've overheard their conversations sometimes. In the next day or two the Xenthos should have escorted me back to the clan. The Guardians are going to take me there just before. Dusk, they are going to kill me there and leave me for our clan to find. It will look like the Xenthos killed me!'

Dusk could not speak for a moment. Were they really capable of this? 'But why — what would be the point?'

He surfaced painfully to take another breath. She winced as the slight swell pressed him against the ceiling. A little of his blood drifted down to them, like smoke through still air.

'Because the Guardians want the Ka-Tse to dominate all the other zeta species. They think that's the answer to the food shortages and a lot of other crazy things. They want open conflict between us and the other zetii species. They think that because I am the Prime Mother's son, the Council...'

She wheeled around. Yes, there it was — a distant familiar cry: 'It is I, Storm Before Darkness!"

CHAPTER 46

"He went to the land
She went to the sea
I'll come back to you
If you give yourself to me."
- Traditional

The fleck of white was distinct now in spite of the distance. It shone bright against the dark band of rain clouds that girdled that horizon, the towers of cloud boiling slowly high into the air above it. There would be rain coming with those clouds, and sharp wind squalls, but for now the fleck was ahead of it all. The sunlight still favoured it and its optimistic brightness beckoned the eye away from the forbidding gloom.

Sky watched it reflectively as he slowly patrolled the shoreline of Forlorn Island. He hoped that the fleck was coming this way as it seemed. It would carry Walkers, and he had become deeply intrigued by them since meeting One Eye.

The "one or two" days that he had suggested Sky stay at the island had lengthened into nearly fifty. He had found that One Eye's irascible façade masked a willingness to have some company, he was just very fussy as to who it might be. And he was an Aligner. He had told Sky stories of a few other visitors; none of whom stayed long. One Eye found most other dolphins tedious companions. He complained that they had few opinions of their own, they lacked insight, were unable to hold an intelligent debate, or that they were simply boring. Sky had been surprised and flattered to realise that apparently, he was not considered to be in these categories. As he slowly gained One Eye's trust he had learned more and more about him. He knew an extraordinary amount about the Walkers, and Sky had tried to find out why. Sky gathered from strands of conversations that he had been in the company of Walkers for some time when he was young, probably as a captive; then he had somehow escaped or been released. Whenever Sky tried to probe, he would stop talking or change the subject. But Sky had gathered that they had tried to make him perform some task for them. It seemed that he had initially been ambivalent about it and had cooperated, but then he had learned something that had completely alienated him from them. He had made the remark on several occasions that there were probably plenty of well-intentioned Walkers, but had clearly implied that they were not all like that.

He seemed to know a lot about the ways in which the Walkers fought each other. The scale of slaughter in their conflicts sounded staggering, and Sky was sure that this was one subject where One Eye was prone to exaggeration. Sky still struggled to understand why they would do this and the old dolphin had no real explanation. Sky had wondered if a faction of Walkers had tried to use One Eye in some way in their efforts to dominate another of their clans, but it seemed too bizarre. He had never dared to ask him as the old dolphin clearly disliked talking about it. On some occasions though, Sky had found that One Eye could be persuaded to say more and Sky had made good use of these, asking many questions about the Walkers and their strange ways.

Slowly, the fleck grew in size, and by mid morning, he could make out the details of it. It was not a typical Walkers' craft; not one of the huge, noisy, metal monsters that thrashed their way across the waters. This was a wind-craft and it leant away from the pressure of the air and cleaved through the water in silence. The way that it rode the swells like a zeta and its use of the wind reassured Sky. Not all Walkers used their machines to force their will on Ocean then. If Walkers existed that were sympathetic to Ocean's rhythms, then surely they might be found on a craft such as this?

It made its way past the shore of the island. Sky drew parallel to it and cautiously surfaced briefly to examine it. It was mostly white, with a tall pole protruding from its centre. Two great sheets of white material were suspended from this pole and they were filled with wind, pushing the craft through the sea. It was not particularly fast and it was easy for Sky to keep pace with it. On its front on each side there was a picture and some strange markings. Although it was highly stylised, Sky recognised that the picture was of a turtle. This seemed a good omen.

Towards the back of the craft a Walker stood in a recess, holding a big circle that moved slightly from time to time. The Walker had some blue material about its lower body, brown skin and grey hair on its head. It had what looked like dark pebbles over its eyes. It had more grey hair on its face, and Sky remembered that One Eye had said that this was a fairly reliable way to tell that a Walker was a male.

Soon, another Walker appeared from a hole and came up. The hairy male disappeared down the same hole. Sky judged that this new one was much younger, with a smooth, unblemished skin. It too went to the circle and held it as it turned back and forth. The new Walker was smaller and more slender than the first one and had long hair growing from its head. Sky liked the way this moved in the wind, like golden seaweed being swept about in a swell. This Walker wore two small strips of red material around its body and had no hair on its face. One Eye had said this sometimes indicated a female, but that the best identifier was that the adult females often had bumps on their chest. The upper red strip did indeed seem to be covering some swellings on the Walker's chest so Sky guessed that this younger one must be female.

Sky was growing in confidence now and he drew closer to the craft, and made higher leaps so that he could see better. Then, during one jump, the Walker turned her head and looked directly at him. Her mouth widened and her white teeth showed clearly against her tanned skin. Cleaners sometimes showed their teeth this way just before attacking, but somehow it did not seem a threatening gesture. The Walker stepped up onto the edge of the craft to look at Sky, shading her eyes with one hand. She stayed like that for some time, as Sky stayed alongside the craft, observing her carefully. During one leap he noticed that the rain squall that had been approaching from behind was nearly upon them. He could see the marks of a blast of air flattening the waves as it sped outwards from the clouds, coming fast, very fast. It hit the Walker craft hard and it lurched over violently. The wind filled the great white cloths from the other side and there was a sudden crack as a rope snapped. Sky watched in mystification as a great pole attached to the bottom of one of the cloths swung across the craft and struck the female from behind. She was thrown hard into the water.

The squall passed and the wind subsided somewhat. The craft carried on its way much as before, the female disappeared below the surface. Sky wondered if she might have entered the water to hunt, but he was reluctant to approach her closely underwater. He watched the craft as it moved away.

The older male appeared from the hole suddenly and looked around. He shouted something several times. It sounded to Sky like "Ah-Na, Ah-Na!" then he moved about quickly, pulling things and turning the circle. Gradually, one of the big cloths seemed to roll away and the craft began to turn. It was now quite far from where the female had entered the water so Sky lost interest in it. But now he was beginning to doubt that her dive into the water was intentional. The Walkers did many inexplicable things, but that had seemed like a very abrupt way to initiate a dive. He looked underwater to see if he could find her. He soon did and watched her from a distance. She was just below the surface and slowly sinking. She was motionless and some bubbles were coming from her mouth. Sky was becoming more certain that something was wrong. It was good to be relaxed during a dive but she was not moving at all. And who would waste air by exhaling at the start of a dive? Then Sky saw a large oceanic shark below the Walker. It had clearly seen her and started to cautiously circle her, moving closer, closer. Sky surfaced briefly. The Walker craft had come back, but had gone past him in the opposite direction now. The male seemed agitated, and was still shouting as before, 'Ah-na! Ah-na!' The female must be in difficulty. Sky dived down again and saw her body had fallen further. Her golden hair gently streamed above her, her face was blank. The shark bumped her with its snout and made a tight turn back towards her. Sky knew it had done this to test its victim, to make sure it was dead or helpless prey. Now it would eat.

Sky hurtled in and butted the shark hard in the side. It whipped around to face him with its jaws wide but Sky dodged at the last moment. It lunged at him but Sky darted aside, away from the Walker who continued to fall. The shark turned back towards the Walker but Sky hit it again. This time it had had enough and it sped off for the depths, looking for an easier meal.

Sky put his head under the Walker and lifted her to the surface. He remembered that she would have no blowhole so he turned her face uppermost so that her mouth and nose were in the air. She did not breathe so he pressed her hard in the chest like he would if he was helping another zeta. On the third attempt she coughed and retched and began breathing. Her eyes flickered open then gradually focussed on Sky. He knew he was in a very vulnerable position now if this was a dangerous Walker. But she did not seem dangerous. In fact, while he supported her there, and she gradually reached full consciousness, she stared into Sky's eyes with a look of great intelligence and warmth, and she caressed him softly with her hands.

Then Sky heard the male Walker's voice. He must have seen them and he guided the craft towards them. He brought it to a stop beside them, and stared over with wide eyes at Sky and the female. He reached down to her, making again the sound 'Ah-na' and some more noises. Sky withdrew cautiously, not wishing to be touched by the male in case he was dangerous, and watched him lift the female into the craft. She was still very weak, but alive.

Sky made one last leap before he left them, and as he fell back to the water he saw them looking at him. The female weakly raised one hand to him, as though in greeting or farewell.

The man cradled Anna's head in his lap and gently brushed her long hair from her eyes. She watched the sleek grey body disappear into the waves then turned to look up at her father, her eyes shining.

'A dolphin. A dolphin saved my life.'

CHAPTER 47

"The undisciplined mind confuses misfortune with mistakes."
- *Saturn Over Antares (12,415-12,438 post Great Alluvium)*

A little way off the south west corner of Forlorn Island under the familiar steep, rocky cape, Sky hung in the water between two tall rock pillars. This had become his favourite spot. The light in the afternoon was lovely, and today, with the sea barely rippled, he expected it to be an especially good day to observe the Shades. He needed something to lift his mood.

As the sun slowly fell, shafts of light sliced down into the depths, wavering gently like searching eyes. Shoals of the bright orange Anthias swarmed around the twin pillars, gently swimming against the waters that the full moon was dragging westwards. The sun behind the Anthias made each little fish burn like a point of fire. Sky had seen real fires burning on the land before; they looked beautiful but dangerous. He had been told that they were very hot and he hoped one day he might be close enough to one to feel for himself. It was good to have something to look forward to.

The incident with the Walkers had given him something to think about. Seeing what they did to Ocean and listening to others speak of them had given him the impression that they were selfish, dangerous creatures with no sense of belonging or responsibility to Ocean. But the female Ah-Na had not seemed like that. He had touched her and looked into her strange eyes. She had seemed gentle and kind, and he had felt a connection with her somehow.

Although One Eye seemed unable to recognise a real distinction between good and evil, Sky was sure that she had been a "good" Walker. Maybe the zetii *should* try and make contact with the Walkers. Maybe there could be some way to warn them of what was happening to Ocean.

Sky was getting frustrated now, feeling there was something he should be doing to help. Most of his days around Forlorn Island had been pleasant enough at first. He and One Eye met and talked on many days, but sometimes they would not see each other for a day or two as they hunted around the island. Sometimes One Eye would not want to talk at all; he would frequently drift off in his mind in a trance-like state. It had taken Sky many days to slowly recognise that the old dolphin had more than reached the first level of consciousness: oneness with Ocean. All of the previous dolphins Sky had known who had reached that level, such as Silent Waters and Cloud Passing, would enter the state deliberately after a prolonged period of relaxation and meditation. You knew clearly when they were in the first level or not. But One Eye seemed to drift in and out constantly; he sometimes stopped using "i" or "me" completely when conversing, using only "we" and "us". This had confused Sky at first, but then he had realised the old dolphin was no longer talking about himself at those times; he really felt part of the Everything, the Universal, of Ocean itself. He had somehow achieved the ultimate goal: to reach the stage where you could "no longer see where the zeta ends and Ocean begins" and Sky envied him. One Eye did not miss the company of others; for him there hardly were any "others", he already felt a part of everything.

Sky was still unclear about what One Eye's relationship was with the Aligners of the Way. He certainly had been an Aligner at one point, and might still be, but Sky had the impression that he was too much of a maverick even for them. Sky had asked him if he would train him in his duties as an Aligner, but he just laughed, saying that if he could just train Sky to think for himself, it would be enough. And he certainly did force him to think about things constantly. To question everything. To accept nothing.

Sky had been diverted from his troubles for a while by the conversations with One Eye, and had grown a strong affection for him. But for much of the time the old dolphin was on another plane to Sky, and now the full weight of Sky's loneliness was descending to crush him again.

He missed the clan; Muddy, Deneb, Dusk. He missed Venus In Mist: another lost chance. Only two females had ever appealed to him, and he had lost both by being too slow, too indecisive. Now he was alone. Probably forever. In frustration he closed his eyes and called aloud: 'What is going to happen to me?'

'When?'

Sky opened his eyes. One Eye was swimming towards him. Sky shook his head. One Eye never gave a signature call. Sky suddenly realised why: of course, he just didn't see himself as an individual anymore. 'I meant, what is going to happen to me in the future?'

'You want to know the future?'

'Well, yes; is it knowable?'

'Which one? Anyway, why would you want to know? What would be the point of life if you knew what was going to happen next? If your future was fixed it would mean that *nothing* you did in the present would matter. Life would become pointless; you'd just be playing a part, waiting to die on an appointed day. How crushing would that be?'

'I can see all that I suppose, but I wish you could just give me a straight answer sometimes.'

'Alright, i will. Here's what your immediate future holds. You're going to leave these islands.'

'Leave? Why? You don't want me here anymore?'

'What i want is irrelevant. The time has come for you to develop to your next stage. You've learned some hard lessons of late, a few of them here. But now i see encouraging signs. You've learned to think for yourself and you seem to be starting to recognise what's important. Maybe you even know what you want. You've started to recognise some of the weaknesses in Ka-Tse society; how all the zetii belief systems are struggling to keep pace with a changing Ocean. Remember when you came here you felt you had some duty to perform? This is it. Go out and do something about it.'

'Like the way the Guardians want to change things?'

'No! They are an anathema to Ocean, they are a *symptom* of the disease, not the cure. There is much of the Way that is good, but the fact that the Guardians can grow as they have shows that the Way must adapt if it is to serve zetii in this world. The zetii need individuals like you to go and tell them what to do. How to face the threat of the Guardians, the Walkers, the changing climate, the lack of food. You have been chosen as an Aligner of the Way. And the zetii need guidance from their Way now more than ever before. '

'But I don't know what to do!'

'At least your mind is free to think! You don't have to be shackled by old thinking any more! You can do it. Find the problems with your mind and the solutions with your heart.'

'How can I help? It's too big a task.'

'Remember this if nothing else: if you want something *badly* enough, if it *consumes* your mind, if it is in your thoughts in every waking moment and fills your dreams, then it *will* happen. Life is full of countless possibilities and little coincidences. Call them luck. If you're focussed on your goal you'll seize each useful opportunity that passes and ride every wave and current that takes you towards your goal. Nature colludes with the driven mind.'

The dolphins faced each other in the water between the columns. Sky swam gently forward and pressed his head for a moment against One Eye's. Quietly he said, 'Thank you, Jeii.' He pulled away again and then froze. There was a sound: sonar. Dolphins were coming, several of them. One Eye must have heard it too but he kept looking at Sky as though this was completely expected.

Then, out of the blue, four common dolphins appeared, travelling fast. They slowed, the leader gave his signature call; Sky replied with his. The leader asked a question, but Sky barely understood a word. To his surprise, One Eye answered in what sounded like fluent Xenthos. They spoke for a while, then he turned to Sky. 'They are scouts with a big clan close behind them. They are rather hostile; it seems that they think the Ka-Tse have broken some kind of agreement.'

'What agreement?'

One Eye spoke some more in Xenthos.

'As i understand it, the Ka-Tse were supposed to send an envoy to spend time with the Xenthos to show good will and to prove that food quotas were being maintained. But the Ka-Tse envoy never arrived.'

'What? Ask them if there is one with them called Trevally Outpaced.'

One Eye translated the question.

'Yes, he's amongst their clan.'

'Please ask them to send him to me urgently; I have to talk to him. Please.'

Soon after Sky was face to face with Trevally Outpaced. The mass of the Xenthos clan, hundreds strong, teemed past behind him as they moved to their next feeding grounds.

Sky looked into the suspicious eyes of Trevally Outpaced and started hesitantly, 'My friend, Deneb Rising, was designated as the Ka-Tse who would meet you and spend time with your clan.'

'Your "friend" insulted the Xenthos race and made me seem a fool to my Council!'

'Deneb is an honourable zeta. He would never break his word.'

'I only know that we agreed a day and place to meet during the Grand Council meeting. We arrived at the rendezvous on time; he never appeared.'

'But, you changed the day of the meeting. Didn't you bring it forward a day?'

'No. The day was never changed. The Xenthos kept their word.'

'Are you certain?'

'Absolutely. We made no changes. Now I go to join my clan.' Trevally Outpaced turned and sped off to join the retreating throng of common dolphins.

Sky turned to One Eye. 'I have to go back to the Dune Coast Clan immediately. Something is terribly wrong.'

One Eye nodded. 'There's one more thing i have to tell you before you go. i told you once before that a zeta stayed here a while ago; that he had been hurt by the Guardians.'

'Yes, I remember you saying. Was he hurt badly?'

'Very badly. Physically and mentally. He told me he had been the leader of their clan and had been attacked by a younger rival.'

Sky stared at One Eye, as this sank in. 'A younger rival?'

'That's what he said. A zeta called Storm Before Darkness. He became the new leader.'

Sky spoke slowly, softly, 'Then the zeta who came here was my father.'

'i thought there was something about you that was familiar.'

'What did he say to you?'

'We did not talk a lot. But he kept saying that he felt betrayed, let down. Felt that Ocean had taken everything from him, he had lost his family and two clans. He said that those he should have been able to trust the most, had treated him the worst.'

Sky was afraid of what the answer to his next question would be. 'And what happened to him?'

'Like i said he was very badly hurt by that other zeta. i did what i could but he was too far gone and had lost his spirit. i'm sorry, he lasted two days, then he died.'

'Storm killed him?'

'Yes.'

'And I never got to meet him again. I hate that Storm Before Darkness!'

'Be careful with hate. It has a way of taking over.'

'I think I really must go now.'

'Yes. Farewell boy. Keep thinking for yourself.'

Sky called a farewell back. He watched the old dolphin for a moment as he swam away across the sand and disappeared into the distance. Then he noticed a curious thing: although the sunlight was bright, One Eye had not seemed to cast any shadow. He shook his head, he must have imagined it. He turned and made off at speed towards his old clan, feeling as though he carried a heavy, cold stone in his chest.

CHAPTER 48

"One Cleaner ate two tuna
Two tuna ate three jacks.
Three jacks ate four crabs
Four crabs ate one Cleaner."
- *Children's jumping song*

Dusk swam away from Storm and the Guardians, still struggling to stop herself from shaking. She had never been so afraid in her life. When she had heard Storm's distant signature call, she had rushed out of the cave without a word to Deneb. Storm was not yet in sight but had to be very close. She had muttered to Rock, 'Excellent: he told me just what we wanted. Now: no word of this to *anyone*.' Then she had swum quickly in the direction from which Storm should come. She met him almost immediately, but she had gone just far enough to be out of sight of the forbidden cave. He had been suspicious at first, but she had flattered him and been flirtatious, and then, best of all, she had told him that in three nights' time the position of the planets would be right to unlock several important songs. This caught his attention. She had realised that he was especially interested in data concerning prey quotas or those containing the number and usual migration routes of other species of dolphins, so she subtly emphasised the presence of all of these in her elaboration.

All the time she was desperate to get away, to get help, but she had to play his game, to win his confidence. At last, she made her escape and now she could fly back to her clan. She had to warn the Council; they had to rescue Deneb Rising and stop the Guardians' plan. Her greatest fear was that one of the two guards would mention her visit to the cave to Storm. She was hoping that their awe of him would make them unlikely to do this, but the thought still terrified her.

She swam as fast as she could, following the coast north then west towards the bay where her clan were still staying. She made frequent, long leaps so that she could see how much further she still had to swim. It seemed to take so long. All the time she was thinking about Deneb. A horrible dread started to creep into the corners of her mind. She had often talked to Storm about the goings on in her clan. She remembered talking about the Gathering and what would happen there, it had seemed natural and harmless to do so. Had *she* given the Guardians the information they needed to kidnap Deneb? Had she brought pain to another of her friends? She screwed up her eyes in pain. If only Sky could be here now.

Finally, she was approaching the bay. She would go straight to someone from the Council to explain and then they would do something. Deneb could still be saved. Then she heard someone up ahead of her using echolocation. A single dolphin, coming this way. Who would be coming so far in this direction alone?

She took a chance: 'It is I, Fades Into Dusk!'

The echolocation stopped abruptly. There was a long pause, then, 'And it is I, Green Wave Falling!'

He appeared from the blue. She felt a wave of relief. 'Jeii, I am so glad to see you. There is an emergency — the Guardians have captured Deneb, they are going to kill him, he is in a tiny cave, he can't breathe, the Guardians will kill him and…'

'Stop! Slow down! Have you seen Deneb Rising?'

'Yes, I spoke with him and he told me their plans. We must go to the clan now and get help!'

'Wait, wait. First you need to calm down and tell me all you know.'

'Can't we go now? Oh, Jeii, I am so afraid of what will happen. When were the Xenthos supposed to bring Deneb back to the meeting point?'

'Tomorrow at noon, so don't worry, we have some time yet till then. Now, I need you to tell me *everything* so that I can properly brief the Council. You cannot possibly access all your memories of important events in your current state, so I am going to help you regress into a memory access trance.'

'But Jeii, there is no time!'

'There is time and in any case you can enter the trance while we swim. Now stay alongside me. Yes, like that. Keep me on your left and stay alongside me. Good, keep swimming. Now, you must have no distractions. Do not use sonar anymore — good. Now close your eyes.'

'My eyes too? How will I see where I am going?'

'I will guide you. It is important that you have your mind as clear as possible if we are to access your deepest memories. I will keep talking to you, helping you to lower your consciousness so that we can access all of your memories of relevant events. Use my voice to keep your station; it is all you should focus on.'

She swam on with her eyes closed, following the sound of his voice. It felt very strange at first. Swimming blind was nothing new; that often happened if the water was murky or if it was dark. But not using her echolocation was disorientating. She heard him use his very occasionally, but mostly he must be using his eyes. She guessed this would be so that he did not distract her. His voice became slow and rhythmic. He kept up a constant monologue, telling her to relax, to withdraw from her consciousness of her surroundings; to turn her mind into itself. He extended the times between their breaths, letting her just brush the surface to take a deep breath before descending just below the surface again. She had to focus her mind's eye inward, taking herself back in time, back to when she first met the Guardians, remember everything, every word, every sight, every sound. All the time they were swimming, swimming, swimming. Her tail beating up and down at a constant rhythm, but her heart rate slowing as he counted out its pace for her in his low, reassuring voice.

She began to relax. He had been right, now she would remember everything. Swimming this way had let her focus on her memories, once she had put her trust in his voice, it had been easy to reach back into her sub-consciousness. Now she was there, following Green Wave's gentle voice, she was going back at the first time she had ever seen Storm Before Darkness, back to the first time...Green Wave's calming voice abruptly stopped in mid sentence.

She crashed into the net at full speed. She opened her eyes in horror and tried to twist free. The fine, almost transparent fibres, wound around her tail flukes and fins like a thousand tentacles. The net was slackly hanging across a gully. Above her in the net she saw the partly decomposed body of a young turtle. That could be her! She looked around desperately, then saw Green Wave watching her from a short distance. He seemed oddly calm. 'Help me, Jeii, I'm trapped!'

He said nothing but continued to watch her carefully. She suddenly realised that he had done this deliberately. He had led her into this trap. She felt as though she was going to vomit. 'Why Jeii? Why?'

He said nothing but continued to watch her dispassionately. She needed air. She swam for the surface. As she neared the silver layer, the silken strands tightened, anchored as they were to the bottom. She was not going to make it! She came to a stop with her blowhole just below the life-giving surface. The net strands held her firm. 'I can make one more effort and just make it,' she thought, but then caught sight of Green Wave again, his eyes fixed on her. It suddenly came to her why he was waiting. She made a pretence of trying yet failing to reach the surface, then sank back again, tired and shaken. He turned as though to leave.

'Jeii, you'll kill me! What of the Way now?'

He span around, his eyes angry. 'I have never killed any zeta! You will die now because of this Walker device, not because of me!'

'But why? To help the Guardians?'

'The Ka-Tse are doomed unless something is done. The fools in the Council cannot see it! The time is coming for a new order. We must still follow the Way, but it was written for the Ka-Tse, not those lesser zetii.' He paused, and looked down at the sand for a moment. 'I do have pity for you, but you have been a foolish meddler, trying to swim with two clans and being true to neither. Now you have a little while to think on that. Know at least that your death will ensure that the rightful zetii will survive the coming maelstrom.' Just then the red sun emerged from behind a cloud, weakly illuminating her. He looked up at it and his eyes smiled grimly. 'See; Senx shows his face for you one last time. Say your farewells.' He turned again and swam off into the blue.

Once he disappeared, Dusk swam desperately for the surface. If she finned as hard as she could she could just clear her blowhole and take a breath. She sank again and struggled desperately against the net; it just seemed to bind her more tightly, tangling around her jaw too. She stopped herself, her self-control as brittle as thin ice. She tried once again to breathe. She finned with all her strength and just made it. She let herself fall back again, her heart beating fast. How long would she be able to keep this up? Not long. This was how she was going to die. She would cling to life as long as she could though. She would use all her training to eke out each lungful of air. She hung in the net. The slight swell rocked her back and forth. The empty eye sockets of the turtle stared at her mockingly. She hated herself but so much wanted to live.

What had she done with her life? She had become obsessed with Storm, a zeta who led a clan that believed that killing other zetii was right. She had caused Deneb Rising to be captured and soon to be killed. His death would then cause open conflict between the zetii so that the Guardians' twisted logic could work its evil. And Sky. Poor, loyal Sky, who had tried to help her, and had taken her punishment. He would spend the rest of his life alone and despised, as good as dead. She wished she could have had the chance to ask his forgiveness, to let him know that she was grateful for what he had tried to do.

She looked up at the shimmering image of the setting sun; far above the taunting surface, up in the beautiful, distant air. With a growing pain in her heart she thought, 'So this is how I am to die.'

She fought her way up to take another breath then sank back exhausted. She gazed hopelessly around her. As the sun finally came clear from the clouds the Shades about her changed from ambivalent messages into clearer ones, taking on first one meaning then another, then finally crystallising: *Fulfilment...Separation...Justice.*

'So there is a reason. This is what I deserve.'

CHAPTER 49

"The first duty is to your lovers and families;
the ultimate is to your clan and to Ocean."

- The Prime Mother in "Times and Places" (from the Albatross Alone collection of plays).

Sky swam through the night, across the great, inky black depths between the islands and the mainland. It was a long swim and he had time to think. His mind wandered back over his days with One Eye, over the often cryptic conversations they had together. Sky had often found it hard to understand the old dolphin's meaning and in the beginning had assumed that there simply wasn't any in many cases. Now, he wasn't so sure. Very often One Eye's words seemed to contain layers of meaning, and Sky had the feeling that he had often been trying to educate him in an oblique way, or trying to develop him in some manner. And One Eye's parting words seemed to imply that he thought that Sky had changed: had grown into something better.

Sky had gone to Forlorn Island because he had felt that he had some duty to perform. He had not really had any clear idea what that was, he had just read it from the Shades that day and it had felt right. One Eye seemed to recognise the truth in it, and had ended up saying he was ready to perform that duty. More, that he *must* do it. He supposed he should try to find a clan where he might meet another Aligner who would train him. But what clan would accept an exile? Now that he knew the final fate of his father, he no longer had the powerful need to find him. Instead he felt empty. Should he be doing something more with his life?

He spent a long time turning the problem over in his mind and gradually started to get a clearer answer. The zetii had to face the fact that the Way was not enough for them any more. The dynamics of Ocean had changed somehow. But the extreme views of the Guardians were wrong too, and that was an immediate problem. They had to be stopped somehow. And then? They still would have to change, and try to find out what was changing them. Sky was sure that the Walkers were largely to blame for creating the underlying problems that they were facing. Did they know? He hoped that they did not. If they were causing all this destruction and were aware of the consequences then they were a truly frightening force. He could not imagine that any intelligent beings would continue to destroy their environment while knowing what was happening. So they *must* be unaware, or at least unaware of the severity of their actions. So, should the zetii try to stop them or try to tell them somehow? He doubted that that was even possible. Still, all these things would have to wait. Right now he had an immediate problem to deal with, and if he got that wrong none of this would matter anyway.

The sun slowly rose on his right in a clear sky and he made out the low line of the land ahead of him. There was little wind, but the gentle deep ocean swell was running towards the land, helping his progress a little. He aimed for the nearest part of the coast, and as the sun eased its way high enough that its rays could penetrate the water, he made out the first hint of the seabed rising below him. Then the first real sign of life: a pair of gigantic Manta Rays passed majestically below him, their great wings slowly rising and falling in silent unison.

The seabed rose quickly as he came closer to the shore. He thought he recognised the area: if he followed the coast to the east now he should reach the bay where the clan had been resident when he left. He turned and continued swimming towards the sun, keeping the fringing reef close on his left. He was tired, very tired, but his mind kept turning over possibilities. Trevally Outpaced had said that the day of the rendezvous with Deneb Rising never changed. But Sky was sure that Deneb had told him that the meeting had been brought forward a day. He had said that Green Wave Falling had told him that. Was this just a simple mistake, or was the Ka-Tse Grand Council being deliberately deceptive? He could not believe that. It was also hard for him to imagine that the Xenthos were lying. He had looked into the eyes of Trevally Outpaced as he had spoken and Sky was sure that the envoy believed that what he had said was true. Sky was so sure that something was wrong that he was now on his way to speak to his old clan, in spite of his banishment. He did not know if anyone would listen to him or even acknowledge his presence, but he felt he had to try.

He swam on, and on his next leap, recognised a feature up ahead. There was the little islet just off the shore that lay just to the south-west of the clan's bay. He remembered that two moons ago he had seen a Walker's net there, draped between the mainland and the island. It seemed a lifetime ago now. As he got closer, he decided to make a detour around the island rather than risk swimming into the net if it was still there. He soon was able to detect the islet with echolocation and soon after to see it underwater. He followed the outer coral wall of the islet and then cut across back to the shore. Just then he thought he heard a faint voice. Yes, there it was again, coming from the gap between the mainland and the island.

He really wanted to get to the clan as soon as possible, but it had sounded like a cry for help, so he reluctantly turned and swam back towards the gap.

Sky made out the net with sonar before he could see it. He recognised that there was something large in the net: a Cleaner perhaps? No, it must be a zeta — this was where the voice had come from, someone was trapped in the net! He came close enough to see the shape now. He announced himself: 'It is I, Touches The Sky!'

The trapped dolphin twitched and then spoke, her voice weak: 'Sky! I thought I would never see you again. Oh Sky, I'm so afraid, and I can't breathe properly.'

He looked at her, stunned. The net was completely tangled about her body, leaving her just able to move her tail. After the effort of speaking, she struggled to surface for air. She could only just reach the surface with her blowhole when she swam as hard as she could, then she sank back down, close to complete exhaustion.

He moved closer. 'Let me help you.'

'No! Be careful or you will get caught too!'

He ignored her and moved in to grasp a section of the net with his jaws and yanked at it. It seemed to make matters worse. He tried to bite through the strands but it was impossible. Dolphins' teeth were never designed for cutting, just grasping prey, and the strands simply lodged between them. Twice he almost became entangled himself but just managed to struggle free.

'Sky stop, please stop! You can't get me out on your own.'

'Then at least I can help you to get to the surface. Try now.'

She swam weakly upwards; Sky pushed her from below, taking care not to entangle himself. With his help she was able to breathe much more easily. He helped her to take several breaths in this way until she had recovered enough to speak properly.

'Listen Sky, you have to go back to the clan and warn them. Something terrible is about to happen.'

She told him about the Guardians' intention to create conflict between the Ka-Tse and other species of dolphins, how they planned to fake the murder of Deneb Rising later that day, making it look as though the Xenthos had been responsible. She told him about Green Wave Falling, how he was helping the Guardians and how he had made her swim into the net, and then left her, sure that she was about to die.

'So you must go, and quickly. Stop Storm somehow! He is dominating the Guardians and he's gone mad. You need to kill him if need be — without him the Guardian clan will fall apart.'

Sky shook his head. 'No, Dusk. Killing is their way and it is wrong.'

'We may not be able to keep the luxury of high morals anymore, Sky. Look, they must be taking Deneb from the cave to the meeting point very soon. You have to stop them killing him!'

'I want to — of course I do — but if I leave you here you won't make it! You are already exhausted; you barely have the strength to make it to the surface!'

'No, you must go; do it for the clan — for all zetii. I've done so much harm already, I couldn't bear this on my conscience too.'

'No! I'm staying here. Someone will come along eventually; then we can warn the clan. I thought I'd lost you before, I'm not going to let it happen again.'

She looked into the empty eyes of the turtle for a long while. Her own eyes had a strange, distant look, but in their depths great emotional currents swirled: sorrow certainly, but also, in other circumstances, what he would have guessed at as joy. She looked into his eyes at last, 'You must go now. I can be strong if I know you are coming back to me. Just promise that you'll return before Senx sets. I don't want to be alone in the dark.'

She swam up to the surface and took a breath, seemingly with little effort.

Sky hesitated, but her eyes smiled reassuringly, pleadingly. He pressed his face alongside hers for a long moment.

'Alright. Be strong. I'll come back before Senx hides his face. Nothing will stop me.'

He disappeared quickly into the blue. She watched him go and closed her eyes for a while. Then, with great effort she swam against the dreadful, heavy embrace of the net and snatched a breath. She sank down again. Her body rocked gently in the swell. She looked in the direction he had gone; closed her eyes once more and at last, spoke softly.

'I love you, Sky.'

CHAPTER 50

"Taking vengeance is like eating sand.
Easily done but serving no real purpose."
— *Clouds Reveal Menkar (8,633 - ? post Great Alluvium)*

Sky reached the arch where the Xenthos should have returned Deneb Rising to his clan as the sun approached its zenith. Of course, no Xenthos would come today — they had already assumed that the Ka-Tse had broken their word. But he knew that a delegation from his clan must be arriving sometime soon. He was surprised that the Guardians were not already here and he looked around desperately, afraid that he had somehow missed them. He decided that they must still be coming and looked for a place to hide among the rocks where he could watch unseen. He did not dare to use his sonar in case it was heard, and so had no warning when a large shape loomed out of the blue towards him, closely followed by another. Two big, powerful, tiger sharks swam towards him, both more than twice his size. The nearest one turned its broad head towards him to investigate, the distinctive dark, vertical stripes on its back clearly visible as it turned.

Sky swam around the beast, not especially concerned. Although the tigers were clearly hunting, they would not be likely to attempt to catch a fit, adult dolphin. As he had expected, once they recognised what he was, the pair turned away again and began patrolling the shallows to the west of the arch. Sky felt relief: for a moment, he had thought that he had been discovered by the Guardians. He quickly concealed himself among the large rocks above the arch. He realised bitterly that he was in almost the same spot as the time he had hidden to watch the Guardian ceremony. This time he made sure that he should be able to escape unseen close to shore if need be. He could then slip back and surface if need be.

He kept thinking of Dusk, trapped in the net and of the treachery of Green Wave Falling. They had trusted him as their teacher and he had fooled them all. He had always been the stickler for following the Way exactly with absolutely no deviation. Yet all the time he must have been a Guardian spy, waiting his chance to betray them all. If there was any one zeta who deserved justice it was him. He had tried to kill Dusk in such a calculating way and he must know the Guardians' plan. To create open conflict between the zetii, so that the Ka-Tse could emerge as the dominant race. It was madness. Sky remembered the lessons in the Academy with Green Wave, the clan Council meetings, the Grand Council meetings. All the time he had been there with his secret plan, telling lies, making schemes. He had even been with Sky when he had first seen that net! Sky realised with revulsion that Green Wave may have already made a mental note of it at that time, in case it became useful for a situation like this. He was not fit to be called a zeta, much less addressed as Jeii! Sky wanted to punish him; to find him and make him suffer like Dusk was suffering.

He did not have long to wait.

Soon he heard the sound of a single dolphin approaching from the direction of his old clan's bay. The dolphin appeared below him, and paused on the sand there, apparently agitated. Although Sky could not see the new arrival clearly from his hiding place, he could make out that the tip of his dorsal fin was missing. It was him! Anger flooded his mind. The old traitor did not know he was there; Sky could dive down now and he would not see him until it was too late; he could smash into him with his rostrum — hurt him, kill him, punish him for what he had done! He started out of the rocks, vengeance filling his mind, but then a small voice — his own — spoke in the corner of his mind: *we'd be just like the creatures we despise*. He had said that once to Dusk; a lifetime ago, when Ocean had seemed a simpler place, with rules that everyone followed. And when she had suggested he should kill Storm he had told her it would be wrong. Yet Storm was another zeta who surely deserved to die.

He paused. It would not help Dusk now if he attacked. And he would be doing just what the Guardians wanted; starting the endless cycle of zeta killing zeta, death leading to more death. But the traitor deserved it. And might not killing this evil zeta prevent the deaths of others in the future? He paused. Then came the sound of the sonar of a number of dolphins approaching. He dropped lower behind the rocks and watched. Five dolphins appeared. The large form of Storm led the way, flanked by Sharp Beak. Close behind, two more big dolphins flanked the battered shape of Deneb Rising. Sky's heart sank when he saw the condition of his friend. He was swimming, but in obvious pain, and he looked pitifully thin and weak. The two guards forced Deneb into a small recess in the reef wall and hovered at its entrance, hemming him in. Storm approached Green Wave Falling and stopped. They were not far from Sky and he could hear them clearly.

'Greetings, Kark-Du.'

'Greetings, old one. Why are you here alone now? You should come at noon with the delegation from the clan. This could ruin things!'

'I know, Kark-Du, but matters were nearly much worse. Fortunately, I believe I have saved us, but I wanted to warn you of an unfortunate development.'

Sky wondered what to do. He could try to swim down and drive the guards away from Deneb, but it looked hopeless. There were too many of them, he would be easily overwhelmed. Below him, Green Wave was still talking.

'The female, Fades Into Dusk, learned of our plans. She was on her way to the Council to warn them, but by chance she met me first.' His eyes gave a little smile.

'How much does she know?' Storm demanded.

'Everything. She had spoken to the prisoner and knew every detail. But do not be alarmed, I have neutralised the threat she posed. We can still proceed.'

'What do you mean, you've "neutralised the threat"?' Storm growled.

'I tricked her into swimming into one of the Walkers' hunting devices. She did not suspect a thing and became hopelessly entangled. When they find her body it will look like it was an accident.'

Green Wave looked pleased with himself, as though expecting praise. But Sky noticed that the smaller dolphin with the long beak seemed to have recognised a change coming over his leader and had stealthily backed away from him. Storm seemed to grow in size; he moved closer to the old dolphin, his eyes blazing. 'Do you mean that she is dead?'

'Yes, Kark-Du; we are safe, she cannot harm us now.'

'You killed Fades Into Dusk?'

'Well, she is dead, but I didn't actually…'

He never finished. Storm launched himself at him, smashing his rostrum into his side. The old dolphin let out a scream of pain and shock. 'No, Kark-

Du, I have saved our plan, you should thank me!'

'Thank you? You hurt her!' He slammed again into Green Wave's side, forcing another scream from him. 'You killed my Fades Into Dusk!' He drove his full weight again into soft flesh just behind his head. The frail form of the old dolphin was thrown against a rock. His eye turned slowly towards Storm in incomprehension. His body jerked spasmodically twice; then was still, a thin trail of blood oozed slowly from his mouth.

Sharp Beak moved over to the body and scanned it. 'He's dead, Kark-Du.'

Storm hung in the water, his head low, near the sand. 'Gone,' he murmured. He reared up again, and with a scream smashed into the inert form of Green Wave again.

'She was mine!'

He sank back to the sand again morosely. Sky watched mesmerised at the strange scene. The smaller dolphin nervously edged forward again towards his master.

'Kark-Du, it is almost noon. What shall we do?'

Storm opened his eyes; wearily, painfully. 'Sharp Beak, help me push this body into deeper water. Then we'll execute the prisoner.'

CHAPTER 51

"Great strength wielded without control marks a coward's mind."
- Hidden Nebulae (11,345 – 11,402)

Sky had watched the scene unfold below him and felt sick. He had just been thinking of attacking Green Wave Falling himself; even thinking of killing him. He had had similar thoughts about Storm, too, had thought of taking revenge on him, revenge for his father's death. That is what it would have been like, that was what it was to kill another zeta — now it repelled him. Once again he was stunned at the violence the Guardians were capable of. Then he roused himself. Storm and Sharp Beak were awkwardly pushing the body out towards the deeper water; they would be back soon. The two guards still had Deneb pinned against the recess in the reef wall. Could he fight them both? He doubted it; they were both huge, strong looking creatures — he needed help. Then he glimpsed a distant shape at the edge of visibility behind him, followed by another. The Cleaners!

He slipped back towards the two big tiger sharks who were still patrolling the shallows. He made a pass close in front of them and then turned back towards the arch. The tigers ignored him. Hunting a healthy dolphin was far too much work. Sky looked around desperately, then realised what he had to do. Nearby was a sharp protrusion of coral. He drove the side of his face against it, opening a wound on the side of his face. The cut burned but there was little blood. He turned again and forced his face harder against the coral, aiming for the same spot. Some of the sharp, brittle coral snapped off, he could feel fragments break off into the wound and this time it really hurt badly. But now there was a steady stream of blood, tinted green by the depth of water.

He overtook the two tigers and made a pass in front of them, and swam with awkward, jerking motions. He went to the surface and splashed about there as though sick and convulsing. The first tiger did not react at first, then it passed through the scent trail of Sky's blood. It immediately turned towards the surface, followed by its companion and they started to circle Sky, evaluating whether he really was easy prey.

Sky could not afford to wait for the tigers to be cautious. He swam back towards Deneb, making a show of swimming spasmodically. The sharks followed, getting more and more interested. Sky was getting close to the arch now, he had to provoke the tigers if this was to work. He swam to the nearest coral head, and, choosing an especially vicious-looking corner, once more ground his wound against it. He cried out involuntarily at the pain. Blood poured forth this time, and now the smell of it made the tigers very excited. Suddenly the big one lunged at him. Sky barely escaped and shot off, keeping just ahead of the monster. The other one joined the pursuit and both were after him at full speed, now frenzied by the stream of blood they were swimming in. Sky flew though the rocky arch, the sharks just behind him. He had just a moment to take in the scene: the two guards turning to look around in shock, Deneb barely visible against the wall, Storm and Sharp Beak nowhere to be seen. Sky barrelled between the two guards, the leading tiger crashed into one of them, his jaws agape, and took in the whole of his head, killing him almost instantly. A huge cloud of blood filled the water. Sky darted into the recess alongside Deneb, as the other shark snapped at the second guard, removing a chunk from his tail fluke. The guard fled, the shark in hot pursuit. The remaining big tiger shook its head violently from side to side, the guard's body flopping limply back and forth in its maw as its teeth sawed through his body. It gave a final violent shake of its head and the guard's head and upper body were severed, the rest of him falling to the seabed. The tiger gulped down its meal and then circled the body, struggling to digest the first half of the dolphin.

Sky turned to the shocked Deneb. 'Quick: go to the clan, tell them what's happened! I'll distract it.'

Deneb started to protest, but Sky shoved him out in the direction of the clan's bay. Then he moved out into the open in front of the shark which eyed him warily. 'Go!' Sky hissed to Deneb.

Deneb took a last look then turned and swam off as fast as he could. Sky watched him disappear; wanting to be sure that he would get clear of the Cleaner. All the blood from the severed body of the guard would attract more of them soon. Sky taunted the shark for a little longer, staying just out of its reach. Then it lost interest, remembering the half eaten body on the seabed. It nosed it again, as though trying to decide whether to try and eat it too. Sky slipped past it, and headed after Deneb as fast as he could across the reef.

Sky was elated. The wound on his head was still hurting badly. But he had done it! He had helped Deneb get away in spite of the odds. Now, he just had to convince the clan…a cry of rage shattered his thoughts and Sky felt a huge blow from above into his back, driving him onto the reef. He was flipped over onto his back and found himself lying in a hollow in the rock with the huge form of Storm looming over him. Storm's eyes were narrow with fury and his voice was icy. 'How dare you! You will die for your interference! Just tell me why you've done this before I kill you.'

Sky's back hurt terribly and he knew that if Storm charged him now he had no chance but he did not feel afraid. He answered with a strong voice, glad that he had ruined the Guardian's plans. 'Because you are insane and have to be stopped. Because of what happened to Dusk. Because you killed my father, the last Kark-Du of your clan.'

'*Your* father! He was not *your* father! What's your name?'

'I am Touches The Sky and he *was* my father.'

Storm looked taken aback. 'Touches The Sky died on a beach with my mother a long time ago. Only I and my father escaped that day.'

'No! I escaped too! But my brother's name was…'

Storm gave a harsh laugh. 'Still Bay. That *was* my old name until I embraced Stone Eyes' teaching and joined the Guardians. So, my little brother survived!'

Sky took advantage of Storm's momentary surprise to right himself and shift himself slightly out of the hole. Storm saw the movement and growled.

'What are you doing? Trying to get away? You think this changes anything? You're not my brother any more — I have many new brothers, every true believer is my brother now, not you. You're from another time, another world. You're weak and foolish like he was and you've ruined everything! It will seem like I have failed and you are responsible!'

His rage overcame him again and he lunged at Sky once more, plunging towards him with his eyes blazing. Sky darted away and Storm just struck him with a glancing blow, but it still hurt. He swam as fast as could; away from Storm, out into the blue, away from the land. He kept near the surface so that he could leap to breathe. It hurt; hurt a lot. Storm must have broken some ribs. But he had to swim or die. Below him, the bottom fell sharply away. Soon they were over the deep waters; darkest blue beneath them.

Storm was close behind him, cursing him, promising to kill him. Ordinarily, he would probably have been able to outpace the big dolphin, but the injury to his back was growing stiff and painful; it was becoming agony to swim. Storm was going to catch him. There was only one place to go.

Sky dived.

He heard Storm follow him, not far behind, using his sonar to track Sky, still cursing him.

Sky forced himself to enter the deep diving trance in spite of the pain. He had never done it before while swimming this fast but this would have to be the best dive of his life or the last one. He visualised his body, the familiar dull red glow representing his conscious extending through it. Quickly, he made the glow dim, from his fins, from his tail, up into his body. He reduced the racing pace of his heart; making it pause between beats, extending the pause each time.

Slow your heart. Slow it or die.

Soon the red glow was just in his head. He was vaguely aware of his tail still driving him ever deeper, but it was far away, and the distant pain was almost a comfort. Now, he was at edge of the fourth level of consciousness. He could hear the sonar of Storm behind him, getting closer. The water became darker, the Shades spoke of *joining, absorbing,* and then: *death.*

Slower still.

They swam on and on into the void. The water became very cold as he passed the deep thermocline. It was almost perfectly black now. He had never been this deep before.

Slower.

He was aware that his body was running out of oxygen, he was struggling to keep any kind of control. He thought of One Eye and wished he could be there.

Beware the worm named Fear.

He knew that the inviting, dark mantle of unconsciousness was not far away; close enough to feel now, close enough to touch.

Slower yet.

A part of Sky's mind could detect Storm closing behind him; he must be only a body length away. He vaguely noticed that Storm had stopped using his sonar. He must be about to attack. It did not seem to matter much anymore.

Dying is not hard at all.

He distantly felt the weight of Storm's body collide with his.

When the impact came, it was not as violent as he had expected. Not really anything. Like the joking push of one friend to another, or the press of a lover against her mate. Dusk used to push him like that sometimes, a long, long time ago. He must be so far removed from the world that he did not feel it. His oxygen levels were so low; he would have been finished soon anyway. He gave into it; stopped swimming.

Let's end it then. Where is She?

Storm pushed passed him, towards the utter blackness of the abyss. The big dolphin's still body sank past him, gently spiralling in the faintest of light. Storm seemed to want to go down there. Sky let him pass.

Farewell, Still Bay.

CHAPTER 52

"I know your skin
I know your eyes
I know your clever mind
Your dancing laugh
Your soft caress
Your leaps, your falls, all mine
I know your moods
All your desires
How you feel when we're apart
I know each element of you
Except what's in your heart"
- The poet Jupiter by Regulas (9,467-9,491 post Great Alluvion).

He swam fast at the surface, flying alternately through clean, cool air and supporting, liquid crystal. Each time he passed from one medium to the next he was chased, but never caught, by a thousand shining diamonds. The water deep, deep below him; a viscous, fluid blue, falling to the still, cold blackness where all zetii eventually go. Above him, the paler, yet still intense blue of the sky. His world; his people's Ocean. Living in one hemisphere, dependant on the other. Yet he felt completely alone in this two-tone blue orb, which rocked gently about the pivot of the bright red light at its join. He swam towards that light as fast as he could, racing it to the horizon.

Soon the sand rose to meet him, patches of rock among it turning to grey in the failing light. And then he could see it: silhouetted against the fiery ball, the tiny islet. Black against the light, piercing into the sky like a Cleaner's fin.

As Senx immersed himself into the distant waters in red fire he could see the net in his mind, painted there by sound. He could make her out, she was still there.

I came before Senx left you, just as you asked me.

Now he can see her, and she — yes, she is moving, he is sure.

I kept my promise my love.

'It is I, Touches The Sky!'

Then he was beside her and realised that although she was moving, it was not through her own efforts. She was rocking gently in the swell, still woven into the net.

With a great effort he lifted her to the surface. Her eye flickered and her blowhole opened and took in little air, but he heard the rasp of bubbles as the little air passed into the water in her lungs and knew what it had to mean. She'd given up, passed out, and water had entered her airways. She was fading.

'Dusk, I tried so hard, I got here as fast as I could.'

She looked at him for a long time then spoke with a great effort, her voice small and far away. 'Sky, dearest Sky. What happened to your face? Did you...stop them?'

'Yes. And Storm is dead.'

Her eyes closed for a moment, then opened again as she continued weakly. 'Thank you. Thank you so much. Then it wasn't all for nothing. Deneb is safe. The clan will take you back. And the Guardians will fall apart without Storm.'

He held her up again and she tried to breathe but convulsed weakly. Some white foam appeared at her blowhole but no air moved in or out.

'Dusk you've got to hold on!'

'Can't. So...very tired. Sky, promise me one...thing.'

'Anything.'

'Find...find the Western Red Mountains Clan. Venus...In...Mist. She wants you. It's the last...'

But there was no more. Her eyes still looked into Sky's with a faraway stare, but he thought she seemed content somehow.

He supported her all through that long night. The sky was perfectly clear and filled with the stars she loved so much. He named those he could and asked her for the names of those he could not. Sang her songs. Reminded her of stories of when they were children. Lifted her to the surface time after time so she might breathe in that cool, precious air, which was sweetened by the exotic fragrance of some night blossom.

But she never did.

Touches The Sky's story will continue in the second part of Dolphin Way: Captured